Nick Harrow

Witch
King

Book 1

Chapter One

TEN THOUSAND STEPS WAS A HELL OF A LONG WAY to climb on an empty stomach. By the time I'd reached Mount Shiki's peak, the gnawing hunger in my gut left me wrung out and exhausted. The site of my shamanic vision quest was near at hand, but the ache in my belly made me want to head back down the mountain for a bowl of my mother's winter root stew.

Instead, I took a deep breath and leaned on my iron war club like a cane to catch my breath. My fur-lined boots had long since given up trying to keep the cold off my feet, and my toes were now as numb as wooden pegs. The traditional loincloth that was the only other item of clothing I was allowed to bring on my vision quest did nothing to protect my nether regions from the mountain's biting chill. My balls wanted to crawl up into my belly to escape the hellish cold.

My foundation core, which I'd strengthened with powerful herbal teas and tinctures during the week leading up to this journey, felt raw and ragged after the long climb up the rugged steps to the holy mountain's peak. Its twin nodes, twice as many as most men had at my age, had been filled with rin when I'd started this climb. That power had kept me alive during my climb, and both nodes were now almost empty. If I couldn't find a place to meditate and restore my reserves of sacred energy, my vision quest would come to a frozen halt.

"A man lives in the world of his choosing." My grandfather, long since dead, had whispered those words to me during one of our many walks in the forests beyond our village. The words had stuck with me ever since, and I felt like I finally understood them.

This was the world I'd chosen.

It was time to stop bitching and live in it, no matter how much it hurt, or how badly I wanted to call it quits. I dragged my sorry ass forward, between a pair of snow-speckled boulders, and into an impossible new world.

The mountain's top unfolded into a vast expanse of snow studded with copses of towering pine trees, stone outcroppings that jutted dozens of feet into the air, and hidden streams that burbled beneath the thick blanket of flawless snow. Birds flitted through the trees, the wind from their wings dislodging flurries of snow from the pine boughs. A fox perked up its ears at my arrival, a white-furred lynx stared at me from the top of a spiny stone, and something much larger shook the forest's branches with its unseen passage.

If I'd had any doubts about becoming a shaman, that was the moment in which they vanished. This was the world I'd always dreamed about. A place of pristine beauty untouched by the hands of mortals.

It was fucking gorgeous.

And it was exactly where I belonged.

"Come out, come out, wherever you are!" I called out, hoping my spirit animal would take mercy on my exhausted state and prance out to wrap up my quest with a tidy bow.

Every animal in sight fled from the sound of my voice, and the birds in the trees took flight as if they'd just gotten word a flock of hungry hawks had been spotted nearby.

I hadn't really thought the call would convince my spirit animal to bound out of the wilderness and leap into my arms, but I would have always wondered how much easier I could have made my life if I hadn't given it a shot.

Fortunately, there was plenty of rin energy on top of Mount Shiki to sustain me while I searched for just the right critter to complete my quest. I hoped for something wise, maybe a snowy owl, or clever, like a white ferret. I'd have even settled for a noble stag, or an industrious mole.

As the sun set on my search and a cloak of purple velvet twilight spread across the snow, I drew in the sacred energy that was so plentiful on top of Mount Shiki. The nourishing power helped me to endure the cold and quelled my body's fierce hunger and thirst. With so much free power for me to cycle through my core, I could survive for a very long time without food or water.

Which turned out to be a good thing, because no blessed animals stepped out from the forest to greet me. Time stood still as I searched high and low for some spirit beast who would bond with me. Though I caught glimpses of my quarry through the trees, faint golden glows that flashed through my spirit sight, I never came close enough to make a connection with any of them. The sacred rin kept me on my feet, but it couldn't totally erase the exhaustion that crept into my muscles and the cramps that knotted my stomach. I couldn't tell how long

I'd been on top of the mountain, but it felt like a long, long time.

And then, hiking through a dense forest with my war club over my shoulders and my spirit as low as it had ever been, I almost fucking died.

One minute I'd been squeezing between a pair of scrubby pine trees, closing my eyes and turning my head to keep from getting my face scratched off by their branches, and the next I was confronted by the gleaming white bones of a few hundred animal skeletons.

The entrance to an enormous cave lay fifty feet ahead of me. The snow in front of it was stained with streaks of red, and the half-eaten carcass of a dead buck steamed in the cave's mouth. A deep, challenging rumble echoed from the darkness. The creature's aura—big, red, and hungry—oozed from the cavern like the shadow of death itself.

"Oh. Shit." Every instinct in my body told me to drop my war club and run like hell back the way I'd come. Far better to starve to death than to get ripped apart by whatever was about to come charging out of that cave.

But another part of me had moved beyond fear. I was too cold, too hungry, and just too motherfucking tired to spend another day tramping around the wilderness with an empty belly. That part of me wanted to stand its ground. It wanted to see what came out of that cave. And, more than anything, it wanted to see if it could best whatever I was about to face.

To my surprise, that possibly insane part of my mind won the coin toss.

"Maybe this is it. Let's see what you've got, motherfucker, because I'm too worn the hell out to back down now," I whispered and hoped I hadn't just made a terrible, terrible mistake. "If you're supposed to be my spirit animal, let's do this thing."

A bear out of my nightmares charged from the cave's mouth. Its fur was the color of fresh blood, and its teeth gleamed like ivory daggers in a mouth big enough to snap my head off my shoulders with a single bite. The bone-white scythes of its claws churned up chunks of blood-soaked earth and hurled them into the sky behind it as it raced across the ground toward me. Whatever else the creature might have been, one thing was obvious.

It was seriously pissed.

The crimson bear was on top of me in the blink of an eye. It lunged forward and snapped its jaws through the space where my head had been before I'd jerked it out of the way. The beast rose to its full height with a mighty roar, and its shadow blotted out the sun above me. My spirit sight snapped into focus on the creature's core, and what I saw there filled me with raw terror.

The bear held a moonbound core in the center of its body.

In all my life up to that point, the most powerful core I'd ever seen belonged to one of the Moonsilver Bat's visiting priests, and he'd only had a skybound core. The bear's core was two full levels above that, five levels above my foundation core, and it held a staggering twenty-five nodes filled to the brim with pure senjin. To top the other scary shit, the killer grizzly had three techniques at its disposal: one for attack, one for defense, and a third for healing or recovery of some sort.

If I didn't do something real clever, real fast, I was a goddamned dead man.

A spike of adrenaline spurred my survival instincts into overdrive. I threw myself back and to the right a split second before the bear's clawed paw could disembowel me.

I scrambled back into the cover of the pine trees. Their boles would keep the bear from charging straight into me, while giving me enough space to swing my club down between them. I did just that, smashing my weapon into one of the bear's paws, and hoped the blow would convince it to go look for easier prey somewhere else.

The crimson bear had other ideas.

It slammed its right shoulder into a tree in front of me, splintering the thick trunk with its massive impact. The beast tore the top half of the damaged tree loose with a single smash from its paw and pushed deeper into the forest after me.

I wisely retreated to a position where the trees were older and sturdier. My gaze stayed locked on the beast's burning-ember eyes, searching for some sign that the creature recognized me and wasn't really trying to tear me limb from limb. It was just my luck to find my spirit animal only to get eaten by it.

The bear tried to bowl over another tree, but the sturdy trunk resisted the attack and the tree remained upright. Enraged, the crimson beast shredded the trunk with its claws, flinging bark and pulp in every direction. It stared at me the whole time it was taking the tree apart, and something passed between us. Yes, this was my spirit animal. And, yes, it was going to kill me if it could.

I wasn't sure what I'd expected, honestly. A cool and wise spirit would have been an ideal guide into the world of shamans. An owl, maybe. Or a raven. Those were supposed to be pretty smart. I'd have even accepted one of the meeker animals, like a swift stag or a cunning ferret. Instead, I'd gotten the most homicidal spirit in the forest. Except maybe a wolverine.

"Can't we talk about this?" I shouted to be heard over the bear's demolition of the pine tree.

The bear stopped, tilted its head to one side, and then squinted at me with an all-too-human expression on its enormous face.

"No weaklings," it snarled. Then it went right back to eating the tree.

That was an insult I wasn't used to hearing. At a little over six feet tall I'd never been the runt of my village. And, while I was no swordmaster like my father, the lessons of my martial arts instructor, Misha, had kept my body plenty strong. If this bear thought I was a weakling, I'd show it the error of its ways. It might kill me, but not without a fight it would remember.

With a roar of my own, I charged forward and slammed my war club down in an overhead smash. The spiked iron's five-foot length gave me plenty of leverage to bring the pain, and that's exactly what I did. The weapon smashed into the bear's left shoulder with a crushing force that sent shock waves rippling through my hands and into my arms. That attack should have shattered even a big bear's bones.

In response, the crimson bear knocked aside the tree it had been eating and lunged at me again. Its head shot through the space it had just cleared and its jaws clamped around my war club before I could yank the weapon out of the monster's reach. The beast reared, dragging me off my feet, but I wasn't about to release my weapon without a fight. I clung to the spiked club like my life depended on it, because it probably did.

The crimson bear whipped its head over its shoulder and sent my club and me sailing through the trees into the clearing in front of its cave. The unexpected maneuver caught me off guard, and I landed awkwardly, then tumbled onto my back in the snow.

That was a very bad place to be with a giant red bear trying to eat me.

I rolled away as the bear charged me again and kicked up to my feet before it could kill me where I lay on the ground. The beast was stronger than I was, and faster in a straight-line dash. My only advantages were desperate cunning and years of combat training every boy and girl in my village had undergone as part of the Junior Guard. I wasn't sure those were enough to turn this fight in my favor.

When the savage animal tried to tear me apart with its claws, I dodged back, counterattacked with a slam from my club, then circled around the fucker to hit it in the back before it could chew my face off. When it charged, I dodged to one side and slammed my spiked weapon into its flank as it passed. No single attack I made was enough to drop the beast on its own, but the dozens of small wounds I opened bled the strength from its body and drained its core of the senjin that fueled its rage.

If the crimson bear wanted a fight, then I'd give it a goddamned fight.

Our battle rocked the top of the mountain until we were both half-fucking dead. I fought my murderous spirit animal until its flanks were foamy with sweat and its head sagged against its blood-soaked paws. The spirit animal's left eye was swollen closed courtesy of a powerful blow from my war club, and its mouth was lopsided with missing teeth. The crimson bear looked like it had fought half a battalion of the Emperor's own guards.

My foe's wounds made me look like the most badass brawler this side of the Iron Arena. Unfortunately, my injuries were just as bad, if not worse.

My torso was covered in deep gouges and brutal bites. A flap of meat hung off my left shoulder, and my right thigh was torn open to the bone. I'd lost so much blood I had to lean on my war club to keep from pitching over onto my face. My hit-and-run tactics had worn the beast down and kept it from killing me, sure, but it had taken its toll in blood and meat from my carcass in the process.

We'd stained the snow red with our blood for as far as I could see in every direction. Hell, from the color of the sun as it set on us, we might have painted the sky with our gore. The seemingly endless battle had knocked over trees and ripped deep furrows in the earth. The fight had left scars on the mountain that would take generations to heal.

And still the crimson bear eyeballed me like it wanted to cut out my heart and eat it. To my credit, I stared right back at it, though my vision was a blurred fog and the last of my blood was scant minutes away from pumping onto the ground beneath my feet.

"Not a fucking weakling." My words stumbled all over themselves on their way out of my mouth. I was punch-drunk and more dead than alive by that point. I thought I deserved extra credit for forming a sentence, proper diction be damned. My core was empty, and I was too weak and too worn out to even try filling it back up.

The crimson bear glared at me from less than a yard away. It could have killed me with a single blow, though the effort would have likely killed it, too. The embers of its eyes had burned low, and its aura guttered like a candle in a stiff breeze. The creature's core was as hollow as mine, all of its sacred energy burned as fuel for our fight. Finally, the bear shuddered, raised its head, and leaned forward until our noses touched.

"Not a weakling," it managed to grunt out, before we both pitched onto our sides in the snow.

Chapter Two

I WOKE IN DARKNESS WITH THE TASTE OF BLOOD IN MY mouth and something warm and smooth pressed up against my naked body. I lifted my eyelids with my fingertips just to be sure I'd actually opened them. That didn't banish the darkness, so either I was blind or I was someplace where not even a glimmer of light could find me. My first instinct was to panic, kick whatever I was under off me, and then try to find a way to get the fuck out of there with all due haste.

Part one of my plan went swimmingly, and my heart and mind raced together toward a stroke and some very bad thoughts about my situation. I wondered if the crimson bear and I had died after coming to our agreement that I was, in fact, a badass. If I was in some sort of hell, that would explain the darkness that surrounded me.

It would not, however, explain the warm, slender body lying on my chest and against my left side. Whatever, or whoever, that was didn't seem threatening, so I decided to investigate that part of the puzzle first.

My hand landed gingerly on a smooth shoulder that, thankfully, felt humanoid. Doing my best not to wake up what could easily be a homicidal spirit who'd dragged me off to its lair to feast on my core, I traced the outline of my cuddle buddy's body. The arm connected to the shoulder was slender and slight, the smooth skin broken only by a random hatchwork of what felt like raised scars along the bicep and forearm.

Goose pimples rose under my fingers, and the arm's owner stirred, mumbled something that sounded irritated and decidedly feminine, and then snuggled up tighter against me. If this was a soul-stealing spirit, it was a sleepy one.

"Hey." I wasn't going to become a shaman lying on my back in the dark, and I desperately wanted to know what in the Frozen Hells had happened. "Wake up."

Mystery girl mumbled something under her breath and buried her face in the hollow of my neck. Her long hair spilled across my chest like threads of silk, and her breath was hot against my throat. She threw a leg over me, which put an intriguing and distracting pressure across my groin, and pulled herself closer with a hand over my heart. Satisfied I wouldn't be able to dislodge her easily, she let out a long, low sigh and fell back into a deep sleep.

Okay, as nice and cozy as that was, I needed to get moving. If the crimson bear really was my spirit animal, I wanted to find it and seal the deal before it changed its mind and we had to fight again.

"C'mon," I muttered and tried to pull the woman's arm off my chest. "I've gotta go."

Surprisingly, her thin arm was impossible for me to move. She didn't tense or tighten her grip; the limb just refused to move no matter how hard I pulled or pushed on it. I might as well have tried to shove a boulder up the side of a cliff for all the progress I made. My struggles went on for a few minutes before she shifted against me and let out an aggravated sigh.

"I'm sleeping here, mortal." Uh-oh. Any creature that calls you "mortal" isn't something to fuck with. "Where do you have to get off to in such a hurry?"

"I'm on a quest." That sounded ridiculous. Only heroes in fables told strange women they were on quests. Then again, only in fables did men find themselves lying naked under equally naked and curiously strong women. "I need to find my spirit animal and make sure it's okay."

"I'm fine." She moved her arm off my chest, though her leg slid across my crotch in slow strokes that made it hard to think about anything else. "But now I'm awake. And bored. Wanna fuck?"

The last syllable was more of a growl than a word. Her hand slipped under her thigh to grab hold of my swiftly stiffening cock, the ball of her thumb swirling across its tip. The sensation curled my toes and tied my thoughts into knots.

"You certainly feel fine." I groaned as her fingers squeezed around me, relaxed, then squeezed again in time with my pulse. "I'm not sure what that has to do with my spirit animal's well-being, though."

"I am your spirit animal, man thing." Her mouth latched onto the side of my throat and she sucked at my skin, tongue hot and squirming against me. Combined with the feelings that flowed from below my waist, she had me teetering on the edge of ecstasy. "And as your spirit animal, I demand some bonding time."

Well, who was I to ignore the needs of my new friend and guide into the world of all things shamanish?

The memory of my time with the crimson bear was a euphoric haze I only remembered in sharp fragments that pierced the muddled veil surrounding my thoughts. The coppery taste of her tongue as it flicked across mine after a meal torn from our prey. The impossibly smooth texture of her skin under my rough palm. The untamed scent of her hair dangling around my face as she rode me with a desperate, ferocious need that threatened to drown us both in crashing waves of ecstasy. The warm, slick grip of her sex around mine as I plunged my body into her depths in a rhythmic cycle that pushed the rin energy from my earthbound core into hers and pulled the shio energy from her celestial core into mine.

She taught me more about fucking, fighting, and feasting than I'd ever known existed. She was an insatiable lover, a peerless hunter, and a patient mentor who grew closer to me with every moment we spent together. It wasn't long before we could hear one another's thoughts as clearly as our speaking voices.

And then, one morning after we'd eaten half a caribou and slept for what felt like a week, I woke up a different person.

"Finally." The crimson bear poked her finger at my solar plexus. "Your core has finally advanced."

Well, I'll be damned. She was right. Somewhere along the way I'd jumped from a puny two-node foundation core to an earthbound core with five bright-red nodes brimming with sacred rin energy. I'd also sprouted a strange, bruised-looking spot in the center of my now deep-brown core, which the crimson bear informed me represented the connection between us. I was turning into a real shaman.

After that, my training in the sacred arts really kicked into high gear. My spirit animal taught me to gather sacred rin energy into my core with much greater speed and efficiency through a trance meditation technique. She showed me how to weave threads of rin from my nodes to activate the Earthen Darts combat technique. And, finally, she blessed me with the gifts of her body, the Crimson Claws and Bear's Mantle.

"Each of those techniques will require a full node of your sacred rin energy to activate, my shaman," she explained to me. "The claws will carve through your opponents' flesh and the mantle will keep you safe from mundane weapons. But the techniques last for only minutes at a time. Be careful, or you'll burn through your rin before the battle is over. And then you'll fucking die and all my time training you will have been wasted."

And all the while, my body grew stronger and my senses sharper. I couldn't imagine how weak I'd been, how blind to the world around me.

Those were the best days of my life, though I have no idea how long they lasted. The sun was useless for tracking the passage of time because it was always twilight outside her cave. Meals weren't much better when it came to marking the hours because I never really felt hungry. We hunted deer, elk, and even a moose or two whenever the mood struck, and gorged ourselves on their meat more for the sensation and taste than any physical need.

Then, without warning, the best time of my life ended the same way it had begun.

The crimson bear tried to kill me.

We were fucking like animals when she changed. One moment, we were moving like a single creature, our bodies united in the shared goal of making us both feel fucking awesome. The next, just as we'd reached our peak and I was thrust deep inside her, she went feral and howled like someone had pulled her guts out with a hunter's knife.

She scrambled away from me like a wild animal escaping a trap, a gleaming thread of our combined juices stretching between our bodies before it snapped into salty beads on the floor of her cave.

"What's wrong?" I shouted and raised my hands defensively. She'd spun to face me, and the look in her eyes was a deadly mixture of raw anguish and murderous hate. The connection between us throbbed with confusion and horror, and I wasn't sure where all this had come from.

"Mortals." The scars that crisscrossed her arms flushed a deep crimson, and her fingernails lengthened into bone-white claws. She curled her fingers as if trying to hang onto the earth, and the natural weapons gouged chunks of stone from the cavern's floor. "They're killing it. I'll destroy them!"

By them, apparently, she meant all the mortals. Including the one standing right in front of her.

The crimson bear slammed into me, her skin toughened into leather and her claws so sharp they screamed as they tore the air. Her roar revealed rows of blood-stained carnivore's teeth, and she did her damnedest to tear my throat out with them. Madness danced in her eyes like wildfire, and her body burned against mine with this new, violent need. If I didn't stop her, she'd kill me.

"Stop, please, stop." I held her wrists out from my body and she writhed in a desperate attempt to escape. When I'd first come to the mountain, the crimson bear had been much stronger than me. But the bond we now shared had gifted me with strength to rival my spirit animal's. She could struggle, but brute strength wouldn't be enough to let her escape from me.

So the bear decided to play dirty and tried to knee me in the balls. The shot was quick, but my reflexes were just a little quicker, and she only clipped the outside of my thigh. She let out one frustrated roar after another, until her throat was raw and hoarse.

"They're killing it." Her voice was ragged, and her body shook with the effort of trying to kill me. "I have to stop them."

"Who?" I pulled my face back from her snapping teeth before they could take my nose off. "Let me help you, damnit."

I leaned into my words and pushed them through the bond we shared. She was a bright and snarling presence inside my core, and I willed myself to be a stable anchor inside hers.

Moment by moment the madness receded from her gaze, until, at last, she fell against me, deep, wracking sobs tearing themselves loose from her body.

"You have to leave." The crimson bear lifted her tear-stained face to show me eyes that were bottomless wells of sorrow. "You have to save them."

"I don't know what you're talking about." I wrapped my arms around her. "I'm not going anywhere. You still have so much to teach me. And I'm not ready to give up all that sexy bonding time yet."

She chuckled at that and leaned back to wipe the tears from her eyes.

"There's never enough time." She offered me a slight, sad smile. "That's the way of the world. Or it was. You've come as far here as you can go. It's time to take what I've given you and use it where it will do some good."

"I don't want to go." That was putting it mildly. The only reason I'd willingly leave that cavern was to hunt down another big old piece of meat to fill our bellies. "And you still haven't told me what happened."

"I don't know, exactly." She frowned and slipped out of my arms to pace the floor. "The sacred energy of the world has changed. It's corrupted. Tainted."

That didn't sound good.

"I'm not sure a low-level shaman is the right guy to fix that." The truth was, it sounded like the kind of job that could get a newbie shaman killed deader than shit.

"You're the only shaman for the job." She eyed me from across the cavern, face hidden in shadow, eyes bright as embers. "You're the only shaman left."

My mind reeled at that. I'd known there weren't many other shamans left since the rise of the Celestial Covenant and the Thousand Gods had come to rule the world of men. I couldn't believe I was really the last of my kind.

"There have to be others." I didn't want this responsibility. I wanted to go back to the good old days of fifteen minutes ago when my whole life was about fucking and eating my fill.

"They killed them." Her voice was as cold and sharp as a knife's blade. "They'll kill the rest of the world, too, if we don't stop them."

"You'll come with me?" That was a relief. She knew a hell of a lot more about this shaman business than I did.

"I'm always with you." Her words rang through my core. "But my place is here. I've given you my gifts, and together we've transformed your core from foundation to earthbound. The rest is up to you."

"I can't do it." That was just the truth. I was a shaman, okay, but I still had the lowliest of all practitioner cores. I could hold five nodes of sacred rin energy, enough to use the totemic gifts of the bear's claws and hide and ignite a simple technique or two. I could beat the shit out of your average guy and hunt like a mad motherfucker, but saving the world was a whole different ball of wax.

"You have to." She crossed the cavern to hold my cheeks in her hands. "There's no one else who can do this.'

"Tell me what, exactly, you think I'll do when I leave this cave." I closed my hands over hers and held on for dear life.

"I can't see the details through the veil between worlds." Her eyes clouded as she looked at something far, far outside the cave. "Something new has risen in the world of mortals. Its afterbirth has unleashed a nightmare disease. You have to kill the abomination and heal the Earth, before it's too late."

I lifted the crimson bear into my arms and carried her out of the cave. I laid her down in the snow under the sky, right where we'd almost killed each other when we'd first met a few weeks back. She shivered, not from the cold—she was impervious to the effects of weather—but with a need so deep it ached in both of our cores.

She threw her legs wide and dragged me down with her ankles hooked around my back. Her teeth clamped on my shoulder as I eased into her and she groaned beneath me. Her tongue, hot and greedy, flickered over my flesh as her teeth pressed into my skin with a pressure a fraction of an inch from pain. Her strong arms looped over the back of my neck, and her hands tangled in the dark mane of my hair. Her hips bucked against mine with an urgent need and our pace quickened.

There was nothing easy or gentle about our last time together. Her nails drew red scratches like broken wings across my back. Our love bites raised bruises and welts from our ecstatic struggles to experience everything our bodies could offer. My shaft sank deeper into the crimson bear's flesh than I'd thought possible, and she groaned and thrust back against me with a frenzied hunger.

I seized the firm globes of her ass and pulled her dripping cleft against me with bruising force. Her smell, wild and feral, flooded my senses and drove me into a berserk fit of lust. My howls shredded the mountaintop silence, sending every animal within a mile of her cave fleeing for their lives.

The crimson bear's eyes rolled back, and she bit her lip with gleaming ivory teeth. Her back arched and pushed me toward her core. With a shout, she pulled her body up against mine, arms clutching my shoulders, breasts flattened against my chest, hips grinding along my length with relentless fervor.

We lost ourselves in that moment, our bodies slamming against and into each other, our breaths mingling in our lungs, our cores colliding and unleashing a burning wave of sacred energy that inflamed our blood. As a flood of pleasure rose higher and higher within us, we were one for a timeless breath.

I never wanted it to end. I wanted to bury myself in her warm depths, to plant myself where she couldn't dig me up and cast me out.

But there was no denying her passion. She came screaming into the night, the muscles inside her squeezing, dragging a final burst of pleasure out of me and pulling me down into a dark and fathomless sea of savage ecstasy.

Later, as we lay beneath the wheeling stars, I caressed the long, red strands of her hair with one hand.

"What's your name?" We'd never needed names for each other before, but I didn't want to leave without knowing hers.

"You're supposed to ask a girl's name before you fuck her a hundred times, you know." She nipped at my throat with her straight, white teeth. "I've had many names, mortal, but I emerged from the heart of creation's shadow as Mielyssi."

"Mielyssi." I liked the way the syllables tasted on my tongue. "Don't you want to know my name?"

"I already know, Kyr." She giggled at my surprised look. "I know everything there is to know about you, my love. You are mine, and I am yours."

"Not fair." I groaned. "When will I know all your secrets?"

"Never." She stood and pulled me to my feet. "That was lovely, Kyr. Now you must go."

"Rude." I crushed her against me, not wanting to hear what she had to say. It wasn't time for me to leave. It couldn't be. Not yet.

Mielyssi slipped out of my arms and guided me back to the cave without another word. She found my club against the wall and lifted it in both hands.

"You'll need this." She kissed the war club's handle and offered it to me. Sinuous threads of silver light unfolded from where her lips had touched the iron, wrapping the weapon with intricate swirls of her essence that glowed briefly along its length before they faded away. "I don't know exactly what's happened down there, but I do know it won't be pretty. If you feed your rin into the channels of my kiss, your weapon can help light your way through the darkness."

"What am I supposed to do with this?" I took the war club from her and was surprised by how light it felt. I was so much stronger now than I had been when I first came to the mountain.

"You're supposed to accept my gift and keep it close. Your responsibility is to heal the world." Mielyssi's voice grew gruff and hungry as she continued. "But your second responsibility is nearly as important. Find the people who poisoned the dream, Kyr. Find them and kill every one of those motherfuckers."

Chapter Three

"**Y**OU'VE BEEN GONE LONGER THAN YOU MAY think." The crimson bear leaned against me at the top of the ten thousand steps that led down to my village.

"How much longer?" A layer of fluffy white clouds lay below us and hid the bottom of the mountain. Anything could be waiting for me down there.

Or nothing.

I wasn't really sure which of those options scared me more.

"I love you, Kyr. But you're not going to be happy about what I have to tell you." Mielyssi leaned up on her tiptoes and pressed her lips against my ear. She hugged me tight, arms around my throat, and a sudden breeze whipped her crimson hair around our faces. "The world you're returning to is not the one you left."

"The world I left wasn't nearly as much fun as I've been having. I'm looking forward to this new one." I chuckled.

Mielyssi didn't return my laugh.

"I told you all the other shamans were gone." She sighed and looked out over the thick layer of stormy gray clouds below us. "They were murdered, Kyr. Hunted like wild beasts."

"That's impossible." The Sevenfold Empire was enormous. It stretched thousands of miles in every direction from the Sacred City at its heart. Millions upon millions of people lived in its cities, and millions more lived in the countryside. Even if there were only a handful of shamans left, hunting them all down would take years, maybe longer. "I haven't been gone long enough for that to happen."

"I'm sorry." The crimson bear buried her face in my long hair. Her heart pounded against my skin and the power of her core flowed into mine with the warmth of the sun. "You were with me for decades, Kyr. Time passes differently in my realm than yours, so I can't say for certain exactly how long you've been away from home. This isn't how I wanted things to be, you have to believe me. The Feral Council thought this was their best chance at recovering after—"

"After what?" My blood had turned to icy slush in my veins. While I'd been having the time of my life, the world I'd left behind had moved on without me. My family, my friends, everything I'd known would be long gone to dust by now, while I still looked as young and healthy as the day I began my climb up Mount Shiki.

"After the world ended." She buried her face in my neck, and a torrent of warm tears ran down my throat.

"This can't be happening." I felt like I'd been dragged out of a nice warm bed and tossed into an icy lake. I'd been more or less prepared to climb down the mountain to kick some ass in the name of good old Mother Nature. I was a hell of a lot less ready to hear that the whole world was fucked, and I'd lost almost everything important in my life.

"I can't stay much longer. The sickness in the dream has already weakened me." She clung to my neck and whispered urgently into my ear. "Find the spirits of forest and stream, search those who remember the old ways. The world you left behind is dead, Kyr. But you can breathe life into its embers. Heal it, and there's still a chance for us."

"Come with me." I didn't want to face this alone. "Together, we can—"

"I'm always with you. Never forget that." She stepped back and held me at arm's length. Her face was red and streaked with tears. Her eyes were sunken in her skull, and her full cheeks had turned gaunt. She was so pale the raised scars on her skin stood out like brands. "I have to go. This world's poison is killing me. You can do this."

"I can't." I didn't want to, either. This was some serious bullshit to put on my shoulders. If I lived to see the end of the day I'd be shocked as hell. "Please."

I don't know what I expected Mielyssi to say or do, but I sure as fuck didn't expect her to laugh at me.

"Oh, Kyr." She shook her head and strands of her faded crimson hair fell from her scalp in withered clumps. "Don't be such a fucking pussy. I trained you for this. Do you think I'd waste my time preparing you to face this challenge if I didn't think you could handle it? Now, shut up, and look behind you at the world that needs you."

"You have to be fucking kidding me." I cast a glance over my shoulder and didn't see a fucking thing. I looked back to the crimson bear.

She was gone. All that remained was the lingering warmth of her lips against my ear, the already fading feeling of her arms around my neck, and the wild, primal smell of her flesh. It was as if Mielyssi had never existed.

The path that had led between the boulders to the snowy wonderland atop the mountain was gone, too. The steps up Mount Shiki's stony flank ended in a wall of natural stone that looked like it had been there for as long as the mountain had existed.

"Fuck!" I shouted into the teeth of the icy wind

I railed against the unfairness of it all for a good ten minutes. An earthbound core shaman didn't stand a snowball's chance in hell against a nightmare that could kill the world. I was still a teenager, for fuck's sake. I was supposed to spend more time banging my spirit animal and learning how to do real magic before I got tossed out on my first big quest.

The mountain didn't care what I had to say, and the wind tossed a faceful of ice at me to show how little of a fuck it gave about my predicament.

"Fine, whatever." Standing at the top of Mount Shiki wouldn't help me. I had ten thousand steps to go down; might as well get moving. Complaining about having the fate of the world yoked around my neck wouldn't get me out of here any faster.

The first thousand stairs were the easiest, and the hardest. I hadn't realized how much I'd missed the warmth of the morning sun until it shone on my face as I took my first steps down the mountain. The air was crisp and clean, and every breath seemed to invigorate me. Despite the madness of the past fifteen minutes, it felt good to be home. This was my world, no matter what had happened to it.

At the same time every step I took was another step away from Mielyssi. I wrestled with the memories of her laugh, her wry wit, and all the ways her body had fit with mine. There was still some piece of her inside me, though that made it all the harder to leave the rest of her behind. If this was what love felt like, it was a wonder anyone ever bothered with it.

That shit hurt.

It still hurt when I'd descended through the cloud layer and lost the sun's light. For a thousand steps I walked under a glowering sky that mirrored my spiritual funk with its churning gray thunderheads. Another thousand steps brought me to the first of the cherry trees that had been trained into a flowering archway above the sacred stairway. Their pale pink and white blossoms told me it was deep into spring, months after I'd first ascended.

No, not months.

Years. Many, many years.

The trees bore that out, anyway. They'd been well-manicured and graceful on my way up the mountain. On the way down, they were tangled and knotted; some of their branches spiraled toward the sky, others twisted down to their roots. There were ugly gaps in their boles left by their dead brothers and sisters, and the arch over the path seemed more of an accident than an intentional design.

Not even halfway down the mountain, and already the world looked like it had gone to shit.

Things didn't get better when I reached the shrine at the stairway's halfway point.

The ebonwood timbers that made up the shrine's frame should have been sturdy and polished to a mirror's sheen. Instead, patches of dry rot riddled the beams, and bloated toadstools sprouted from the wood like cancerous tumors. The shrine's door was missing, the iron hinges rusted away to rotten orange-red stubs, exposing the interior to the elements. Drifts of fresh cherry blossoms were the only spots of color in that drab, gray space. The thick prayer rug that dominated the center of the shrine was moth eaten and its colors leeched away by the colonies of sickly yellow mold that covered it like leprous ulcers.

A slanting beam of sunlight shone through a gap in the roof's warped wooden slats to illuminate even more damage. The cherrywood altar that should have held spirit tokens had cracked apart to reveal the desiccated shell of a swallow's nest. The urn of holy oil meant to light the paths of wayfarers had fallen to the floor when the altar collapsed, and its contents were now a black scab on the stone floor. A few prayer scripts surrounded the altar's remains, so old and weathered they had the soft texture of rotting cloth and crumbled to dust at my touch.

"This is fucking insane." The ruined shrine drove the truth of the crimson bear's words home. The world I'd left behind was gone. Everyone I'd ever known was dead. I tried to imagine a world without my father's stern words or my mother's kind face. It was impossible for me to wrap my head around the idea. I'd felt like I was with Mielyssi for weeks, maybe. It couldn't have been decades.

And, yet, my eyes weren't lying.

The strength and endurance I'd gained during my time with the crimson bear carried me down the last five thousand steps at a run. I wouldn't believe I'd lost everything until I'd laid eyes on my home village. If it was still there, then this all had to be some kind of delusion brought on by too much red meat and too much sex with a bear spirit.

I was in such a rush to reach the village that my feet skidded off the front edges of the last cherry-blossom-strewn steps, and I had to catch myself on my war club to keep from falling flat on my face. The air at the bottom of the stairway was thick and foul with a reeking mist that made it hard to see more than a few yards in any direction. If it hadn't been for the enormous iron towers that marked the way to my village, there's no telling how long I would have wandered through that vile fog.

Shit just kept getting better.

A long chain bridge led from the plateau on Mount Shiki's eastern flank to the stony edge of Floating Village, where I'd grown up. The bridge's surface was made up of heavy starwood planks that dangled from a pair of massive chains on a single braided strand of spider silk cord. The chains were mounted to two towers on either end of the bridge, their deep foundations sunk like the roots of ancient trees into the mountain and the slab of stone that my hometown sat on. An identical bridge on the west side of the town connected it to the Cliffs of Hedoran.

Those two bridges supported Floating Village above a deep ravine and gave the town its name. It was an impressive bit of engineering, though no one had ever been able to explain why, exactly, our ancestors had found it necessary to create an airborne village days away from the nearest real town.

The ancient engineers had done a hell of a job, anyway. The bridge hardly creaked as I crossed it, though the fierce wind that blew through the ravine caused the wooden beams to bounce and buck along the length of spider silk cord. After a few nail-biting minutes, I reached the edge of Floating Village and stepped onto more or less solid ground.

"Hello!" I called. A whippoorwill responded with a haunting cry and flapped through the dense fog that covered everything like a poisonous cloak. "Great. Looks like no one's home."

The old path that had once led from the bridge to the village square had long since been obliterated by with dense patches of coarse sawgrass that reached my thighs. Twined usulang vines hid in the weeds and threatened to trip me every other step.

If the path was a disaster, my hometown was in even worse shape. The wooden buildings weren't just neglected, they were destroyed. Black scorch marks climbed the few walls still standing. Doors had been wrenched off their hinges and tossed into the street for fungus and lichens to feast upon. Ugly yellow blight weeds had infested the village's cobbled paths, overturning stones to make room for more of their sickly siblings.

Even the ground had changed. The once-firm soil of Floating Village was spongy and dotted with deep puddles filled with croaking frogs and black snakes that swam in endless circles around their mirror-smooth surfaces. It was as if nature had gotten tired of humanity's failings and decided to reclaim the world for herself once more.

"Hello!" I shouted again when I reached the village's center.

I needed someone, anyone, to answer me. The whole village couldn't have been wiped out, not even if I'd been gone decades. There had to be something left.

"Welcome back, heretic." A tall man clad in green jade armor stepped through the fog. The sulfurous mist steamed away on contact with the thick plates that protected him. The man's face was hidden behind a demonic brass mask that left only his eyes and lips visible. Golden sigils hovered above the surface of the armor, marking the warrior as one of the Emperor of the Sevenfold Sun's Jade Seekers. These soldiers served humanity's supreme ruler personally. "We've waited a very long time for your return."

More Jade Seekers appeared around me as if summoned from the mist. They all held crescent-bladed spears adorned with sparking talismans. They moved in perfect unison and surrounded me like a noose. They were clearly professional fighters, ready and willing to do violence on my poor body at the slightest provocation.

What was most disturbing about the warriors, though, wasn't their scripted armor or fine weapons. In fact, it wasn't something they had at all. It was something they lacked.

The Jade Seekers all had seabound cores, a full level above mine, and should have had ten nodes to store and channel sacred energy. But these assholes had zero nodes.

That was all kinds of goddamned wrong. Everything that lived needed at least a single node in its core to absorb and process its life force. With no way to absorb and use that power, a nodeless person would wither and die before they could draw their first breath.

My spirit sight dug deeper into the mystery in a flash. Each of the Jade Seekers had a single connection spot at the heart of their cores. It was much like the bond that tied me to the crimson bear, but it was incredibly strong. I sensed a horrible presence behind the connection and withdrew before I could attract its attention. Who, or what, the Jade Seekers were bound to was a mystery that could wait until after I was out of danger.

"I don't want any trouble." I leaned on my war club and raised my free hand to show the warriors I meant what I said. Starting a fight with five of the Emperor's handpicked hunters seemed like a good way to get a blade through my guts. Even if I beat them all, doing so would mark me as an outlaw. I'd be hunted by their kind to the end of my days. "This was my home. What happened here?"

"This is no one's home," one of the Seekers snorted. "The Moonsilver Bat Kingdom broke faith with the Emperor. What you see here is the punishment for that treachery."

None of the words that spilled out of the man's mouth made any goddamned sense. My kingdom had safeguarded the dream meridians for thousands of years. They were the priests who'd shown the other kingdoms how to master the senjin energy that flowed through the world. Hell, my ancestors had helped to found the Empire of the Sevenfold Sun. The idea that my people, even ones I'd never met, would betray all of that wasn't just ludicrous, it was impossible.

"You're wrong." I shook my head vehemently. "There has to be another explanation. My people—"

"Enough of your babbling," the first warrior coughed and spat a wad of phlegm at my feet. "After a hundred years, this damnable watch is finally over. Let's kill the last of the Moonsilver scum. I want to go the fuck home."

"This isn't necessary." None of my options here seemed good, so I held my ground and tried not to look too threatening until I could find an opening to make my move. "We don't need to fight."

"This won't be a fight, savage." The warriors were almost within striking range. "You're already dead. Lie down. Save us some trouble and yourself a lot of pain."

"Last chance," I warned the men. I didn't want to commit the crime of fighting Jade Seekers, but if they thought they could kill me without a struggle, they were out of their fucking minds.

The crimson bear's spirit stirred within my heart as my new enemies moved around me. They shifted position and hefted their spears, ready to stick me like a pig. Any thoughts I had of a peaceful outcome vanished. They were here to murder me.

Fuck. That.

I channeled two nodes of rin energy into my techniques. The instant I activated the shamanic gifts, the crimson bear's power blossomed inside me. I felt a toothy grin split my features and a deep-throated growl rumbled in my chest. My nails hardened into the brutal Crimson Claws and my skin stiffened into the Bear's Mantle, as thick and durable as boiled leather.

The soldiers glanced at one another, then back at me. They adjusted their grips on their spears and swallowed hard. They'd been prepared to kill a young man armed only with a primitive weapon.

They weren't so sure about a pissed-off shaman.

"Drop your weapon and face your sentence," their leader choked out. "Don't make this harder on yourself than it has to be."

Nick Harrow

The bear inside my core roared a challenge at the men who dared to threaten her mate. The world turned red, and my throat ached for the taste of blood.
It was time to kill.

Chapter Four

M Y SPIRIT ANIMAL'S WRATH BOILED IN MY VEINS and propelled me into action against my enemies. I dodged a clumsy thrust from a nervous Jade Seeker and shattered his spear with a swipe of my war club. Before he could recover, I raked my claws across his face. If he'd been earthbound, the attack would have killed him instantly.

Unfortunately, the seabound warrior's core gave him the strength to survive my swipe, even if he might have wished it hadn't.

The natural weapons tore furrows through the Seeker's flesh. Blood gushed from the deep wound above his brow and filled his eyes in a blinding torrent. Tattered streamers of raw meat hung from the left side of the warrior's skull, their ends drizzling the swampy ground with sticky blood. Greasy patches of pale bone gleamed through the grisly wounds I'd inflicted.

The warrior groped at his wounded face with trembling fingers. When the tips of his fingers found the shredded ruins of his upper lip and nose, he dropped his weapon and shrieked in agonized terror. If he survived, that asshole would spend the rest of his life avoiding mirrors. Served him right for trying to stick me with the pointy end.

If the Jade Seekers had been smart, they would have immediately started poking holes in me. They outnumbered me, and their spears gave them a serious reach advantage. Even with the gifts of the bear, I couldn't have fought off four skilled warriors at the same time without suffering some serious wounds, at the very least. Fortunately for me, the sight of their screaming friend's ruined face made the enemy warriors hesitate while they pondered their own possible mutilations, and their chance to kill me slipped right through their fingers.

I shattered the knee of another Seeker with my war club and knocked him into the mud. Before his friends could react to my latest violent outburst, I leapt over the fallen warrior and sprinted into the fog as fast as my supernaturally speedy legs could carry me. I had to get clear of the Seekers and give myself space to figure out my next move without a bunch of assholes trying to kill me.

From behind me, the Emperor's warriors shouted for help.

Apparently, they had friends.

Awesome.

I wove a serpentine course through the ruins of Floating Village, and my childhood memories warred with the changes that had happened while I'd been bedded down with Mielyssi. Entire sections of the village had been torn down, rebuilt, and then torn down again. I recognized a few landmarks, like the Moonsilver Bat's temple, but there was much, much more that I didn't recognize at all. There were even the scattered ruins of buildings that had once stood several stories tall, something I never would have imagined when I'd left my hometown to chase down my dream.

The world had moved on without me. My parents had grown old and passed away believing I'd died trying to become a shaman against their advice. My unfortunate fate had probably been used to convince my friends to listen to their parents.

If only those friends had known I'd spent years in the embrace of a horny spirit animal, they might have realized that sometimes it pays to pursue your dreams, however crazy they might seem to someone else.

Hoarse cries of anger interrupted my thoughts. There were at least a dozen other men out there in the fog, maybe more. With the men still in the town square, I rounded up the number of my enemies to an even twenty. I would have been flattered that the Emperor had thought so highly of me to send such a large force if I wasn't more concerned that one of those motherfuckers would soon cut my head off my shoulders.

The vile mist that blanketed the village did an excellent job of hiding me from the hunters, and the clatter and clang of their heavy armor both announced their presence and drowned out the quiet pad of my soft-soled boots against the earth. That combination let me slip through the first wave of reinforcements without being spotted, and I hunkered down in the shadow of a burned-out shell of a building to get my bearings.

The number of voices in the fog grew by the second, and I revised my count of their numbers up to thirty, then forty. Floating Village wasn't very large. If they kept adding to the hunting party, they'd be able to encircle the whole damned thing and cut off my escape routes. My only hope of survival lay in getting the fuck off this hunk of rock and into the wilderness. Out there, the skills the crimson bear had taught me would make it impossible for even experienced woodsmen to find me.

There were only two ways out of Floating Village. The first was the east bridge to Mount Shiki. That exit was a no-go because Mielyssi sealed the top of the stairs behind me. The second way was the wider suspension bridge to the west that led to the Cliffs of Hedoran. If I made it across that bridge, I'd be a stone's throw from Ruliko's Wood.

That was a big fucking if, though.

It's not like you've got a choice.

Mielyssi's voice jolted me like a bee sting. The voice had been so faint that I might have imagined it. It was also completely right—the only options I had were to go for the bridge or wait until the Seekers finally surrounded me and slit my throat.

The bridge it was, then. I slipped out of my hiding place, my heavy spiked war club over my right shoulder and ready to swing, and made my way toward the western edge of the village.

There were far more Seekers in the mist than I'd counted. Flashes of scripted jade armor lit up the gloom in every direction, and they'd formed a circle of searchers that closed around me with every passing second.

And as they grew stronger, my techniques started to fade. In a handful more minutes, the protection from my shamanic powers would be gone, forcing me to spend more rin to reactivate them. With only three nodes still filled, I couldn't afford that. Once my core was empty, I'd have to rest and restore my rin before I could accomplish anything.

Time was always, always, too goddamned short.

I prowled inside the noose of hunters, invisible and silent to my pursuers, looking for a gap I could slip through. All I needed was a hole a few yards wide, and I'd be gone like a ghost. After minutes of frustration at the orderly advance of the Seekers, I finally found a weak point. Just in time for my techniques to wear off. Looked like I had to do everything the hard way.

One of the warriors had sheltered on the downwind side of a crumbling stone wall to light the brown twist of his cigarette. I recognized what was left of the place as the ruin of Old Lady Lyri's candy shop. I'd spent countless afternoons there, running errands for a handful of sticky sour treats.

I'd never imagined I'd have to kill a man in its shadow.

The guard had raised his helmet's green visor to puff on his smoke. It was the last mistake he'd ever make. Blinded by the orange flare of his cigarette and the cloud of thick, gray smoke it spewed, he didn't see me emerge from the shadows.

My war club smashed into the Seeker's face and buried its spikes deep in his gray matter. The impact of the skull-cracking blow vibrated through my weapon with stinging force and nearly shook it loose from my grasp. I tightened my fingers around the weapon's handle and ripped it free of the dead man's head. The spikes pulled the Seeker's skull open to reveal the shredded mass of his brain through the crushed wreckage of his sinuses.

The guard collapsed onto his face, and the pulped goo inside his skull sloshed out and splattered on the weed-choked cobblestone path like a dropped bowl of pudding.

"Gross." I carefully stepped over the mess I'd made. If I slipped in the corpse's brains the other Seekers would be on top of me before I could escape. That would be embarrassing as hell.

Before the fallen Seeker's companions realized he was down, I loped into the ruins through the gap I'd created and headed for the bridge. The disgusting mist clung to my skin in oily beads and turned my breechcloth into a sodden strip that slapped against the insides of my thighs with every step. I hoped the world outside Floating Village wasn't cloaked in this fucking mess.

After five nerve-racking minutes of fleeing through the ruins, I finally saw the bridge looming out of the mist ahead of me. Its chains, each as thick as my waist, were attached to mighty iron towers at the near end of the suspended structure. The rusty chains faded to indistinct streaks as they rose through the heavy mist toward the enormous support pillars at the center of the bridge. Despite all the time that had passed since I last saw the massive thing, it was still intact and ready for me to run over it to freedom.

As soon as I killed the two Seekers who guarded it.

The one on my left fiddled with something in his belt pouch, while the warrior to my right pierced the gloom with a hawk's penetrating glare. They stood yards apart and faced away from one another to cover all angles of approach to the bridge. That made my job a little easier, since I'd have a few seconds to fight one of them without the other one jumping into the battle. It also made things harder because I couldn't take them both out at the same time.

"Ah, well," I whispered to the tiny peep frogs who'd gathered on the swampy ground around me while I watched my targets. "Beggars can't be choosers."

I bided my time and stayed as still as a rat under an owl's shadow. The guards grumbled at the weather and muttered to one another without moving from their posts. During the half hour I watched the bastards, they didn't take a break to shit or piss, and neither of them allowed themselves to be distracted from their watch for more than a handful of seconds.

"Fucking professionals." The frogs chirped their agreement that the world was a much safer and more pleasant place when your enemies were incompetent scumbags.

The sounds of the other guards grew fainter by the moment. As near as I could tell, their circle would reach the village's center in another fifteen minutes. When they met up there, they'd know I'd slipped through their net and they'd come back this way, pissed as hell.

I needed to get across that bridge, right fucking now. I debated using my techniques for a few moments, then decided against spending any more rin. The seabound warriors were tough, but I had the advantage of surprise and a few other tricks up my sleeve. If I really needed the techniques, I could always pull them out for an encore presentation of ass-kicking.

The guard on the left was closer to me, and I charged at him with my war club raised high over my head. The enhanced speed and strength of my earthbound core let me cover the ground between us in the blink of an eye.

Surprised by my sudden appearance out of the gloom, the Seeker fumbled his spear into the mud at his feet. He raised his hands in a feeble defense and cried out in alarm.

Fucker couldn't even have the decency to die without making a racket.

My war club hammered the top of the Seeker's head and shattered his jade helmet with a surprisingly musical tinkling. The ruined helmet still saved the man's life by turning away just enough of my blow to send the war club's spikes into his armored shoulder rather than through the crown of his skull. The impact was strong enough to drive the man to his knees and open ugly black cracks in his heavy armor.

It just wasn't strong enough to kill him, and now the battle was two Seekers versus one shaman. Not exactly awesome odds.

The second bridge guard liked the way the fight was shaping up and dove right into the fray. He jabbed his spear at my guts in a blur of punchy strikes that put me on the defensive. He pressed his advantage and shouted for his friend to grab his weapon and flank me.

That wasn't cool.

Facing two trained Jade Seekers with enhanced cores at the same time was a surefire way to get stabbed, so it was time to even the odds. I dug my toes into the mud, clenched my war club in a two-handed grip, and eyeballed my foes.

The one on my right, who still had his helmet, was a little more eager than his partner. He advanced with quick, even steps and kept his spear aimed at my heart. His maneuver pushed me away from the bridge and gave his partner time to retrieve the weapon he'd dropped.

His wounded buddy, who had a bloody nose, two black eyes, and—judging from the way he wobbled as he walked—a concussion, advanced more slowly. He looked ready to back his friend's play, but he clearly didn't want me to ring his bell again.

His hesitation to get up close and personal with me was the only real hope I had of winning this lopsided fight. I feinted toward the uninjured guard, who dodged back from the whistling sweep of my spiked war club and raised his spear to protect himself. It was a perfect defense.

Just like I'd hoped.

The warrior's switch to defense gave me the necessary space and time to channel a node of rin from my core to activate Earthen Darts. The technique erupted in front of my target, hurling darts of hardened earth straight at his face.

Or, at least, that's what the technique would have done if the entire area hadn't been saturated with brackish water. Instead of sharp missiles meant to pierce the Seeker's helmet and kill him dead, the technique threw sprays of reeking mud that splattered across the man's visor. Effectively blinded, the warrior cursed and scraped at the goo with the back of one gauntleted hand. That hadn't gone quite the way I'd expected, but the mud splash had taken one of my enemies out of the fight for the moment.

I'd take it.

The wounded fighter got his balls back and charged toward my left side. He was clumsy and slow from the head wound I'd given him, and the tip of his spear wobbled drunkenly. What he lacked in finesse he made up for in raw aggression. Mud sprayed from around his heavy jade boots, and he roared a wordless battle cry as he covered the distance between us at a full-on sprint.

I pivoted on my left foot and slipped away from his attack.

The Seeker shot past me, feet churning the mud in a futile attempt to stop his headlong rush.

I spun and slammed my war club into the base of the warrior's skull. His head shattered with a wet crunch and his body sagged to the wet ground, threads of tainted senjin unravelling from his core.

The blinded Seeker had decided the better part of valor was to back the fuck away and try out whatever dirty tricks he had up his sleeve. His right hand dug in the pouch at his belt, furiously searching for something to save his miserable hide.

There was no telling what he had in there. I charged at him, determined to finish this fight before the Jade Seeker could unleash a script grenade or some other damnable device that would blast me into a fine red mist.

The bastard found what he needed before I could pulp his face. It was much worse than any weapon I could have imagined.

He raised a thin bone rod into the air and snapped it between his fingers.

An unearthly wail exploded from the shattered spirit siren. Birds burst into frenzied flight, frogs dove into puddles of water, and even the mosquitoes suddenly had other places to be. The sound was bone chilling and so loud I knew my ears would be ringing for the next hour.

"Fucking asshole." I closed with the Seeker and grabbed his still-raised arm with my left hand. Before he could react, I wrenched the captured limb around behind him, seized his elbow with my right hand, and expressed my displeasure with his little stunt by twisting my hands in two very different directions.

Violently.

The Seeker's shoulder and elbow gave way inside his armor with wet pops, transforming his arm into a limp sack filled with meat and bone. The scream that tore itself free of his throat was nearly as loud as the spirit siren's wail. I hoisted him over my head by his groin and wounded shoulder, hauled him to the edge of Floating Village, and tossed his sorry ass into the ravine.

Angry voices burst from the mist behind me. The siren's shrill cry had summoned the Seekers, and they were closer than I'd hoped. Another two minutes, three at the most, and they'd be on top of me.

It was time to get the hell out of town.

The bridge from Floating City was twenty feet wide and ten times that long, and when the wind blew it bucked like a bee stung stallion despite its enormous size.

It was very windy just then.

"Of course," I growled and stepped onto the undulating bridge. Thirty seconds later, I'd made my way halfway across the bridge despite its best efforts to throw me off its back to my doom.

A slow clap from the far side of the chasm mocked my achievement.

My tormentor emerged from the mist surrounded by a brilliant blue aura that told me he was the proud and powerful owner of a skybound core. That put him two levels above me and meant I was in for a very serious ass-kicking if I didn't come up with a truly awesome plan in the next few seconds. The arrogant asshole strode across the dancing bridge as if its surface was as still and stable as a marble slab. His armor was thicker and heavier than the other Seekers, its jade plates etched with glowing scripts, and his helmet was crowned by a pair of antlers that shed radiant sparks like autumn's leaves with every step he took. His aura glowed like molten gold around him, and his core was a dazzling sphere of roiling flame. This dickhead looked like something out of a storybook and scared the living shit out of me. He didn't look any less terrifying to my spirit sight.

His skybound core was two full levels above my training, and just two levels short of Mielyssi's power. He had an offensive and defensive technique, as well, though I wasn't sure how he could use them when his core held no nodes. Like the other Jade Seekers, he was bound to something or someone much more powerful.

If this guy got his hands on me, my quest to save the world would come to a sudden and painful end.

"It is the Emperor's will that the Moonsilver Bat Kingdom be annihilated." The nightmare that continued walking toward me had pronounced the death sentence of my entire kingdom with the casual, bored air of a man with much more interesting things he could be doing. "Thank you for coming down off that damned mountain so I can finally put an end to this endless vigil."

"Or, you could step aside and let me go about my business." The cocky words sounded a lot braver than I felt. The two nodes of rin I had left in my core wouldn't be enough to dent this guy's armor.

"Kyr Nissil." He spat out the syllables of my name like they tasted bad. "You are the last of the Moonsilver Bat's people. You are condemned to death by the word of the Midnight Emperor. Kneel and accept your fate."

"Nope." Before he'd started talking, this piece of dog shit had had me rattled. As soon as he started in with the death threats and the proclamations from his boss, my spine stiffened and my balls grew three sizes.

This guy, the voice of some authority from a thousand miles away, thought he could push me around on my home turf? This was exactly the kind of asshole that had made me want to be a shaman in the first place. I'd go down swinging before I'd give in to this officious dickface.

"Know that your petty resistance only adds to your crimes, boy. Your honor will be tainted by your cowardice and criminal ways, even in the afterlife." The obvious commander of the Jade Seekers reached for the hilt above his right shoulder with both hands. "Please, feel free to continue debasing yourself. It will only make my pleasure at your death that much greater."

The prick's armor was twice as thick as the plate worn by the other Seekers, and that had only cracked with all the weight of the crimson bear's power behind it. The scripts that blazed across its surface would add to his defenses. I wouldn't be able to beat his protection with my war club or my bear's claws.

The asshole hadn't left me many options.

I charged. There were two nodes of rin left in my core, and I burned them both to stiffen my hide against his attacks and give me something to grab hold of him with if shit went south. The techniques might not win the fight, but they could keep me from getting my head knocked off on his first swing. That'd have to be good enough.

Confident his armor would shield him from whatever damage I could dish out, the Jade Seeker didn't even try to defend himself as he drew his sword.

I reached him at the same moment that enormous sword's point was at its zenith. The blade was the color of lightning and it moaned with a young woman's lusty voice. It was a powerful weapon, the kind of thing a hero out of myths would wield when he went off to slaughter demons. Its presence was terrifyingly awesome, and the sight of it made me want to piss myself and run far, far away. Even scarier, his offensive technique flared to life, surrounding the blade with black flames.

So, yeah. I couldn't let the sword touch me.

From the Jade Seeker's casual posture, he knew the effect his weapon had on his enemies. He probably expected me to give into that fear and let him slice my head off. I was a simple savage who couldn't possibly pose any threat to him.

"Surprise, motherfucker." I dropped my shoulder on the last step of my charge and threw all my weight behind it. In the same instant, I shoved the shaft of my weapon between the asshole's legs and bent all my bear-given strength into him.

The combination of my supernatural strength and the war club's leverage threw the heavily armored man off-balance. His lead foot skidded out from under him and he flung his left arm out to try to balance himself. Unfortunately, the weight of the massive weapon in his right fist dragged him even further off kilter.

The Seeker howled and fell backward through the gap in the bridge's support chains. He swiped his enormous sword at me with one hand, and I stepped aside to let the clumsy attack slide past my face.

It was his other hand I should have been worried about.

The bastard flung a kunai at me as he fell. It sailed through the air and punched into my flesh just to the right of my navel. A wave of cold pain washed through me, and my earthbound core throbbed with frigid agony.

My legs wobbled beneath me, and I only stayed upright by bracing myself on my war club. Weakness spread through my body from my core, and all I wanted to do was lie down and sleep off the pain that threatened to overwhelm me.

The other Seekers had reached the end of the bridge. They'd be on top of me in seconds.

I staggered toward the cliffs, left hand clutched to the blade stuck in my guts, war club dragged along behind me.

"Don't run from me, you coward." The fallen warrior's fingers had caught the edge of the bridge. By some miracle the weight of his armor hadn't dragged him to his death. Just my fucking luck. "I am Jiro Kos, first hunter of the Midnight Emperor, Lord Commander of the Jade Seekers. You will face your doom at my hand."

"You already know my name." I dug the kunai out of my side and flipped it onto the planks in front of him. If I hadn't been wounded, if the other Seekers had been just a little farther away, I would have stomped that cocksucker's fingers into bloody goo. There just wasn't time. "Fuck you."

Chapter Five

THE JADE SEEKERS HAD A PROBLEM.

Their Emperor had told them very plainly to murder the ever-loving shit out of me. Also, their commander was hanging onto the edge of a bridge a thousand feet above the floor of a very rocky ravine by the slipping fingers of one hand. A man could chase me, or he could save his commander. He couldn't do both.

Every man in that unit had to weigh that choice before they could do either one. That gave me a handful of seconds to drag my sorry ass farther along the bridge while they argued about who, exactly, should do which job.

My side ached where the kunai had punched through my skin, and my core felt as raw as a whore's cooch during parade week. If I could evade the Seekers and meditate to cycle more rin into my nodes, my body would stitch itself back together. The stronger my core became, the more powerful its ability to heal itself. Earthbound should be a high enough level to deal with that little poke.

I hoped.

The wound hurt out of all proportion to the inch-wide, half-inch-deep hole the kunai had poked through me. The ridiculous pain and ache in my core worried me. That bastard Jiro Kos had done something to me.

Something very, very bad.

I forced myself to run the last twenty feet to the far end of the bridge despite the gnawing ache of my wound. It took all the willpower I could muster to push myself to widen the gap between my poor abused body and the tips of the spears behind me.

My dream of vanishing into the woods slithered out of my grasp. The Seekers were too close to me, and I was too weak to lead them on a chase long enough to lose them. I struggled to think through the blinding pain that radiated from my side with every step. My thoughts scattered like frightened birds from the agony, and every plan I dredged up seemed worse than the last. It was time for something desperate.

The Jade Seekers jeered at me, certain they were about to turn me into a pincushion. The tips of their spears danced in front of my blurred vision. So very, very close.

And yet, so very, very far away.

A single rope of woven spider silk secured all of the bridge's timbers to the enormous chains. That cord was no thicker than my thumb, but it was incredibly resilient and so strong it was said even war mammoths couldn't pull it apart. The woven strand had withstood centuries of neglect and weather. It had a dull silver solidity to it that looked like it would last forever.

And it came apart with a single swipe of my claws.

The bridge to Floating Village, the last link to my home, disintegrated like a child's poorly made toy. The severed spider silk cord unraveled, and the heavy timbers it had supported plunged into the foggy abyss.

Along with all of the motherfucking Jade Seekers and their leader.

The warriors screamed as they fell, and scavenging birds mocked them with cries of their own. The sudden change in the bridge's tension wrenched the enormous chains that had held it aloft, and the ancient iron groaned. Its links shattered and rained broken iron into the ravine, pummeling the Seekers and dragging the bridge's ruined supports into the depths.

I sagged with relief. The Jade Seekers were gone.

And so was Floating Village.

I wanted to honor the fallen ruins of my former home. I tried to think of something wise to say, something that would be a proper homage to all the souls who had lived and died here.

"Goodbye." Sorry, that was the best I could do with the pain in my side.

I sat down on the stony ground and took a good look at the hole Jiro had punched in me. It wasn't surrounded by radiating black lines, and the blood that leaked out of it was still bright red. That ruled out the scariest poisons I knew.

First things first. I needed to restore my rin and let its power heal my wounds. While my breathing technique could gather sacred energy anywhere, the rocky, windswept cliffs wouldn't have much power to offer. I limped away from the stony precipice and down the rutted caravan trail that led into the forest. A few agonizing minutes later, I was surrounded by towering pine trees.

And the smell of cooking meat.

My nose led me off the path and between tightly packed evergreen boles. The pain in my core radiated through me with every step, making me feel as brittle as old glass. I needed rin to heal, but the lure of food was too strong to resist. I'd eat, restore my rin, then heal myself.

Step one of my masterful plan went off without a hitch. I discovered the camp of the Jade Seekers, and no one rushed out to try to kill me. With any luck at all, they'd all gone into the village to find me and were now lying in a pile of broken bodies at the bottom of the ravine.

I ate big bites of roasted forest pig right off the spit at the heart of their camp. It tasted so good I didn't even care about the hot grease that scalded my lips. The succulent pork filled my belly nearly to bursting and restored some of my flagging strength. Fighting Jade Seekers is hungry work.

Next, I parked my ass on a flat stone near the fire, closed my eyes, and took in a deep breath. My nostrils picked up the sweet, meaty aroma of the pig. Beyond that I detected the scents of oil and leather from a tent off to my right. The clean aroma of running water came from a spring deeper in the woods, and the pine trees themselves flooded the small clearing with their crisp, fresh perfume. A trickle of rin flowed into me along with the forest's smells.

The sacred energy coiled inside my core like a snake ready to strike. It writhed in a restless circle that ratcheted up the pain in my center to a blinding fury. The energy that should have soothed my soul and helped cure me erupted with fever-hot spikes of agony. Every beat of my heart carried fresh jolts of pain to my head, where it took root and bloomed into a killer migraine.

What the fuck was going on here?

I focused my spirit sight on my core and groaned at the magmic ball of orange and black inside me. Rin, the masculine energy of the spirit world, should have been purest red. If I'd had any shio, the feminine energy, it would have glowed a deep, clean blue. And if I combined the two sacred energies into senjin, the blood of dreams, it would gleam like a polished mirror.

Unless it was tainted. Then the senjin would be as black as tar.

"Fucking asshole infected me," I growled and staggered to my feet.

Jiro Kos's weapon had injected a trace of corrupted senjin into my core, which explained why I felt so shitty. Adding rin had triggered a chain reaction between the two types of energy and filled me with destructive energy. If I didn't purge the foul corruption from my core, soon, it would eat me from the inside out.

"Feverfew to bring down the heat," I muttered as I prowled through the deserted camp in search of an infirmary tent. The Jade Seekers had been here for the long haul; they had to have some supplies I could use. "Ginger to soothe the energies. Narisin oil to purge the sickness."

I tore through the first, second, and third tents without finding anything other than second-string weapons, a few scraps of dried jerky, and the personal effects of the Jade Seekers who, thanks to me, would never need them again.

I searched more tents until my head felt like it would burst and my skin was slick with sweat from the tainted senjin burning inside me. My core was a knot of agony that consumed my strength at an alarming rate. If I didn't find what I needed very soon, I'd end up on my face, praying for death to free me from the torture.

"Jackpot," I groaned when I found Jiro's tent. On the outside, it was the same oiled canvas as the other tents, but on the inside it looked more like a luxury apartment.

Jiro traveled with every creature comfort he could cram into his private space. Chests overflowing with foods kept fresh by powerful scripts painted around their rims. A cot enchanted with sigils that kept it soft and comfortable, no matter the outside conditions. Cones of eternal essence that could erase a man's most terrible moods and ensure a good night's sleep. A cool, springy rug that covered the tent's floor and felt amazing against my bare feet.

And, there, in a rack against the far wall, were enough elixirs, pellets, capsules, and tinctures to cure a small army of whatever ailed it.

The medicine labels swam in front of me, jumping around like a pack of drunken monkeys. I couldn't make heads or tails of what was on the rack, and I'd be dead long before I could open each bottle or packet and puzzle out what it contained. Desperate for a cure, or at least something to buy me time to find a cure, I let my spirit sight guide me to the most potent sources of sacred energy.

Most of the bottles were bland gray smears, useless by themselves. A few glowed like bright red spikes, a sure sign they were dangerous if not outright poisonous. The blue blurs I needed were all gathered together on the rack's lower shelves.

"Finally," I slurred. My numb fingers fumbled with the brightest of glowing phials. I pinched the large vessel's neck between my thumb and forefinger, dragged it out of its resting place, and promptly fell on my ass.

I had no idea what was in the phial, and I didn't care. The brilliant sapphire-blue glow inside it promised some sort of potent healing power. It had to be good enough. The phial's wax lid cracked under pressure from my thumb, and I tipped its contents into my mouth.

Or tried to anyway.

Blue smoke drifted out of the bottle and flicked across my lips like the warm, wet tip of a woman's tongue. A whiff of the sea—salty and wild—tickled my nose. The smoke flowed into my nostrils when I inhaled, and out through my mouth. It lingered on the bare skin of my chest and pooled in the spaces between my abdominal muscles like warm water.

"He's sick." A woman's voice, light and lilting.

"He's dying." A second woman, this one's tone firmer and harder than the first.

"His core is infected with the vile power." Soft fingers traced the outline of my core around the aching heat of my solar plexus. "Help me, Aja."

My blurred vision gave way to fever dreams. The smoke separated itself into two clouds, one the pale blue of a spring sky, the other sapphire shot through with crimson threads. The lighter portion settled over my body, cooling my flesh and growing heavier and more solid by the moment. It took on a woman's shape, lithe and translucent, long strands of cloudy hair hanging around her stormy eyes. She straddled my belly and pressed herself flat against my chest like a living blanket.

A hand formed from the sapphire cloud, and its slender fingers unknotted my cord belt and flung my breechcloth away. Those same fingers formed a warm fist around my cock. Each finger tightened and relaxed in an undulating pattern that made me forget, at least for the moment, that I had a ticking supernatural time bomb stuck inside me.

I was too stunned to protest, not that I would have stopped the pleasure coiled around me for any reason.

The pale blue woman on top of me lowered her face to mine and caught my lower lip between her teeth. Her cool breath gusted into my mouth and flowed down my throat. The heat in my core lessened instantly, and the threads of pain stitched through my flesh frayed and began to dissipate. She breathed in, sucking my breath deep inside her, and the weight of her body on mine became more solid, more real. Her hips bore down on me, the firm mounds of her breasts flattened against my chest, and her hands roamed over my face as if she needed to memorize every curve and plane.

Maybe I was delirious. Or dying. Fuck it. If this was how my life ended, I'd go out with a smile.

I tangled my hands in the blue woman's white hair and pulled her mouth to mine. Her lips were like splashes of seawater, her tongue a flicker of lightning that danced between my lips with increasing urgency. We kissed with wild abandon, fierce and hungry, and she pressed her body against me as if desperate for contact between us.

The hand below my waist vanished with a suddenness that left me gasping. It reappeared without warning and entwined its fingers through mine. The deep blue hand pulled my arm down below the woman on top of me, who lifted her hips and let out a faint, eager moan as my captured hand slipped between her legs.

The mist woman raised up and leaned back, coating my hand with slick heat as she ground against my fingers. Her body grew more substantial with every second, and her blue skin glistened with fine beads of sweat that flickered with mesmerizing firefly patterns. Her deep blue nipples jutted toward the tent's ceiling as she arched her back, and the damp ends of her long hair brushed against my thighs. She grabbed my free hand and pulled it to her chest, holding it tight over her galloping heart.

Slick fingers slipped away from my other hand, and a taller woman with blazing red hair appeared behind the mist woman. The newcomer's face and heavy breasts were flushed a red so deep it almost matched her hair, and her plump lips parted in a wicked grin that showed me twin lines of straight, white teeth.

"Be one with us," she moaned, and knelt beside me. Her hand, still dripping wet, slid down the length of my prick in a slow stroke, then back up again. The sensation was an excruciating tease that pulled my thoughts into a spiral of animal need.

I squeezed the breast of the woman astride me, then traced the outline of her dark nipple with the pad of my thumb. The first two fingers of my other hand slipped inside her to meet the downward pressure of her hips. She tightened around my fingers and moaned as her muscles pulled me in deeper.

"Now," she begged. "I need this."

The redhead leaned over me, her hand still working with an agonizingly slow rhythm. Her hair formed a curtain around her face, and all I saw was the fiery glow of her tiger's eyes. Her breath was hot and wild, a predator's scent that drove me insane with desire. I lifted my head and nipped at her lower lip with a guttural growl.

"Now." She shifted her hand's position as the mist woman raised her hips off my fingers.

Wet warmth enveloped my cock, and I thrust my hips up to meet the blue woman's weight. We cried out together, and I found the redhead's eager sex with my wet fingers and stroked the swollen bulb of her clit with my thumb. I kissed the flame-haired woman in a bestial frenzy, and she met my passion with her own bruising lust.

The world vanished from around us. I didn't feel the tent's plush carpet, or the clammy chill of the mist-choked air. My universe narrowed to a tangle of fingers and heaving breasts, of hungry mouths and grinding hips. The women shifted positions so fluidly and frequently it felt like I'd sometimes start a thrust fucking one and end deep inside the other.

We burst into a ragged chorus of groans and gasps. I came in gouts of pleasure that tightened every muscle in my body. My shaft and fingers were surrounded by quivering flesh that clung desperately to me as rapturous pulses spread through the three of us in an endless torrent of mind-bending ecstasy.

We collapsed in a panting heap, the women flanking me, their legs draped over my thighs, their hands tracing the patterns of the scars my struggles with the crimson bear had left on my shoulders. The white-haired woman nuzzled my throat, her lips tracing a line between my ear and the hollow of my collarbone and back again. The redhead stared at me with brazenly appraising eyes.

"You've lain with the crimson bear." She said the words as if they were the most obvious thing in the world. "And you're still alive. Impressive for a mortal."

"What the fuck are you talking about?" I had no idea how she knew about Mielyssi, but I wasn't going to confirm her suspicions until I knew more about her and her motives.

"The smell," the redhead said and took a deep breath to emphasize the point. "It's earthy and wild. I've never smelled anything else like it. Can you introduce us?"

"No." I let out a deep sigh. It was going to be a long goddamned time until I made it back to Mount Shiki. "How do you know what she smells like?"

"It's one of my gifts." She shrugged. "If you see the bear again, tell her I appreciate what she taught you."

"Thanks." I stroked the woman's red mane and plucked tangles from it with my fingers. The mention of the spirit animal teased a grin from my sleepy memory. The sex with her had been more ferocious and dangerous than what I'd shared with these women. Not better or worse, just different from the healing pleasure I'd just experienced. "I'm her shaman, Kyr."

"I'm Aja." She propped herself up on one elbow. "That's Ayo. How do you feel, Shaman Kyr?"

"Just Kyr," I said. Somehow the two of them had used sex to split the corrupted senjin into purified rin, which now filled my core's five nodes, and shio that glowed inside them. "I feel great. How about you?"

"Alive." She showed me her predator's grin. "We were in that bottle for far too long."

"You can say that again," Ayo chimed in from my left side. She, too, raised up on one elbow and stared at me with glowing crystal eyes. "It's been a long time since we've felt better. Our cores are filled again, and we have bodies. Your core looks good, too. We cleaned you right up."

"You'll have to show me how you did that." I knew a lot of shaman tricks, but fucking corrupted sacred energy out of someone wasn't on the list of things the crimson bear had taught me.

"We will." Aja bit down on my earlobe. "After."

"After?"

"After we do that again." Ayo shoved Aja's leg off me and straddled my hips.

"Now?"

"Unless you want us to die." Aja raked her nails down my chest just shy of drawing blood.

"We definitely can't have that." I squeezed the taut muscles of her ass in both hands. "At least not until you teach me that trick."

Chapter Six

I WOKE THE NEXT MORNING WITH AYO AND AJA sleeping on either side of me, heads on my chest, their hair spilling down my torso in a vivid clash of blue and scarlet. They breathed slowly, evenly, and perfectly in sync with one another. I was surprised to find my breath in time with theirs, as well. Our little cuddle puddle felt less like three distinct bodies than a single creature with six lungs and three hearts.

Which, by the way, all beat in perfect rhythm, too.

That was weird.

It also raised my hackles and made me wonder just how much crazy I'd stuck my dick in. Before I made a move to wake the lovely, and possibly insane, creatures sprawled on and around me, I needed to know more about them. My spirit sight roamed over their naked bodies and showed me some very interesting details about them, starting with the fact that they weren't even remotely human.

Ayo was a river spirit with two nodes in her core, both now filled with shio. The vibrant blue connection in the center of her core identified her as a familiar bound to a feminine practitioner of the sacred arts. Aja was a hunting spirit and also had two nodes and a familiar's binding within her core. It was hard to be certain, but it appeared they were both bound to the same practitioner, which explained how close they seemed to be. Both spirits had a technique, but I couldn't get a read on what those techniques did.

The pair reminded me of Mielyssi in many ways, though they weren't nearly as powerful. Unlike humans and other higher-order creatures, spirit cores weren't categorized by level or type. A spirit's power was measured solely by the number of nodes they contained, and the only thing that limited that power was the age and experience of the spirit. Some of the most ancient spirits were said to be more powerful than even the Emperor, and some priests claimed he was nearly a god himself.

While knowing what kinds of creatures I'd been in bed with the night before was enlightening, it didn't tell me all that much because they were also familiars. A mist spirit could be as benign as a warm spoonful of honey, but if she served a killer, then her master's demeanor could bleed into her personality. More worrisome, one of the spirits was a hunter.

She could easily have been sent out here to hunt me.

"You think very loudly," Aja grumbled. She shifted her position, and the soft weight of her breast settled against my side. "Please stop."

"They can't do that." Ayo sat up, stretched, and yawned. Her lean frame glowed with the inner vitality of her crystal-clear core. She shook her hair out in the most distracting way possible, breasts swaying in the first rays of dawn, which found their way through the tent's open flap. "It's what makes mortals so adorable."

"Who sent you?" The question sounded a lot ruder out loud than it had in my head.

Aja frowned at me. She dragged her nails through the tangles in her red hair as she considered an answer, opened her mouth as if about to speak, then returned to grooming herself.

"It's complicated." Ayo adjusted her legs and sat cross-legged next to me. She smiled when my gaze drifted to the velvet shadow between her thighs, and a faint blue blush crept into her cheeks. "We're bound servitors."

"But our mistress can no longer communicate with us." Aja rested her hand on the flat of my stomach and walked her fingers along the lines of my muscles. "We've been away from her so long her thoughts are less than whispers to us now."

"Though we've not been gone as long as you." Ayo corralled her white hair and tied it into a sloppy braid to get it out of her face. "Our mistress has been waiting a very long time to see you."

"You aren't making any sense." I rubbed my face with the palms of my hands and let out a frustrated sigh. "If the crimson bear is right, I've been gone for decades. And yet the minute I show up in my old village a bunch of assholes try to kill me and the two of you ambush-heal me. Thanks, by the way."

"You're welcome." Ayo bounced happily and clapped her hands together. "Surely you can see that this isn't a mere coincidence. The stars were aligned to announce your coming to our mistress, and she sent us to find you."

"We'd planned to go up the mountain after you." Aja's hand stopped moving and she shuddered. "That asshole Jiro Kos captured us before we could reach the second gate. The things he planned to do to us..."

"The Jade Seekers are the Emperor's agents." I furrowed my brow and tried to make sense of this. "Why would the ruler of all humanity send his most trusted servants out to murder a neophyte shaman and capture a couple of spirits?"

"The world has changed." Ayo leaned into me, her head resting on my shoulder. She took my hand in hers and pressed my knuckles against the swell of her breast. "It's sick. There isn't much time left before this world dies."

"The world can't die." I sat up and drew my knees up to my chin. I didn't want to hear this bullshit. It was all too much to take in at once.

Aja adjusted her position and leaned on my right shoulder to mirror Ayo. The pair of them wrapped their arms around me and held on tight. I'd be a liar if I said their bodies pressed against mine didn't make me just a little more willing to hear them out.

"You're a shaman. You know this strange mist that clings to everything is foul." Aja stroked my arm with one soft hand. "You can't deny that there is something very wrong happening."

I struggled to avoid the truth of what the spirits said. I concentrated on the way they felt against me, their breasts pressed into my arms, the heat of their breath against my skin. Any distraction was a welcome one if it kept me from contemplating this horrible new world I'd been cast out into.

Because I did feel something evil in the air. It squirmed against my spiritual senses and left a strange crawling sensation in my core. There was a darkness out in the world, coiled up like a centipede in the bottom of a water jug, just waiting for its chance to fuck my life right in the mouth.

"What am I supposed to do about it?" I wrapped an arm around each of the spirits. "If the Jade Seekers are villains now, that means the Emperor and the other leaders are, too."

"The last true emperor has been in his tomb for more than a hundred years, Kyr." Ayo kissed the side of my neck and cupped my chin in her hands.

The Emperor had been a man in his prime when I'd left for my vision quest. Given his access to life-extending senjin treatments, he couldn't have died from natural causes.

"I'm no hero." I was a kid. A strong kid with more experience and shaman powers than your average teen, sure. That didn't make me the star of some legend about saving the world. "I can't march across the Sevenfold Empire and kick in the Emperor's door to have a chat about how to fix this. I'm not a hero."

"Then you better learn to be one." Aja's fingers tightened on my bicep, and the tips of her nails poked into my skin just shy of making me wince. "Our mistress will soon be dead. She read the auguries and sent us to find you because there is no one else who can do what needs to be done."

"What is it she thinks I can do?" I couldn't take sitting down for even a second longer. My stomach was empty, my bladder was full, and my thoughts were chasing themselves in impossible circles. I surged to my feet and stormed out of the tent. I didn't want to hear any more of this shit. Everyone wanted to lay the burden at my feet, but I didn't see anyone around to help carry the load.

The latrine's sour stink was easy to pick out with my sharp senses, and I stomped over to its edge to take a piss in peace. I owed those spirits my life, there was no denying that, but the words that spilled out of them sounded like bad fairy tales. I didn't know what had gotten into me when Mielyssi had told me the same thing. Everything had seemed so much more believable up on the mountain. Down here, it all seemed like bullshit.

The crimson bear had kept me as her personal fuck toy for decades. My village had changed so much it was almost unrecognizable, and there'd been no sign of the people who'd lived there. I could accept that, as much as it was starting to annoy me.

But the world couldn't die.

That was just crazy talk.

"You can save it." Aja planted her feet next to mine and crouched down to unleash a torrent of piss into the latrine's trench. "They hunted down all the other shamans, trapped the witches with spells to rob them of their power. Even those tree-fucking druids got it in the neck when the Midnight Empire clawed its way to power. But they couldn't kill you, Kyr. Because you were hidden from them."

"I'm one shaman. I heal wounds. I treat diseases. The crimson bear gifted me with claws to fight and a hide tough enough to turn aside a sword. I'm strong, and tricky, and mean enough to kill when I have to be. But none of that makes me a hero." I shook the last drops off my dick and stared out into the misty forest. This place had once been pure and pristine, as clean as winter's first snow. Now the ground was mushy with rot and the air was fouled by the reeking, ever-present mist. "I cannot save the fucking world."

Aja finished her business and stood to face me. She pressed her chest into mine and the hard nubs of her nipples pressed against my skin like accusing fingers.

"Someone has to." Her eyes held my gaze with a fierce challenge.

We stood nose to nose for a string of moments that stretched out into what felt like hours of uncomfortable silence. Aja's breath tickled my face and the heat of her naked body so close to mine made me want to throw her down on the ground and ravish her. Fiery sparks danced in her eyes, and her lips drew tight over her teeth. She reminded me of the crimson bear, who I'd never been sure meant to fight or fuck when she looked at me like that.

In the end, the two activities had been much the same.

"Let it go, Aja." Ayo stood a few yards away, her arms crossed over her chest, one leg crossed in front of the other. Her skin seemed paler at the edges of her form, almost translucent. "We'll have to search for another."

The redhead dashed away from me and wrapped an arm around Ayo's waist. The blue-skinned woman looked at the other spirit gratefully and visibly sagged into her for support.

My spirit sight swept over the woman, and a cold stone of dread settled in my heart.

Ayo's core was empty.

Mortals could survive without rin, shio, or senjin in their core. They'd grow tired until rest replenished their sacred energy, of course, and they'd need more food and rest to sustain them while their nodes were empty. A few martial artists even learned to live with an empty core, claiming it freed them from worldly fears and allowed them to stare into the heart of the Void without flinching.

Most people thought those guys were full of shit.

The point was, humans didn't need the sacred energies to survive.

Spirits did.

"Bring her to the tent." I rushed past the spirits, thoughts racing. I didn't want to run off into the-devils-only-knew-what trouble with these two, and I also didn't want either of them to die so soon after they'd saved my life.

While the spirits shuffled toward the commander's tent, I looked over the medicine rack. A few phials of shio would have been just what the doctor ordered. Unfortunately, the Jade Seekers hadn't needed any feminine energy to power their armor or fighting styles, and so hadn't brought any of it with them.

They had, however, brought along enough other medicines for me to come up with a temporary fix for Ayo's problem. Sex could fill her nodes with shio, but she needed something more advanced to keep the scared energy from leaking away too quickly.

"Sit her down on the cot." I scooped up a handful of packets, phials, and tins and knelt next to Jiro's bed. The instant Ayo settled onto the cot's edge, I cracked open the first waxed packet and handed it to Aja. "Help her take all this. Chew the leaves, then swallow them."

Aja opened her mouth to say something, then clenched her jaw and did what I'd asked.

While Ayo munched on the hifir leaves, I pulled together what I needed. The medicine at my disposal had enough sacred energy in it to stabilize the spirit, even if it wasn't exactly a perfect cure. I fed her two pills from a tin of gulvas essence, a few sips from a phial of mourndew, and eight stalks of sinmint weed.

"Thank you." Ayo chewed on the final stalk and grimaced at the bitter taste. "This is horrible."

"More horrible than your core bleeding out?" The mixture of herbs and medicines I'd fed her had returned a single node of unrefined shio to her system. Hopefully that would stabilize her until I could determine why her core had let so much of her life force drain away.

"No." Ayo sighed. "I'm sorry you had to deal with this."

Aja rubbed the blue spirit's back and eyed me seriously. She wrestled with some inner struggle that showed itself clearly on her face, then spoke up.

"We're on borrowed time. The bonds to our mistress are stressed and leaking." She leaned against Ayo and kissed the top of her blue head. "She needs more energy than we can give her, and it drains us."

Well, fuck.

If their bonds were sprung, the spirits would need regular infusions of energy to sustain them or they'd fade away to nothing. There was a way to repair the damage they'd suffered, though it was dangerous and likely to fail. The crimson bear had showed me many ways to treat wounded spirits during my time with her, and this one was the most dangerous. If I fucked up, they'd die, their mistress would end up with a crippled soul, and I'd be lucky if I only ended up a dead man.

The wisest choice was to part ways with these beautiful, damaged creatures and wish them well on their journey. Getting involved in whatever madness followed them would just get me killed.

I'd never been terribly wise.

"I can't save the world." I rested my hand on Aja's shoulder. "But you saved my life. The least I can do is take you back to your mistress and help fix you up."

"She's in the Lake of Moonsilver Mist." Ayo clutched my hand with the desperate strength of a frightened child. "You swear you'll come all that way with us?"

If I remembered my geography, that lake was a bit of a hike. Overland, it would take us more than a week's travel to the south before we reached it. But if we took the Deepways, we could cut that trek down to two days, three at the outside. The spirits would need more energy during the trip, but I thought I could handle that.

Three days of regular carnal activities with a pair of spirits who gave the crimson bear a run for her money in the supernaturally attractive category sounded pretty perfect. Maybe their mistress could even answer a few of my questions after I worked my magic on her.

"I swear." I gestured around the tent. "Grab whatever you think will be useful and let's get the fuck out of here."

Chapter Seven

W E SPENT THE NEXT FEW HOURS TEARING THE Seekers' camp apart looking for anything even remotely valuable. Our efforts netted us a few dozen dinged, dented, and rusted weapons, some leather scraps useful for repairing jade armor and not much else, the overcooked remnants of the pig I'd left on the spit the night before, and the herbs and other medicines I'd been able to salvage from Jiro's tent.

"It's not much," Aja said with a frown. "You'd think a force of this size would have had more supplies."

"It's more than we had before we searched the place." I tried to look on the bright side, but the truth was, I'd expected at least some trail rations amongst the tents. The fact that there'd been nothing of the sort meant either the Seekers had been receiving regular supply shipments from their home base or the hunting around here was so bountiful they didn't feel the need for preserved foods. I hoped it was option two, because I was an excellent hunter.

If, on the other hand, there was a supply caravan headed here, they'd likely come up through the Deepways. It would be awkward as hell to run into more Jade Seekers on our way to the station.

"I can do something with those." Ayo scooped a few scraps of leather off the pile and started knotting them together.

"I'm going to put together some medicine for the trip." I headed back to Jiro's tent. "Take whatever you need. We'll leave as soon as I finish in here."

"I'll make sure no one sneaks up and kills us while you two are playing arts and crafts," Aja called after me. I couldn't tell if she was joking or not.

Inside the commander's tent, I mixed up a batch of herbal powder and fashioned it into a dozen tablets with the help of the pill press I'd found behind the medicine rack. I would have liked to have brought the equipment with me, but it seemed more than a little impractical to lug a hundred pounds of machinery along on our jaunt. If we needed more pills than we had on hand, we were fucked anyway. Even with my medicines and enough sex to leave us all blissed out of our gourds, the leaking bonds would kill the spirits in a matter of days.

With that cheery thought in my mind, I gathered the supplies I'd foraged into a bindle I'd made out of Jiro's pillowcase, and returned to the campfire.

"What do you think?" Ayo asked as she turned around to show me what she'd been up to.

She'd fashioned the leather armor repair scraps into a top and skirt that only loosely qualified as clothing. While her new outfit covered the parts of her body you weren't supposed to expose to the general public, that was basically all they covered. Ayo's slender blue body seemed more naked than it had before she'd put the clothes on, and my breath caught in my throat at the sight.

"You look stunning." There wasn't another word for it. She looked beyond amazing. "Maybe too stunning."

"He's right." Aja had made some adjustments to the outfit the other spirit had created for her. Strategically placed scraps of leather covered more of her skin, though she'd still attract every eye we passed. "Every man and most women that see you will want to fuck your legs off."

Not that the rest of us were dressed any more conservatively. My shaman dress code, a simple belt of hemp cord, a leather breechcloth, and not another stitch of clothing, was going to stand out wherever we went. Unfortunately, wearing more clothes wasn't an option for me. I needed the air to touch my skin and for my feet to touch the ground to use my abilities and restore my core's rin. The more clothes I wore, the weaker I became.

"Let them stare." Floating Village had been on the outskirts of the Moonsilver Bat Kingdom, so it was unlikely we'd stumble across any other travelers before we reached the Deepways. Once we arrived there, there'd be so many other strange and exotic sights, a mostly naked shaman and his sexy spirit companions wouldn't attract more than passing attention.

I hoped.

"The road would be easier," Aja grumbled after I'd led them through the forest for an hour. The spirits had more trouble navigating the undergrowth between the narrowly spaced trees than I did, it seemed.

"Easier for the Jade Seekers to spot us, maybe." I pushed aside another tree branch and plucked a handful of bright yellow cymberries from a bush. Their sweet pulp was made bitter by the mist that clung to their skins.

I tossed the half-eaten berries aside with a disappointed frown. "We're taking a more direct route."

"Are you sure you know the way?" Ayo asked sweetly from behind the red-haired spirit. "The lake, and our mistress, is more to the southeast."

"I know a faster way." I'd spent my childhood dreaming of far-off lands and cities whose names I'd only ever heard on the lips of traders who'd reached the Floating Village by traveling through the Deepways. One of them had shown me a map of the mystical transport system, and I'd studied it until the dozens of stations closest to my home were burned into my memory.

The Deepways were miracles of senjin science built by the Yellow Serpent Kingdom during the Second Age. Over the thousands of years since it was first created, the marvels of sacred energy technology had expanded until there was a station at every major dream meridian intersection. Those stations harnessed tremendous amounts of senjin energy and used it to propel enormous carriages between one station and the next at truly mind-blowing speeds. The network of stations had been critical to the growth and prosperity of the Empire. Even if everything else had fallen into ruin while I'd been on top of Mount Shiki, the Yellow Serpents would never allow such a vital piece of sacred technology to fall into disrepair.

My plan was to hike overland to the Cragtooth Station west of my former hometown, trade away the medicines I no longer needed for passage to the Looptail Station north of the Lake of Moonsilver Mist, then walk the rest of the way to the spirits' mistress. If everything went just right, we could cut a week-long trek down to just three days. Maybe two days if we got lucky and ran into a friendly wagon headed our way.

When we stopped for a late lunch, the spirits were already looking rough around the edges. Ayo's skin had taken on a dry, almost scaly, texture, and Aja's fiery red hair had faded to a dull pink mottled with white patches.

"Here." I opened my bindle and gave each of them a hunk of roast pork and a single pill I'd created with the equipment in Jiro's tent. "Eat and take the pill. I'm going to meditate to pull some senjin into my core, then we can have some fun and refuel the two of you for the next part of the hike."

"What is this?" Aja frowned at the tightly pressed tablet.

"It's an all-natural mixture of herbs and shaman spit. The important part is that it will slow down the loss of shio from your core. Sit. Rest. Eat. Swallow the pill." I gestured ahead of us. "I'm going over to that giri tree to do my thing. I'll be back in a few minutes."

The spirits flopped down on the ground and tore into the hunks of meat like they hadn't eaten in months. It was a good thing my mad shaman skills let me go without eating for days at a time because the spirits looked like they could eat a pig a day all by themselves.

The tree I'd picked for my meditation spot was thick-boled with drooping branches that provided excellent cover when I crawled under them. The fallen needles around its trunk made the ground extra comfortable, and it only took me a few seconds to fall into a deep meditative trance.

My earthbound core could hold five nodes of rin energy before it was filled. With practice and more knowledge, I'd eventually have a seabound core that could store ten nodes of rin energy. With a lot of luck and the right skills, I could reach even higher levels of mastery and push my core up the ladder to seabound, skybound, and beyond. The crimson bear had claimed there were nine or ten core levels, though even she thought that was unlikely. She was the strongest creature I'd ever seen, and her core was only firebound at the fifth level. Trying to imagine a core twice as powerful as hers was mind-boggling.

Sacred energy was plentiful this close to a dream meridian. The turbulent flow of senjin rumbled against my shaman's senses, and red lances of rin speared through drifting clouds of shio in my spirit sight. The crimson rin was easiest for me to absorb into my core. Its masculine energy resonated with mine, and rays of power drifted toward me with every breath I took. I could have filled my core with rin in a matter of minutes.

Unfortunately, that wouldn't have done either of the spirits any good. They needed shio to maintain their cores, and that power was beyond my ability to control.

Senjin, on the other hand, contained both masculine and feminine power. While it would be much harder to draw into my core than rin, the spirits and I could pull the more complex dream essence apart with some good old-fashioned sexy times.

I reached out for the senjin in the dream meridian with my spirit. It was like sticking my hand into a honey-spraying firehose. The sacred energy was warm and thick and so powerful it threatened to sweep me away in its unearthly current. Raw potential hummed through my body. I steeled myself, emptied my mind, and took a deep breath.

Of burning sewage.

My core screamed in protest as the foulest energy I'd ever experienced slammed into my spirit. I'd expected a slow, steady stream of intoxicating power and had instead swallowed a tidal wave of vile rot. My core filled before I could tear myself free of the meridian. All five of my core's nodes filled with an essence so toxic it left me dazed and wretching. The poison burned a thousand times hotter than the wound from Jiro's mercurial kunai. My core felt ready to burst at any moment.

"Fuck." I dragged myself to my feet and staggered back toward where I'd left the spirits. The world reeled drunkenly around me. Color bled out of reality, only to be replaced by dark shadows and sprays of purple light. A flock of passing birds transformed into a thundercloud before breaking apart into searing streaks of blood-red lightning. Finally, after an eternity wandering through a twisted hellscape of hallucinations, I found the spirits. "Poisoned."

The crimson bear's presence pushed through the dark venom that clouded my thoughts. As always, her primary concern was survival, and she knew exactly what that required.

Aja's red eyes met mine and went wide with surprise at the burning need she saw within me. Sparks of animal lust kindled in the depths of her gaze, and she started to rise from where she sat next to her sister, her hands busy with the knots that secured her scant clothing.

There was no time for that. I grabbed her by the waist and spun her away from me. I pushed aside the thin patch of leather that covered her sex, and my fingers brushed against Aja's damp heat.

"Yes," she moaned, and shoved her hips back toward me. She reached back through her legs, grabbed hold of me, and jerked me forward with savage strength.

I plunged into the red-maned spirit with a guttural groan. Aja's body closed around mine, and she threw her head back and cried out as the burning heat inside me joined our cores together in a knot of searing ecstasy. Her fingers clenched into fists and tore tufts of grass from the forest's floor with every thrust. She turned her head to stare hungrily at me over her shoulder, panting, her cheeks and throat red with desire.

Time ceased to have any meaning. Our bodies slammed together in perfect synchronicity, every motion triggering a fresh wave of pleasure. Our cries tore the still air of the woods, sending birds into panicked flight and deer bolting from where they'd grazed among the trees. Primal passion drove us harder, faster, as a desperate need raged inside me.

Blue arms wrapped around me from behind. Ayo crushed her chest against my back. Her smooth skin was cool against the infernal heat that radiated from my core, and she gasped when the power washed over her. She kissed the back of my neck, then swirled her tongue across the knob of my spine. She pushed her hands down the length of my torso, her nails dragging over the skin as if she wanted to claw her way into my core to get at the tainted senjin that way.

Ayo's slender hand slipped between the taut muscles of my stomach and the smooth curve of Aja's ass. The blue spirit's thumb and forefinger circled the base of my cock, a slippery band of friction that amplified every other sensation to nearly unbearable heights. She squeezed and relaxed her grip in time with my thrusts, adding an exquisite counterpoint to the velvet throbbing pressure of Aja around me. Ayo's other hand reached around me to close over my grip on the redhead's hip, urging us faster, harder. Our cores pulsed together, and the edges of reality blurred until all sense of time and place vanished.

The three of us were all that existed, all that would ever exist, all that could exist.

Aja whimpered and stiffened, her body suddenly rigid as a wave of pleasure shattered her thoughts. A soul-deep groan oozed from her throat as she spasmed around me, her nails digging furrows in the earth, her pulse pounding against mine.

Ayo bit down on my shoulder, an intense flash of cold that snapped the bonds of my self-control. I drove deep into Aja, cum gushing from me in thick spurts, frenzied thrusts lifting her knees almost off the ground. The spirits clung to me, their bodies slick with sweat, shuddering as pulses of ecstasy hammered us closer together and connected our cores in a flash of power.

The crimson bear roared inside me. She'd experienced every second of that encounter and heartily approved of almost all of it.

What she didn't like was how the experience left her wanting more. To the eternal spirit, that hour of animal lust had passed in the blink of an eye. By the time she'd roused herself from her slumber and felt me fucking the spirits, it was over. She wanted more.

"Soon," I promised in a hoarse whisper.

I eased back from Aja and sat, stunned, on the ground. The bonds between our cores had faded with our pleasure, but their purpose had been served. My core was filled to bursting with pure rin. The spirits crawled to my side and reclined on either side of me, their heads resting on my chest, their arms curled around my waist. My spirit sight showed me their cores as brilliant sapphire lights, nodes filled to capacity.

"The crimson bear taught you well," Aja teased, her voice soft and dreamy. "Are you sure you're still mortal?"

That was a good question. If I'd been gone for decades without aging, maybe I wasn't strictly mortal. But all that time was in the hunting grounds of the gods, where time flowed to a different rhythm than the people of the Sevenfold Empire experienced.

"Does it matter?" The question was as much for myself as the spirit.

"Not if you keep doing that." Ayo lifted her head and kissed the hollow of my throat.

"When we stop for the night," I promised as I stood and pulled the spirits to their feet. "But we need to hurry if we're going to get to the Deepways station before dark."

"I could run the whole way there." Aja flexed her left leg, then her right.

Despite the aggressive exercise we'd all shared, the three of us had more energy now than we had before we'd banged ourselves silly. The sacred energy that filled our cores invigorated our muscles and purged the weariness from our bodies. Buoyed by that energy, we made excellent time to the station.

"It's just over this hill." I urged the spirits onward. Their cores still glowed with nodes of shio energy, though the initial rush of power had worn off an hour before. They'd need to be replenished before our ride on the Deepways carriage was over. That would be an interesting experience.

They followed me up a hill whose top had been smashed flat by some ancient energy artist. A focusing beacon rested on the hill's flat top, its enormous senjin crystal dark and covered in thick, thorned vines. The grass had grown up around the structure's base, and there was no trace of the power couplings and capacitors I'd seen in the illustrations a trader had shown me.

"No," I groaned. "No."

The Deepways station was below us. The senjin lanterns that surrounded it no longer shed pure silver light. Instead, viscous shadows dripped from their cracked lenses, and the earth beneath them was covered in the rancid, blistered caps of poisonous fungi. The open mouth of the carriage cavern was clotted with weeds and rogue saplings with leaves the color of sun-bleached bones.

There wasn't another soul as far as we could see from our perch. The stalls clustered around the cavern that should have bustled with merchants hawking exotic wares from far-off lands were empty, their shelves rotted away to nothing. Signposts announcing the various routes and times of departure were cast down, the metal posts choked by coils of black ivy that spread over the ground like cancerous lesions.

The Deepways station, the best hope we had of reaching the Lake of Moonsilver Mist before the spirits bled out, was dead.

Chapter Eight

A COLD EMBER OF RAGE LIT UP THE DARK CORNERS of my heart. I'd counted on the Deepways to reach the lake before the spirits bled out. If this station was as dead as it looked, I'd have to figure out some way to make up the time we'd just lost.

"What happened?" Ayo asked. "Was there some sort of accident?"

"Let's find out." I had the same questions as Ayo, and I really didn't look forward to getting the answers.

From a distance the lanterns had looked like they were leaking shadows onto the ground below. When we got closer to the station, though, it became obvious that wasn't exactly the case. Thick, black vines had climbed up the posts and wrapped their oily tendrils around the lanterns. The strange plants were covered in a sickly sheen and had sprouted bloated fruits dotted with red nodules the color of raw beef. Clusters of those bulbous growths dangled from the lanterns and oozed a tarry ichor from their pulpy mass into black puddles coagulated around the bases of the lamp posts.

"Gross." Aja stopped to sniff at one of the puddles of black goo. "This is what I meant when I said the world was dying. Things like this have been sprouting up all over the place."

It was hard to argue with the spirit's dire prediction when faced with such grotesque evidence. Whatever these plants had once been, tainted senjin had transformed them into something foul and grotesque. The presence of such obvious corruption told me that it wasn't just the meridian we'd been following that was corrupted. I switched to my spirit sight and found swirls of pitch-black taint in all of the meridians that converged on this Deepways station. The vile energy was so thick here it had manifested in the plants.

This is worse than I'd imagined. Mielyssi's voice rippled through my thoughts, distant and faint. *I wish I had better advice to offer than be very fucking careful and don't get any of that shit on you.*

"Don't touch anything," I cautioned the spirits. The crimson bear's warning had confirmed my worry about the sticky goo that stained the grass. The tainted senjin I'd taken into my core had nearly killed me. If I hadn't had the spirits to fuck its diseased power out of me, I'd never have survived. If they became infected, too, there wouldn't be any safety valves to save us the next time it happened.

"No need to worry about that," Ayo said. "This stuff stinks. I wouldn't touch it with Aja's finger."

"You want to go for a swim?" the red-haired spirit asked with a feral grin. "I can arrange that."

Ayo cowered away from Aja with an exaggerated look of panic stretched across her beautiful features. They both laughed and followed along behind me as I led them around the worst of the corruption.

Their resilience in the face of all the bullshit they were faced with lifted my spirits. If they could joke while their cores leaked away their vital essences, the least I could do was put on a brave face and try my damnedest to get them back home to their mistress.

Fortunately, it wasn't hard to see the danger spots. They shed a purple-black radiance that kept triggering my spirit sight. My stomach churned at what I saw, and more than anything I wanted to get away from this place. But, first, I had to scavenge whatever we could from the station. The corruption would make any animals I could hunt or plants I could forage inedible, which meant we'd need some sort of trail rations to reach the lake. More medicinal supplies would be good, too, because what I had on me wouldn't keep Aja and Ayo up and running for more than a few days. Anything else we could find, like a map or some clothes for the spirits, would be a bonus.

My shopping list grew longer with every step, and I hoped we'd be able to fill at least some of it. The traveling merchants who'd visited Floating Village had told me the Deepways were used to ship all sorts of cargo. The wealthiest merchants with the most precious goods would seal their wares inside scripted containers to preserve them so they'd be fresh when they reached market. With any luck, our search would net us a few of those that we could crack open and loot.

After navigating a zigzagging route around the corruption hotspots that dotted the open plain around Cragtooth Station, we finally reached the entrance. The sun had sunk near the hilly horizon by that point, and its bloody rays hardly put a dent in the blackness beyond the building's yawning doorways.

The structure was bigger than it had looked from the hill. Thirteen evenly spaced doors pierced the wall ahead of us. Seven of them were triple the width of the others, large enough to allow wagons and large cargo crates to pass through with room to spare. The ground in front of the doors was overgrown with weeds and blades of black grass, though large numbers of cracked cobblestones jutted up from the earth like broken teeth.

It was hard to believe that hundreds of men and women had passed through those doorways every day. Wagon trains had picked up cargo to haul to distant villages, horse hooves had clattered across the stones as they carried riders too far-flung destinations. This Deepways station had once been a center of life in the Sevenfold Empire. That it had fallen into utter ruin filled me with a deep, unwholesome dread. If the rest of the world was as bad off as the station, my job would be a hell of a lot harder than I'd imagined.

The spirits sensed my discomfort and leaned against me to provide the simple comfort of contact. Their cool shoulders against mine reminded me that while I'd lost my past, I'd found the first pieces of a puzzle to build a different kind of future. It wasn't what I'd ever imagined, or wanted, but the crimson bear had always told me that mortals were spectacularly shitty at predicting the future.

"Let's stick together until we figure out what we're dealing with in here." I hooked my arms over the spirits' shoulders and pulled them closer. "We're looking for metal boxes or chests. They'll be covered in scripts, and some of those might be dangerous. If you see one, don't touch it until I can examine it for traps."

"I've been reading scripts since before you were born, mortal," Aja said with a huff. "You don't have to tell me how to handle them."

"Oh, you're a century old, are you?" I asked.

"You know what I mean," Aja grumped. Then her voice softened and she leaned her head against my shoulder. "Sorry. I get snippy when I'm nervous."

"Don't be nervous," Ayo chirped excitedly. "This will be exciting. There's bound to be all kinds of treasure in here!"

"Let's hope." We'd reached a door, and I pulled it open to let the dim light of the fading sun inside.

The interior of the station was far larger than I'd expected. It was crowded with stalls and desks, chandeliers dangled from its ceiling, and strange plants had grown up through cracks in the tiled floor. On the opposite side of the building from the doors, an enormous staircase plunged into the earth, and I glimpsed a much larger, deeper chamber down there.

Or at least part of a bigger chamber. The fading light could only reach so far past the end of the stairs, and everything after that was cloaked in pitch darkness.

"Anybody bring a torch?" I asked.

The spirits shook their heads, and I cursed at myself. As a shaman of the crimson bear, I saw just fine in low-light conditions. True darkness, though, blinded me just as much as any other person. I wouldn't be able to see much once I got down there.

Let there be light. I fed a trickle of rin into my weapon and prayed that the crimson bear's offer of a light through the darkness wasn't just a figure of speech.

The instant my power reached the channels, sinuous lines sprang to glowing life along the length of my war club. The remnants of Mielyssi's kiss grew brighter by the moment, until they shed a thirty-foot globe of near daylight around us.

"Neat trick," Ayo said.

"Uh, yeah," I said.

You're welcome.

The crimson bear's voice rang in my head, followed by a faint chuckle that left me wanting her more than ever when its echoes died. I wondered what other tricks she might have imparted to my club and wished there was a way for me to ask her.

I had no idea how long the light would last and decided to make the most of it. I descended the stairs into the lower level of the Deepways with the club held high.

Rats and squirrels scurried away from the light, disappearing into holes in the floor and nests under the desks and inside the stalls. I didn't see anything of value on our way to the stairs, and my spirit sight didn't find any glowing spots of sacred energy, either. Someone had cleared this place out. I only hoped the deeper parts of the station hadn't been so thoroughly looted.

"There's something down here," Ayo whispered. "I can feel it. It's so dark. So alone."

"Well, hopefully it can't feel us." I still had enough energy in my core to activate the crimson bear's techniques, if it came to a fight, but I'd rather not tangle with some unknown foe in a deep fucking hole in the ground. "Let's look over here."

Unlike the upper floor of the Deepways station, the area at the bottom of the stairs hadn't been overrun by wildlife or rampant weeds. The light from my war club spread thirty feet in every direction without hitting a wall. The silver glow showed us ranks of evenly spaced columns that supported the roof, orderly lines of colored tiles on the floor to guide passengers to their destinations, and scattered standing desks with heavy iron boxes chained to their bases.

The real prizes, though, were the gilded capsules of the Deepways carriages that rested in eight sunken berths ahead of us. My gut told me that if anything valuable had been left behind when this place was abandoned, it would be in those golden transports.

I'd just reached the closest of the carriages when whatever Ayo had detected smashed into the back of my head. Black wings buffeted my ears while its claws tangled in my hair and its beak stabbed at the top of my skull.

"Intruders! Intruders!" the flying monster screeched raucously in a rough-edged voice that was almost as painful as the bloody holes it had punched in my scalp. "Guards! Alert!"

"Get the fuck off me!" I shouted.

For all the noise the infuriated creature made, it wasn't very big or strong. I reached behind me, grabbed it around the neck, and yanked it off my head with a yelp. Its clenched claws had ripped out bloody hanks of my hair, and its beak pecked at the back of my hand with a ferocity out of all proportion to its actual size.

"Release me, intruder!" The creature in my hand appeared to be a talking raven. I'd seen weirder things during my stay with the crimson bear, to be sure, but I hadn't expected to run into such a vocal critter after I'd left Mount Shiki.

"Stop, goddammit." It would've been easy enough to snap the thing's neck, but that would have been a dick move. The angry creature was only doing its job, and it must've been down here alone, in the dark, for a very long time. Besides, I was a shaman. It was my job to protect nature's children, not slaughter them because they annoyed me. "I said stop!"

"That looks like it hurts." Ayo fussed over me while I wrestled with the bird. She gingerly probed at the bloody spots on my scalp with one finger. "The cuts aren't deep, but they're going to sting for a while, and we should watch them for signs of infection."

"Release me!" the black bird croaked. "Begone! I am the guardian of the station, and I will not allow you to ransack its carriages!"

"Oh, come on." Aja rolled her eyes at the raven's raucous protests and spread her arms out to encompass the empty station. "Anyone who owns any of this has long since abandoned it. Finders, keepers. Now get out of our way before I wring your neck myself."

The bird glared at Aja but shut its beak.

"I'm going to let you go. And you're not going to stab me in the head with your beak anymore. Nod if you understand me." The bird and I stared at one another, its black eye as cold and expressionless as a marble. It gave me one small nod of its head. "Good."

The raven fluttered to the top of the nearest carriage, and watched us anxiously. For the first time, I noticed it had three legs and was suddenly very glad I hadn't killed it. Three-legged ravens were sacred beasts that some claimed were messengers of the gods. Offing one of those for doing its job would've racked up some very bad karma indeed.

"Look, we don't want any trouble," I said to the raven. Maybe if it understood what we were doing here, it wouldn't try to snatch me bald-headed again. "We'd hoped to take the Deepways carriage to the stop closest to the Lake of Moonsilver Mist."

"And I'd hoped not to have to do this job for a hundred years without relief." The raven's claws ticked against the roof of the carriage as it shifted from one leg to another to another. "I guess none of us are getting what we want today."

"We need supplies." I eyeballed the raven, and it eyeballed me right back. Despite the creature's small size, it looked ready to fight me if I tried to get past it.

Rather than try to bull my way past the bird to reach the carriage, I decided to use my awesome shamanic powers to do some scouting. There wasn't any point in dealing with this creature if there wasn't anything on the carriage.

Unfortunately for the bird, my spirit sight immediately spied a deep, azure glow coming from inside three of the carriages. That glow was a sure sign of concentrated shio sacred energy. The kind that would be used to power preservation scripts. I was sure what we needed was inside those vessels.

"My spirit companions are sick. I need to return them to their mistress before the illness takes them." The raven didn't seem impressed by my sob story. "Unfortunately, their mistress is far to the south, and we don't have enough supplies to carry us that far. I'd normally hunt and forage for food, but the land is so corrupted that's no longer an option. There's no harm in letting us take a few items from these carriages. No one's coming back to claim them."

"The harm is to me," the raven croaked. "If I let you steal from what I'm sworn to protect, my duty bond will punish me."

"Maybe there's something I can do to help you." As a shaman, dealing with the mystical connections between creatures, spirits, and mortals was my stock in trade. If I could figure out how to free this creature from a bond that had long since outlived its usefulness, then

I'd earn some good karma and get the provisions we needed.

"I doubt there's anything you can do." The raven flapped its wings in agitation. "My bond is to the station manager. The last one, Yala Kinrey, told me she'd send another raven to relieve me when she reached Madrus Lota, but that was obviously a lie. I've been stuck guarding this place and it's been thirty years, eight months, and fourteen days since I've seen another soul."

Well, shit.

I pulled Aja and Ayo back toward the steps to the upper level. I needed their advice, and I didn't want the raven to overhear our conversation.

"We should kill it," Aja said the second we reached the staircase. "If there's anything that can help us in those carriages, we need it, and there's no sense in letting some stupid bird get in our way."

"That's a three-legged raven," I said, my voice serious. "I don't know what your mistress taught you, but that's a sacred beast. Some people say they're the messengers and agents of the gods. Killing the raven would let us get into the carriage, sure, but it's going to piss off whoever created it. Are you willing to have one of the Celestial Bureaucracy gods pissed off at you?"

Before I'd climbed Mount Shiki and spent decades knocking boots with the crimson bear, I'd only ever paid lip service to the immortal deities that made up the Celestial Bureaucracy. It wasn't like they showed up in Floating Village to chastise those who broke their laws or offended their priests. But experiencing the higher spirits' realms for myself had changed my view of the world. There were forces at work that mortal eyes couldn't see, and I took them very seriously now that they'd flipped my whole life upside down.

"We may as well start walking," Ayo said. Her eyes shimmered with unshed tears. Her core was nearly empty, and she knew she'd never survive the walk back to her mistress without more help than I could give her. "Even if we don't make it back, you can still reach our mistress and help her."

"I'm not giving up that easy." I mulled over our problem and tried to come up with a solution. "There's a bound sacred beast between us and supplies we need. We can't kill it. We also can't sneak around it because the raven will get hurt if we steal anything. That's just as likely to piss off the Celestial Bureaucracy as bashing the bird's brains out with my war club."

"We have to set it free," Ayo urged me. "It wants to be away from here, I can feel that. If you remove its bond, the raven will leave us in peace."

"That's the plan." I looked at each of the spirits in turn. "Did your mistress ever tell you anything about that?"

"No." Aja furrowed her brow. "She's very private. We were never around for her workings."

"Of course she didn't let you see any of her secrets," the raven called to us. "You're her familiars; she wouldn't want you to know how to break her bonds with you any more than my masters wanted me to break mine."

"You can hear us?" I asked.

"I can hear anything in the station." The raven cawed and hopped to the end of the carriage. "You might as well come over here to talk. I'm going to eavesdrop on you, regardless."

"You could've said something," I grumbled and headed over to the golden vessel.

"Then I wouldn't have been able to eavesdrop on your secrets." The raven clucked its tongue.

I leaned on my war club and considered the raven. To my spirit sight it glowed a rich blue, swirled through with streaks of pure silver senjin. It was a powerful creature, and if it hadn't been for the corrupted energy that radiated from the dream meridians all around us, it probably would've been even stronger.

My connection to the crimson bear wasn't the same as a bound spirit. We were partners more than master and servant. She gave me techniques I wouldn't otherwise have, and she could influence the world of mortals through me. There was a give and take there that didn't exist with bound spirits, who were basically slaves to their master's whims.

There were other kinds of connections, too. Sorcerers could bind demons using the sevenfold rituals handed down by the lost gods. Wizards could summon elementals and bind them to their cores to power their spells thanks to ancient thaumaturgic rites. Shamans could have familiars, though we tended to treat our bound spirits with more respect than the other practitioners.

That gave me an idea, though I wasn't at all sure that it would work.

"I'm going to try something that you're not going to like." This was risky, but I needed what was in those carriages to get Ayo and Aja safely to their mistress. If it came down to fucking up a sacred beast or watching the spirits die, I'd risk the bad karma and wrath of the Celestial Bureaucracy.

"Take your best shot, kid." The three-legged raven didn't seem concerned about me in the slightest.

"But you better make it a good one. Otherwise, my bond will make me peck out your eyes and shit on your brain."

Before the raven could make good on its threat, I focused my spirit sight until its core glowed in my mind's eye, so close to my core I could touch it.

"What kind of pervert are you?" the crow squawked. "Stop digging around in my core. I'm not your average crow for you to jack around with."

"I'm trying to fucking help you. Sorry if you don't like it." I didn't much like it, either, to be totally honest. Messing around with a sacred beast bordered on the blasphemous, and if I fucked it up there'd be no end of trouble in it for me.

But if I got it right, I'd get all the loot I wanted from the carriages and hopefully earn the raven's gratitude. Before I could come to my senses, I made my move.

Chapter Nine

FOR MY NEXT PARTY TRICK, I STRETCHED A THIN strand of rin from my core's first node toward the raven. The bird tried to hop away, but I was faster. The loop of sacred energy closed around its core with a faint sizzle.

"Don't you dare," the raven squawked. "I don't want to be your pet!"

"Do you want to stay down here for another thirty years before someone else finds you?" The bird's protests were more frantic than fierce, and I suspected it was more afraid of what the bond would do to it if it didn't fight me than it was of becoming my familiar.

The three-legged raven's core nearly slipped away from me several times before I found what I was looking for. The shell that surrounded the bird's spirit was bright blue, with a single dark spot on one side. That spot was surrounded by a ring of silver script that I assumed was the binding itself. I turned the core this way and that looking for other connection points and didn't find another one.

Perfect.

"Don't fuck with that," the bird squawked. "It has warding seals on it that will go off if you tamper with it."

"Settle down." I had no intention of tampering with the bird's bond. What I had in mind was more effective than that. And more dangerous. If I messed this up, the bird might end up free, but I would almost certainly end up very, very dead. "Try not to struggle."

Before the raven could react, I pushed my rin into the shadowy connection point. This would never have worked while the bird's master was still alive, because an active master could easily deny a new connection to a bound spirit. But the station manager was long dead, and there was no one around to stop me from doing my thing. It was, as Aja had said, a case of finders, keepers. I only needed to forge my binding to the connection point, and the raven would be free from its duty.

I took a deep breath and willed my rin to form a binding seal around the dark spot on the bird's core.

And it would have worked, too, if the sneaky fuck who'd set up the duty bond hadn't been so goddamned clever.

The asshole had bound the bird not to a person, but to the station itself with a contingency that the binding was under the control of the station manager. And, while that manager was dead as a doornail, the station wasn't.

"Stop!" the raven squawked. "You're going to get us all killed!"

"A little late for that." The bond I'd forged to the bird would keep us tied together until either I'd won my battle against the station, or I was dead.

A thread of silver senjin speared out of the darkness and smashed into the raven's core like a blast of lightning. The script that surrounded the connection point flared to life, the symbols spinning faster and faster as sacred energy flooded into them.

I tightened my mental grasp around the black bird's spirit with a grunt. The script pushed against my spirit like a gale force wind, but it wasn't strong enough to sever the connection I'd forged. Unfortunately, I felt a tremendous amount of senjin behind the attack. It couldn't overpower me with brute strength, but it could wear me down with its constant, unrelenting attack.

And the instant it threw me out of the bird's core, the warding seals would kick in and do something really nasty.

"Aja," I groaned. "Can you sense this senjin thread that's trying to kill me?"

"I think so." The spirit went silent for so long I had to look over my shoulder to make sure she hadn't left. While I struggled against the core's death trap, she sniffed the air. Finally, she cleared her throat and spoke again. "I have its scent now."

"Find its source and kill it." The effort of holding onto the raven's core for dear life wrenched a long, pained groan from deep inside me. "Hurry!"

"I'm going with her," Ayo called. "Give me your club for light."

"Fine, take it, but go!" I didn't want to be short with the spirits, but the spiritual battle had me worried. Senjin pulsed through the thread into the bird's core, and it came closer to knocking me loose with every moment that passed.

Steal its fire. Mielyssi's faint voice trickled through my thoughts like a cool, refreshing stream.

The connection I'd forged with the three-legged raven gave me access to its core.

A core rapidly filling with senjin.

I drew in a deep breath and pulled senjin through the rin thread I'd tied to the raven. A river of senjin gushed through the connection and into my core, where it stormed around inside me with bruising force. There was so much of the pure power I couldn't hope to contain it all.

Oops.

Before the flood of pure dream energy could overwhelm my core, I sealed the rin thread against it. I immediately emptied two of my nodes by activating the Crimson Claws and Bear's Mantle techniques, and my core split some of the senjin into its rin and shio components. The rin settled into the space I'd created for it, while my masculine core shed the feminine shio energy in opalescent droplets that oozed from my pores.

That maneuver didn't do shit to help me. My core was still dangerously overloaded. I wasn't sure what would happen if I couldn't shed the senjin, and I didn't want to find out. It was time to make a mess.

"We're both going to die," the raven croaked. "Oh, Blood God, what did I ever do to deserve such a miserable existence? Thirty years trapped in the dark, and now this so-called shaman strolls in and tears my soul apart!"

"You're gonna have to shut the fuck up," I gasped. "Can't concentrate with you running your beak."

"Well, excuse the fuck out of me, Mr. Breaking and Entering," the raven muttered.

With a shout, I unleashed one node after another to trigger the Earthen Darts spell. The floor around me exploded into jagged shards that flew up into the darkness, where they shattered against the ceiling. A stinging hail of gravel fell down around me, pelting my head and shoulders, pinging off the raven's back, and rattling against the top of the carriage in a seemingly endless barrage.

When my nodes filled again, I emptied them again, this time by forcing the sacred power into my blood and muscles. My strength and endurance surged, and I used my newfound vigor to push back against the trap. It was a constant struggle, but stealing the senjin from the trap was working.

Sadly, there seemed to be an inexhaustible amount of the shit. No matter how many times I emptied and refilled my core, there was more senjin flowing into the raven. It was like trying to bail the ocean with a fucking teaspoon.

"I should have just killed you," I groaned.

"Oh, the Celestial Bureaucracy would have just loved that." The raven shielded its head from the gravel with one wing. "And if I ever get back there, I'm going to tell them just how much of an asshole you are."

I turned my attention back to the senjin, draining and refilling my core, shattering more rock, and generally trying to not motherfucking die.

"Found it!" Aja's voice was chased through the subterranean station by dozens of echoes that made it hard to tell where the hell she was. "It looks like some kind of script plaque. What do you want us to do?"

"Disable it!" I shouted. "You said you can read scripts, so find the power circuit and shut it off."

"How?"

"Scratch it, break it, I don't give a fuck!" My voice cracked with the effort of taming the senjin that wanted to murder the shit out of me. "Just make it quick!"

"Okay!"

A moment later, Cragtooth Station was hit by a lightning bolt.

The brilliant flash blinded my physical eyes and overwhelmed my spirit sight with a chaotic stream of silver senjin threads. The unfettered energy spiraled off in a thousand different directions, unfocused and unconstrained. The insanity only lasted for a second, and that was more than enough for me.

"You killed me!" the raven screeched and flapped its wings. "You've condemned me to the lowest of the Frozen Hells where maggots will feast on my burst eyes forever!"

"You're not dead, you big baby." The senjin burst had been impressive, but it hadn't done any real damage. Released from its script, the reservoir of power had rushed back out into the world to be absorbed back into the earth, air, plants, and wildlife.

Or, more likely, to be corrupted by the rot that spread through the world.

"Everybody okay?" Aja ran over to me, Ayo hot on her heels. "That was a little more spectacular than I expected."

"You did good," I said with a lopsided grin. "It could have been much worse. And, yes, we're all fine here. More or less."

"I'm dead." The raven croaked and flopped over onto its back, head lolling, eyes closed tight. All three of its legs poked straight up into the air in a reasonable imitation of rigor mortis.

"You'll be fine." The old duty bond was gone, blasted apart like the senjin that had powered it. Mine was the only connection that remained.

Now that the raven and I were bound together, the edges of our thoughts brushed together like tentative fingertips. The bird scratched at the surface of my thoughts, and I showed it that I meant it no harm.

It recoiled when I stroked its ruffled emotions, then settled its core against mine with a shuddering sigh. For all its protests about not wanting to be a pet, the raven had been alone for a very long time. It had almost forgotten what it was like to be around other creatures. It craved the simple contact of another living being.

"That was way too close." The raven righted itself and flapped off the roof of the carriage to land on my shoulder. Its talons were sharp, but the creature did a very good job of not skewering me. "Now what happens?"

"Serve me as my familiar." I said the words softly, so quietly only the raven could hear. "Accept the bond between us of your own free will."

The bird eyeballed me and pensively adjusted its position on my shoulder.

"What if I don't want to be your familiar?" the raven asked.

"Then you're free to go. I don't need a slave bitching and moaning all the time." I meant it, too. I could have forced the bird to serve me, but that was pointless and cruel. We'd spend the rest of our lives squabbling, and there was no sense in that.

"You really mean it?" The bird poked its beak into my hair and plucked out the remains of a leaf I'd picked up somewhere. "You won't force me to do it?"

"It's up to you." I shrugged. "We could learn a lot from each other, I bet, but if you've got shit to do and places to be, then get the fuck out of here and let us get on with our looting."

"Maybe you're not so bad after all." The bird hopped off my shoulder and flapped over to the carriage again. "Let's do this thing."

And, with those solemn and sacred words, the three-legged raven became my familiar.

"Now that we've got that out of the way, let's go shopping, ladies." I led the way onto the carriage, which was packed with a dozen or so heavy metal crates. Scripts crawled across their surfaces like knots of fucking snakes, and their power glowed like a bonfire in my spirit sight.

"This one's full of gemstones." Ayo had moved to the back of the carriage to start her search. "Looks like a level-three warding script and a level-four locking script. Probably not worth the risk to try to unravel them."

"We've got a bunch of preserved food here," Aja said. "Level-one locking script, no wards."

"You two weren't kidding about your skill with scripts." I hadn't even known scripts had levels. Maybe after I healed their mistress, she'd be inclined to give me some private lessons. And maybe I could return the favor and teach her a few things I'd learned between the crimson bear's thighs. "Let's go through the rest of these, figure out what we've got, and take whatever we can carry."

"Don't get yourself killed," the raven squawked. "I'm really looking forward to seeing some sunshine again. If you die, I'll be stuck down here guarding your corpse until it rots away."

"I'll try not to inconvenience you," I said.

"And we wouldn't leave his corpse down here," Ayo said, her voice surprisingly solemn. "He's a shaman. We'd be sure to take him outside where the animals could eat him."

"That's comforting." I shook my head. "Let's get an inventory of this place and get out of here before you make any more funeral plans for me."

It only took us an hour to get through the contents of the carriages. There was a lot of food, though most of it wasn't terribly portable. The preservation containers held lots of fresh meat, some fruit, a wide variety of very spicy peppers I'd never seen before, some kind of sour vegetable that not even the spirits recognized, and pounds of fragrant, glossy black beans.

"Coffee," the raven groaned. "Oh, coffee."

"What is that?" I asked.

"The black blood of the earth. Elixir of the gods." The raven hopped from foot to foot outside the carriage. "Please take some. I'll show you how to use it. It's been so long since I had coffee."

At the end of our search both spirits had new sets of boots that were serviceable if a little ornate for our needs. They'd also found some light leather armor to replace the scraps they'd been wearing. Surprisingly, what they found still seemed sexier than serviceable, but I wasn't about to complain.

"Yeah, try that on." The raven bobbed his head toward Ayo. "I want to see that."

"Knock it off." I was surprised to feel a thread of animal lust through my bond with the raven. "Keep your beak to yourself."

"Spoilsports," the raven grunted.

The spirits also loaded up on bracelets, rings, and necklaces. The jewelry was all gold, studded with a few gemstones. It looked nice, but it was also practical. We could sell the hardware or trade it for whatever we needed, provided some bandits didn't try to swipe it off us first.

I wondered if there were even any bandits left in the world, then decided there had to be. After any sort of disaster, the vermin were the first things to begin thriving again. It wouldn't surprise me at all if the only people left out there were bandits and soldiers.

We also found two packs and a satchel. We loaded them up with as much food as we could comfortably carry. Most of the other items were impractical to haul around, which is why they'd been on the carriage in the first place. I did find a tome of power, the *Formation Manual of Borders and Boundaries*, which seemed out of place amongst the rest of the goods.

I opened the book's cover and squinted to make sense of the spidery text on its pages. Most of the scripts were too advanced for me to understand, though the index page was perfectly clear.

Wall of Sanctity: Restricts the flow of sacred energy into or out of its boundary.

Wall of Wind: For protection against projectiles and harmful vapors.

Wall of Earth: For protection against physical assault.

Wall of Iron: An impervious barrier.

Wall of Mortality: A deadly barrier.

Wall of the Void: A barrier between worlds.

My core wasn't yet advanced enough to use any of the book's knowledge, but I couldn't bring myself to leave such a treasure behind. I shoved its waterproof sleeve into my satchel for safekeeping.

While the spirits went off to change their clothes out of the raven's sight, I examined a map engraved on a thick copper panel bolted to the wall of one of the carriages. It showed the station and its environs, including a winding river that headed south to the Lake of Moonsilver Mist. The map also identified several towns and settlements in the area, though I didn't have much confidence they'd still be there after all this time.

"My name's Yata, by the way." The raven had perched on my war club. "Not that my new shaman even fucking asked."

Chapter Ten

W E LEFT CRAGTOOTH STATION UNDER THE light of the full moon, and the dark pools of corruption that dotted the plains around us looked even creepier under the silver glow of the night sky.

"I am not sleeping anywhere near this place," Aja said. "It's unclean."

"No argument there. We'll head west until we're clear of the corruption before we break camp." I hadn't gone two steps when Ayo called out to me.

"Kyr, the Lake of Moonsilver Mist is southeast of here." The spirits stood stock-still, their hands on their hips.

"I know. But the Hunjis River is to the west. It runs into the lake, and the map in the station showed tons of trade ports along its length. We can hire a riverboat pilot in one of those towns to take us to your mistress." I'm more than just a pretty face.

The spirits' dubious looks gave way to cautious optimism.

"If those trade ports are still there," Yata croaked from its perch on the head of my war club. "That map hasn't been updated in at least thirty years."

"My mistress has had dealings with merchant ships traveling the Lake of Moonsilver Mist," Ayo said. "There have to be at least some trading ports left, and following the river would be easier than tramping overland, in any case."

"We aren't getting any closer to our goal yammering about what we're going to do." Aja leaned up on her tiptoes and kissed me on the cheek. Her new jewelry jingled and jangled like distant wind chimes. "Your call, Kyr. Let's get moving."

"West it is." I pointed toward the horizon and started walking.

We didn't reach the forest until the full moon was well up in the sky. It wasn't midnight yet, but it was getting close. The hike across the hilly terrain under the moonlight was more exhausting than I'd anticipated. The spirits were nearly out of shio in their cores and were seriously dragging ass. Even Yata, who had spent the whole march perched on my weapon's tip, seemed exhausted by the time I had a small fire going. While the others watched me with weary eyes, I plucked some green branches from nearby trees for makeshift skewers and got our dinner cooking over the fire.

"I'll stand watch." My familiar flew up into the branches above us. "I don't need to sleep, so you won't have to worry your pretty heads about getting a good night's rest."

After we wolfed down our meager dinner, I gave the spirits more medicine to help their cores retain the sacred energy they needed to survive, then we got down to the always exciting business of refilling our cores. I'd wisely placed our camp farther away from the dream meridians, so when I drew the tainted senjin into my body with slow, careful breaths, it didn't immediately try to kill me.

The spirits and I worked closely together to make the whole process a lot more manageable, and more pleasurable. The crimson bear woke the instant we began exploring one another's bodies, and waves of primal lust radiated from her into me. The spirits noticed the change immediately, and it spurred on their own desire. Gentle caresses became more urgent strokes, the flow of energy into me and through the spirits spiked with my quickened breathing, and our hearts pounded together.

My core had filled with senjin, and the burning pain only heightened the sensual pleasure that radiated from every inch of my body. A wave of carnal need washed my mind away, and the crimson bear roared her approval. I yanked Aja's clothes away from her body, grabbed her hips, and pulled her down onto me, her face to the fire. She moaned and bucked like a wild creature, the surge of power that passed between us driving her away from the death that awaited an empty core and toward a life of savage passion.

I pulled Ayo down to me almost before she could shed her own clothing, and parked her ass on my chest, her knees even with my shoulders, her feet flat on the forest floor on either side of my head. My tongue probed the velvet opening of her sex, and she melted against my mouth and tangled her fingers in my hair. She tasted like the sea, wild and untamed.

It went on for what felt like hours, a carnal delirium that dragged us down into crashing waves of pleasure. We collapsed at last, spent, our bodies slick with sweat and sticky with the fluids we'd smeared over each other in our hunger for more. I don't know how long

I slept after that, but it wasn't anywhere near long enough.

"Get up." Yata woke me with a tap of its beak on my forehead. "Sun's been up almost an hour."

That was strange. Most days I woke before the first rays of daylight brushed against my shaman's senses. Even after I shook loose from sleep's embrace, though, I felt sluggish and had a hard time dragging myself out from the cozy space between the still-sleeping Ayo and Aja. There was a warm weight at the heart of my being that made it hard to rouse myself.

What the fuck was happening here?

"Thanks for the wake-up. Can you keep an eye on these two for a minute?" The bird nodded and croaked out a caw, and I headed away from our small camp to answer nature's call.

With my business completed, I hiked a bit deeper into the forest and examined myself with my spirit sight. My body was in perfect shape, though all the physical activity of the last couple of days had left me on the verge of dehydration.

My core though, looked strange.

Bright blue-green swirls flowed over my earthbound core's surface in brilliant contrast to its normal deep brown. Crimson sparks of power danced along the borders between the two colors, radiating a soothing warmth that made me want to curl up into a ball and sleep for the next week.

"Holy shit," I gasped. "My core's advancing."

Under Mielyssi's training, I'd advanced my core from foundation level to earthbound, expanding its capacity to five nodes and bonding me to the crimson bear. Though it hadn't seemed like it at the time, the single advancement had taken decades of training under the tutelage of the most powerful spirit I'd ever encountered. I hadn't expected to advance again for years, maybe longer.

And, yet, here I was with my core covered in swirls of glowing aquamarine light.

"Fuck." I had no idea what to do.

"Just breathe," Yata croaked from a tree limb above me. "You're not going to die."

"How do you know?" My core didn't hurt, exactly. It felt like someone had filled it with a few dozen pounds of cold lead. The heat from the sparks between the brown and blue flowed through me in soothing pulses that left me weak and wobbly. The combination made me feel woozy and disoriented, almost drunk.

"I don't know how I know anything about this." Yata sounded irritated and confused. It flapped down out of the tree and landed on the ground in front of me. "There's a lot of stuff in my head that I didn't put there. Must be a perk of our bond."

"That's comforting." It was not. Trusting a surly three-legged raven who didn't know where its information came from seemed like a fantastic way to get screwed over by the universe.

A cool breeze blew across my brain, and I clamped a hand over my head to make sure the advancement hadn't blown the top of my skull off. My stomach lurched and the world tilted on its axis around me. My eyeballs rolled in their sockets, completely out of my control.

And, then, just as suddenly as it had begun, the advancement ended. My core was no longer earthbound, but seabound.

The shell around my spirit was now the color of fresh seawater in my spirit sight, an almost luminous blue-green dotted with ten nodes. Five of those glowed with an intense red light I recognized as rin energy, while the other five were a ghostly white. There was also a new bruised-looking spot on the opposite side of my familiar bond with Yata. It looked like I could form a new bond if I wanted, though that was the furthest thing from my mind. Being tied to the raven was more commitment than I really wanted.

"Love you, too," the bird cawed. "You've also got space for a new technique in there. Better find a teacher."

"That would be nice, but I'm the last shaman." I stretched and marveled at how easy the advancement had been. I'd worried it would be more difficult without the crimson bear by my side, but maybe I was a natural. "Not sure where I'll find someone to teach me shaman shit now."

At least not until after I'd saved the world and traipsed back up to the summit of Mount Shiki.

The new core filled me with a sense of strength and power beyond anything I'd ever experienced. I stood and hefted my club, marveling at how light the heavy spiked weapon felt in my grip. I swung it with one hand, and it whistled through the air like an arrow fired from a crossbow. It took hardly any effort to lift, and scarcely more than that to swing.

"Nice swing," Yata cawed and preened itself. "Be careful, though. You don't know your own strength."

"Thanks for the warning." I hoisted the club over my head and started back toward camp. Yata flew to the top of a tree ahead of me. "I see the river up ahead. Little less than half a day's march for you and your trollops."

"Don't let them hear you say that. They'll cook you for dinner."

"Those slowpokes can't catch me." The raven tossed its head and took off again.

"Hey there, stranger." Ayo was tending to some skewers of meat when I returned to camp. "We thought you might have gotten tired of us and skipped out."

"And break my promise?" I scoffed at the idea. "Never."

"You look different." Aja raised an eyebrow, then scrutinized me with greater intensity. "Oh, wow. You're seabound now."

"Yep, just advanced." I struck a pose and flexed my newly improved muscles. I wasn't bigger, exactly, but my muscles were more defined and symmetrical. I'd always thought heroes in paintings looked so buff because they took care of themselves, but now I knew they cheated. Advancing your core made you stronger and hotter.

"That was fast." Ayo tapped her chin with her index finger as she considered something. "I bet it's all the purification we've been doing. The tainted senjin is hard on your core, and it takes a lot of effort to get it cleaned up."

"I hadn't thought of that." I'd been too busy trying to stay alive to notice the details. It was also hard to focus on that sort of thing because saving my skin involved a pair of gorgeous spirits and lots and lots of frenzied fucking. "Now that you've brought it up, we should definitely keep purifying senjin."

"How about now?" Aja licked her lips and stretched her arms over her head. "I could use a top-off."

"Later." The spirits still had full cores. The herbs I'd given them helped slow their leaks, which would help us make better time. The sexy times that kept them alive did nothing for their mistress, and I'd promised to try to save her life. We needed to get moving to do that. "But when we get to our next stop, I will definitely take you up on that."

"Where are we headed?" Aja plucked a skewer of seared meat off the fire and dropped it onto a flat rock we'd used as a serving tray the night before.

"There's a river village not far from here. Map had it marked as Ulishi. We can get a pilot to take us downstream from there." My stomach growled at a whiff of breakfast. "With any luck, we'll be able to ride the river all the way down to the Lake of Moonsilver Mist."

"Sounds good." Aja took a mostly raw hunk of meat from the skewer. She blew across the steaming slice for a few seconds, then gobbled it down. Blood dribbled down her chin, and she wiped it away with the back of one hand. "How long will that take?"

"If everything goes right, shouldn't be more than two days." I tried not to think too hard about how many more things could go wrong in two days' time.

"Fingers crossed," Ayo said.

"And toes," I added.

After breakfast, we covered the fire with dirt, gathered up our belongings, and headed out.

The terrain, rolling hills on a gently descending slope, would have made for a very pleasant hike if the air hadn't been soggy with gloomy, reeking mist. The stuff was relentless and left our skins slick with a layer of greasy moisture. I doubted I'd ever be dry again.

Yata did a great job as a scout, though, which kept us from getting turned around in the dense fog. The three-legged raven flew high above us, coming down only to let us know when we needed to change direction or give us an update on how far we were from our destination. I wasn't sure how it could see through the fog, but it hadn't failed us yet.

We decided to skip lunch to get to the river town faster and finally reached our destination a couple of hours after noon.

The river was a hundred feet wide, its surface black and turbulent. White caps dotted the water where it crashed over submerged boulders or tumbled around fallen trees. Sampans plied the treacherous waterway, their sleek hulls cutting through the water under the expert guidance of their pilots. The boats ranged in size from barely large enough to hold a single crewman to long vessels capable of carrying significant amounts of cargo. The sampans arrived at or left the village in a confusing swirl, and their pilots cried out with greetings and curses as they glided past one another or nearly collided.

Relief welled up inside me in a dizzying rush. Seeing the village, hell, seeing other people, after the disaster at the Deepways left me nearly breathless. Since I'd returned from Mount Shiki, the only other humans I'd encountered had been very intent on killing me. The simple sight of other humans going about their mundane, ordinary lives filled me with a powerful, almost painful, sense of gratitude. While there were still pockets of normalcy in this world, it wasn't yet doomed. I took a deep breath, closed my eyes, and let the moment sink into my bones.

"Be careful here," Yata croaked as it landed on my shoulder. "The Deepways conductors always said the river pilots were outlaws and cutthroats."

"Outlaws, for sure." The riverboat pilots were part of an unofficial, but still powerful, criminal organization that was said to stretch across the continent. It was well known that they'd do just about anything for the right price, and only paid lip service to the rulers of the Sevenfold Empire. At least, those were the stories I'd heard a hundred years ago. It was time to find out just how badly my information had aged. "And outlaws are just what we need. Come on."

We headed downhill to the river, and more of the village emerged from the mist. Its buildings rose from the river on thick stilts. Swaying rope bridges and rickety wooden planks connected the aerial structures, and their inhabitants moved between them with practiced ease.

More stilts, thick as old tree trunks, jutted from the river's center. The buildings atop these were taller and wider than their cousins nearer the banks, and ladders hung from their sides to just above the water line. Passengers from brightly colored sampans clambered up the stilts like monkeys rushing up the sides of trees, while pilots moored their boats to stout docks that emerged from the dark waters.

Despite its seemingly precarious position on the mighty river, the village had clearly been around for a while. Its buildings were weathered and stained by the hands of time, and obvious signs of wear and tear marked every surface. It looked seedy and rundown, and I couldn't have been happier.

"Give me your jewelry," I said before we reached the river's edge.

"Good idea." Aja stripped the gold and jewels from her body and handed them over. "I wouldn't want these river scum to kill us and dump our bodies in the river for a few bracelets."

"Nobody's getting murdered." I was confident I could protect my group from an outlaw or two if it came to that, though I hoped there wouldn't be any violence. "My father always said these pilots were smugglers, mostly. That works in our favor."

"How?" Ayo handed me her jewelry and I added it to Aja's in my satchel.

"We need to get smuggled." I grinned. "Look, the Jade Seekers that captured you were in my village to kill me. These pilots don't want any Imperial attention, and they're good at getting illicit cargo from one place to another."

"Now that you put it that way, I see your point." Aja bumped my shoulder with her fist. "I guess there's more in that hot body than just a healthy sexual appetite."

"Thanks." I chuckled and hoisted my satchel back over my shoulder.

We headed down the hill to the river's edge, with no idea just how much trouble we were walking into.

Chapter Eleven

"OUTTA THE WAY, GRUB!" A RIVERBOAT PILOT, dressed in sleek black shorts and a striped, red-and-yellow short-sleeved shirt, barked as he hustled past me and made his way down the dock. The captain scampered up a long, rickety ladder to the village overhead. His black ponytail danced along his spine with every rung, and a few seconds later he'd vanished onto the balcony twenty feet overhead.

"Rude," Yata croaked. It flapped its wings and flew up to the balcony railing.

"That's very high." Aja glared at the ladder as if willing it to shrink down to a more manageable height. "If you fall, it'll break your leg. Maybe your neck."

"It's not that high." I looked up at the top of the ladder, then back to Aja. "Are you scared of heights?"

"I'm not scared of anything," Aja growled. She crossed her arms over her chest. "But this seems unnecessarily risky. If someone falls, we'll be delayed."

A gaggle of riverboat passengers flooded past us and shot up the ladder one after another. They were all children, and if any of them had seen more than twelve summers, I'd have been surprised.

"I'm a shaman. If someone falls, I'll fix them up and we'll be back on the road in no time." I held out one hand to the spirit. "Come on. You'll be surprised how easy it is to climb."

"No." Aja didn't move an inch. "There has to be another way."

"This is the fastest way to the lake. We just need to hire a pilot, then we can climb back down and—"

"You go. I'll stay here."

The idea of leaving Aja down here didn't sit well with me. If anything happened to her, I'd lose my mind.

"Out of my way." Ayo shot past me and scrambled up the ladder. She looked down from the top and shouted, "It's easy!"

Aja glared at me, then tackled the ladder with more violence than agility. She kept her eyes locked on the wooden stilt in front of her face and wrapped her arms around it every time she went up a rung.

"Blood God," a man cursed as he hopped out of his boat with a bundle of deer hides over his shoulder. "Is she trying to climb that ladder or hump it?"

"Shut your fucking mouth," I snapped.

The pilot glanced at me with anger in his eyes. Too bad for him I was a solid foot taller and thirty pounds heavier than he was. He looked away, wisely deciding that the better part of valor was not getting his shit kicked in by a mostly naked shaman.

"Geez, Kyr," Aja called down from the balcony. Her face was red and her eyes wild. "Don't be such a baby. There's no reason to be afraid of a stupid ladder."

I gawked at the spirit, considered a comeback, and let it go. We're all afraid of something; there wasn't any point in riding Aja about her fears. If razzing me made her feel better, that was a victory I could let her have.

Climbing the ladder with my war club was tricky, but I managed it without breaking my neck. Ayo took the weapon from me when I reached the balcony, and Aja slapped my shoulder with a grin.

"Let's find that pilot," she smirked and sauntered off with her hips swinging.

"She gets like this," Ayo whispered to me. "She's not afraid of anything, really, but sometimes she gets nervous."

"And then she gets cocky when she gets past the fear. I get it." I'd felt much the same after I'd sent the Jade Seekers to one of the Frozen Hells. There was something about ducking death's claws that made a person feel pretty awesome about their skills.

The elevated parts of the village were even more chaotic than the river's traffic. People passed one another on the narrow rope bridges, cursing as the unstable walkways swayed from side to side and threatened to dump them into the water far below. The planks were only used by the brightly dressed pilots, who ran along them with suicidal speed without even looking down.

"Now what?" Aja asked. Her wild-eyed confidence was fading to caution, and she was very careful to keep her eyes off the river.

"Excuse me," I called out to a riverboat captain as she reached the balcony.

"Fuck off, lander," she growled and stormed past me in an obvious hurry to be somewhere else.

"You should kill one of these people," Yata suggested. "Maybe that would convince the rest of them to be more polite."

"This way." I chased after the rude woman. If pilots were anything like the merchants I'd known growing up, the first thing she'd want to do when she made landfall would be to get a drink. And wherever she was drinking, there'd be plenty of other pilots doing the same.

A few minutes later we pushed through the swinging doors of an enormous bar over the center of the river. It was the noisiest, most crowded building I'd ever been in. I couldn't tell if I was excited by the buzz of energy in the air or nauseated by the overwhelming smell of cheap alcohol and cheaper cigarettes. The heavy mist that covered the world couldn't compete with the dense wall of steel-gray smoke that filled the bar, and I couldn't help but cough as we crossed the threshold.

"Get out of the goddamned way, lander," a man growled as he bulled through. "I need a beer and a slice of pussy."

Ah, yes. This was definitely the place.

My eyes adjusted to the dimly lit interior and showed me a clientele predominantly dressed in light, garish clothes. The waitresses that plied the pilots with booze, cigarettes, and pipes loaded with sticky black balls wore skirts so short the bottom halves of their swaying ass cheeks jutted proudly from below their hems. Most of the serving girls wore garish necklaces and jangling bracelets, and not another stitch of clothing.

"And you were worried about us attracting attention," Aja snorted. "At least my tits are covered."

"Sort of." I searched the crowd for a pilot who didn't look too drunk or crazy. "Let's try this guy."

My target wore a blue vest covered with overlapping embroidered circles of gold thread. His long mustache hung in oily strips on either side of his mouth, the braided ends so long they threatened to dunk into his bowl of soup as he shoveled spoonfuls of piping hot broth into his mouth.

"Not interested," he grumbled when I drew up to his table. Greasy brown broth spilled over his lips and into his beard as he spoke. "I said fuck off!"

The crimson bear bristled in my core, furious that anyone would speak to her shaman like that. She wanted me to drown this fucker in his bowl of soup. I wanted that, too, but it seemed like a bad first impression to make on the other pilots.

"Sorry to have disturbed your meal," I muttered and stepped away from his table.

"Over here." A fat man with so many rings in his nostrils I was surprised he could breathe waved at us from a few tables over. He waited for us to reach him, then steepled his fingers and leaned forward until his belly shoved the table a few inches toward me. "You three look like you're in need of a good river man. Am I right?"

"I'm looking for a pilot to take us downriver," I said. Up close, it was obvious the guy was either very drunk or very high. His glassy eyes were out of focus, and his mouth hung open like he didn't have the energy or coordination to keep his jaws together.

"How far?" He puffed on his pipe and unleashed a cloud of black vapor that smelled like wildcat piss.

I jerked my head away from the vile smoke, careful not to let any of it climb up my nostrils. There was no telling what effect that shit would have on me if I got a good whiff of it.

"I need to get to the Lake of Moonsilver Mist." I dodged another black cloud. "How much?"

"Fifty," the man's words left his mouth in swirls of ebony smoke. "In advance."

"Fifty imperials?" That was enough to buy a fucking horse and all the tack to go with it. Who the fuck did this asshole think he was trying to rob?

"Fifty celestials!" the man barked and jabbed his pipe's bowl at my face. "Imperials, bah. Stupid grub."

Celestial coins were worth ten times imperials, or at least they had been before I climbed Mount Shiki. This guy's price was enough to buy a decent house back in my village. I bristled at the thought of just how hard this guy was trying to fuck me.

"Goddamned thief," I growled.

"What did you call me?" The man's eyes were suddenly as clear and sharp as a pair of glass knives. "My price is fair, you naked fucking savage. I oughta carve your spine out for your bullshit insinuation otherwise."

The fat man shoved back from his seat and stood up. He wasn't quite as tall as I was, but he had close to fifty pounds on me and an ugly knife in his hand.

"Whoa, easy." I was sure I could take the bastard in a fair fight. I was also sure I'd still get some nasty cuts and attract all the wrong kinds of attention in the process. "I was just surprised by the price, that's all."

We eyed one another over the table, the threat of violence thick in the air. The spirits stood on either side of me, tense and ready to spring into action if push came to shove. I wasn't sure what Ayo could do in a fight, but Aja looked like she could do some damage if she was backed into a corner.

"Get away from that fat fuck, kid." A woman's voice, brash and bold as a trumpet blast, sliced through the tension around me. "He's too jacked up on lilis tar to pilot piss out of his dick, much less a sampan downriver. Come with me before someone sticks a knife in you."

The speaker strode past me confidently, without so much as a glance for the pilot squared off in front of me. She was tall, and her long legs made the pair of tight black shorts she wore seem like they covered almost nothing. Like the other pilots, her shirt was so bright it made me want to squint. Unlike the other pilots, though, she left her dark hair loose, and the tangled curls spilled down her back almost to her waist.

I glanced at Aja and Ayo, shrugged, then followed the pilot through the crowded bar.

She tossed coins onto the trays of passing waitresses as she wove through the full tables, and the servers grinned and bobbed their heads in thanks. By the time she'd reached a surprisingly empty booth in the bar's far corner, she'd shelled out at least twenty coins. It was clear this woman was a regular, and just as clear that the staff liked and looked out for her as thanks for her generosity.

"Gotta watch who you talk to," she chided me and took a seat with her back to the wall. "That fat fucker is Guasil. He traffics in sweet flesh like your little friends here. If he'd got you alone on the river, the last thing you'd have seen was his knife opening that pretty neck of yours. Blood God, tall boy, sit the fuck down before I get a crick in my neck from staring up at you."

"And you're telling me all this out of the goodness of your heart." I sat down on the rickety bench on the opposite side of the booth. Ayo dropped in next to me, and Aja pulled an empty chair from a nearby table and planted it on the outside edge of the table.

"I'm Jaga, and I'm telling you because I could use the coin, and you could use a pilot who won't try to steal these sweet pieces of ass for the slave market." Jaga leaned back in her chair and put her hands on the table.

Her fingers were festooned with heavy rings, and the metal bands clinked against the table. "You told Guasil you wanted to go to the Lake of Moonsilver Mist?"

"That's right." I tried not to let my inexperence at haggling show on my face. "How much?"

"Not fifty fucking celestials, that's for sure." Jaga clucked her tongue against the roof of her mouth. "Let's say twenty imperials, and you help me with a little issue I have."

"Seems reasonable." Twenty imperials was still a decent chunk of change, but it seemed a lot less like a ripoff than Guasil's price. "Unless the favor's going to get me killed."

"Probably won't." Jaga leaned over the table and gestured for me to come closer. She didn't speak again until I'd lowered my head toward hers. "I've got a buyer for materialized senjin containers. I need help filling them."

"Sounds dangerous." Unless Jaga was a practitioner, the only way she could fill senjin containers was to spend time near the dream meridians. I'd seen the corruption that oozed into the earth from around those lines. There'd be no telling what kind of trouble might crop up if she was intentionally gathering corrupted senjin.

"Probably." She shrugged and leaned back. "But that's the offer."

This ride was a hell of a lot cheaper than the first offer, but it would put me and my companions in serious danger. Materialized senjin affected the world around it, and legends said that powerful sacred beasts often sought the energy to consume its power. Would corrupted sacred energy draw corrupted creatures to it? I didn't know, but fighting monsters was not high on my list of shit I wanted to do before I died.

I also wasn't sure partnering with someone who collected tainted senjin for a living was a great plan. Whatever Jaga's customer was going to do with the poisoned sacred energy couldn't be good. I'd come back to save the world, not let someone use its poison for dark purposes.

"No thanks." I leaned back in my seat and crossed my arms. "I won't get my people killed to line your pockets."

"Ah, well." She shrugged and gestured for me to get away from her table. "If you change your mind before tomorrow morning, I'm docked down below. Gold-prowed sampan with a red cabin. Can't miss it. Now fuck off so I can eat and drink in peace."

No other riverboat pilots stepped forward after Jaga's rude dismissal. Left to my own devices I fumbled through one negotiation after another as the sun sank lower and my energy flagged. The spirits weren't doing much better. Their cores were running dry, and we'd have to recharge before we slept. That, at least, was something to look forward to.

"Thirty imperials," the last pilot said as I flopped down in the rickety chair opposite him. "I've heard your other negotiations, and you and I both know this is the best price you're going to get here."

"Deal." This fucker's deal was more expensive than Jaga's, but he didn't want me to get us all killed fucking around with tainted senjin. Plus, I was too worn out to keep doing this. I needed to recharge and sleep. "My name's Kyr."

"Mokar," the pilot said. "Pay me now, and I'll meet you on the east shore at first light. My boat's blue with a green cabin. Two silver stripes on the prow."

"Half up front, half tomorrow," I shot back. I was tired, not stupid. Before he could object, I dug a gold ring out of my satchel and slapped it down in the center of the table. "You'll get another just like it once we're on the river."

Mokar glared at me for a second, then scooped the ring off the table and stuffed it into a pouch that dangled from his belt.

"Consider me hired, then," he said.

"Thanks." I rubbed my eyes and held out my hand to seal the deal. Mokar glanced at it, shrugged, and we shook on it. "Is there someplace we could stay?"

"You can rent rooms from Mama Buko," the pilot said. "She's the next building over. Her place isn't quite as big as the bar, but you can't miss it. Look for the blue torches."

I thanked Mokar again, promised to be ready at the shore by dawn, and guided the exhausted spirits to our next stop.

Mama Buko took one look at my group, shook her head, and wagged a finger at me.

"If you want to hire out a hole, you pay my girls." She pointed her lacquered purple nail at my eye. "Don't bring those sluts in here."

Aja growled like a hungry wolverine and shoved her face into Mama Buko's.

"We're not whores." She clenched her fists so tight the knuckles crackled. "How much for a goddamned room?"

The innkeeper stepped back and spread her arms wide.

"My apologies. You look very much like whores playing dress up in that armor." She stepped toward a rack of keys hanging on the wall and scooped a ring off the peg board. "Five imperials for the three of you."

I opened my satchel, careful not to reveal the extent of its contents, and plucked out a golden ring with a cat's eye agate mounted in its prongs.

"Will this do?" I put the jewelry in Mama Buko's outstretched hand and hoped she'd accept it without argument.

"Hmm." Her eyes flickered as she shifted into her spirit sight and inspected the ring. "Real gold. Gem's flawed, though. Fine."

The gold in the ring weighed more than twenty imperials, but there was no point in arguing. Jewelry wasn't as easy to trade as cash, and I wasn't in a position to bargain. After the physical effort of the past few days and the stress of negotiating with greedy sampan pilots, I was too exhausted to care that I was getting ripped off.

We found the room that matched the number on the key, and I managed to find the keyhole after only three tries. The script on the key triggered a matching script in the lock, and the door swung open. Yata fluttered into the room ahead of us, squawked once, and then perched on the windowsill.

Aja shoved the door closed behind us and pushed me toward the bed. We were all tired and hungry, but there was another, more desperate appetite that needed to be satisfied before we could worry about food or anything else.

"Come here, you," Ayo said, her voice low and husky. She shoved my breechcloth aside with one hand

and dropped to her knees in front of me. Her mouth closed over my cock almost before her knees hit the floor, tongue swirling in a hot spiral around its head, and she sucked until my knees buckled and I had to sit on the edge of the bed.

Aja pounced on the straw mattress next to me, closed her hand around my balls, nails gently grazing the sensitive skin. I grabbed the back of her head and pulled her into a fierce kiss. My tongue flickered over hers, tips brushing against one another. She sucked it deeper into her mouth and thrust her breasts toward me. With a snarl, she unbuckled the straps of her armor and shoved it to one side.

Despite everything that had happened, I had to admit that life was pretty fucking great.

Chapter Twelve

DESPITE MY FILLED CORE AND THE DAY'S physical activity, my sleep was fitful. The wound in my side had mostly healed, thanks to the constant cycle of rin and senjin purification moving through my body, but it started aching not long after midnight. The pain came and went, sticking around long enough to wake me up before it faded away.

It was annoying as hell.

But not nearly as annoying as what happened next.

In the darkest hours before dawn the smell of smoke and the piercing sound of screams dragged me out of an especially exciting dream about my time with Mielyssi. She growled inside my core at the sudden interruption, and I wondered just how much of that dream had been something else entirely.

"Fire," Yata croaked from its perch on the sill. "Two buildings to the west. Doesn't look good."

I jumped out of bed, raising annoyed shouts from Ayo and Aja, and joined Yata at the window. The fire had consumed part of a building's roof and sent its occupants scrambling outside with whatever possessions they could carry clutched to their chests. They shouted with fear and confusion and pointed excitedly toward something I couldn't see down on the river.

"Find out what's going on," I said to Yata. Then to the spirits, "Grab your shit, we need to get the hell out of here."

"Do you know how long it's been since I slept in a real bed?" Ayo groaned. "It's probably nothing to do with us. Let me sleep."

I wanted to believe the spirit, but I couldn't. A niggling voice of doubt at the back of my mind warned me to trust my instincts and get moving. Better to run like hell and be wrong about the trouble than to stick around and get my throat slit.

"Not now." I grabbed my war club and ran to the room's door. I hesitated before I opened it, listening for any trouble outside. We weren't the only ones awake, but I didn't hear any screams or sounds of real trouble in the inn. I eased the door open and peered out into the hall.

"What's going on?" A woman in a red robe brandished a knife, as if that would convince someone to answer her.

"Fire," I said and looked down the hall to see if there were any other signs of danger. I let out a sigh of relief when I didn't see any threats.

"Shit. That's bad." The woman in red's knife vanished into her sleeve, and she crossed her arms under breasts that threatened to spill out of her robes. "If it spreads, we'll all be swimming."

At the sound of Yata's wings beating against the windowsill, I ducked back into the room and shut the door.

"Jade Seekers," the three-legged raven squawked and ruffled its feathers. "Their leader has a giant sword that moans—"

"Like a woman." My heart sank at the news. I'd dropped Jiro a few hundred feet into a rocky ravine. I had no idea how the bastard had crawled out of that, much less how he'd found where I was staying.

"Ah, motherfucker," Aja snapped. "That's the fucker who caught us looking for you."

"Yep." I slung my weapon over my shoulder and grabbed my satchel. "We have to get gone, like, now."

I left the hotel room at a brisk walk that was just shy of a run. I didn't want to attract attention; just another sleepy guy trying to figure out what the fuck had woken him up. Not that I thought that would hide me from Jiro Kos for long. If he saw a mostly naked man with a pair of hot spirits, he'd be on top of me in the blink of an eye. I had to be gone before that happened.

We threaded our way through the crowds gathered outside the inn, and I pulled my shoulders in and hunkered down to keep from towering over the rest of the crowd. I hoped that would be enough to keep Jiro from spotting me as he burned the city to the waterline.

My stomach clenched at that thought. Everyone who called this village home would suffer because I'd decided to stop here. They were criminals, sure, but they didn't deserve this kind of trouble. If Jiro found me, he'd probably kill a bunch of them for harboring a fugitive. If he didn't find me, he'd still murder everyone out of sheer spite.

Goddamn, I wanted to kill that guy all over again.

"This way." I pushed through a knot of pilots and broke into a jog. I needed to get to the shore and find Marok.

I spied his boat a few minutes later, docked in the midst of a few dozen other sampans. All the pilots were on deck, eyes wide in the firelight.

The blaze was spreading, and if someone didn't put it out soon the whole village would be ashes by sunup.

I scrambled down the ladder to the riverbank and ran to the boat. Yata fluttered along beside me, and the spirits hustled to catch up to my long strides.

"Marok," I barked as I ran up to his boat. "We need to go."

"It's still hours to dawn," the pilot protested. "Far too dangerous. We'll leave in the morning."

"I can't wait until morning." I struggled to keep my voice even, but from the look in Marok's eyes, I hadn't succeeded.

"What's the hurry?" The pilot didn't even attempt to keep the suspicion out of his voice. He pointed at the fire. "Are you running from the assholes who did this?"

The last thing I wanted to do was explain to a smuggler that the Jade Seekers were on my ass. At best, he'd use that as an excuse to jack up the price, and at worst he'd sell me out to the hunters.

"It's complicated."

"Complicated costs a lot more than simple," he said with a smirk. "And no one gets on my boat with secrets. Hazardous cargo has a way of blowing up in my face."

"I can explain." I reached for my satchel. I'd pay whatever he wanted if we moved right fucking now. "Once we're downriver."

"I don't think so."

"Fuck," I snapped and paced the shore. Moored boats formed an archipelago of sampans that stretched from one side of the river to the other.

Without another word from Marok I ran past his boat and onto the deck of another vessel. The spirits raced after me, and we jumped from one sampan to the next, leaving bobbing vessels and shouting captains strung out behind us. Yata circled above us, nearly invisible against the night sky.

"You're really making friends today," Ayo shouted as we dodged past an irate captain and his gaff hook.

"Fuck 'em," I shouted back.

"Where are we running?" Aja asked. She dodged under a swung oar, then leapt onto the next boat.

"Toward the second-best offer we got." I blocked a pilot's rowing pole with my war club and kicked him into the water. "Sorry!"

I found the boat I was looking for in the middle of the river. I jumped onto its deck and raced to the door of the low-slung cabin at its aft.

"Jaga!" I shouted and banged on the wooden door like my life depended on it. "You still need someone to watch your ass while you harvest senjin?"

"Shut the fuck up!" The pilot groaned from behind the curtain. "Blood God, what fucking time is it?"

"Before dawn." I shoved the door open and felt my cheeks redden when I saw Jaga standing naked in front of me, her hand raised as if she'd been about to open the door. A vivid blue tattoo encircled her breasts, and a pair of golden rings through her left nipple glinted in the firelight.

"Never seen big tits before?" Jaga asked, hands clutching her head. She tilted her head back, eyes wide, and sniffed at the air. "Mother of fuck, is Ulishi on fire?"

"Yes." I opened my satchel and grabbed a fistful of chains and rings from its guts. "I need to get out of here, now."

"Fucking hell." Another voice groaned from inside the cabin, and a pale-faced man with rings through both of his nipples staggered out of Jaga's bed. He wobbled from side to side, then caught himself on the cabin's wall. "I've had too much to drink to deal with this shit."

"Then get the fuck off my boat, you limp-dick cocksucker." Jaga grabbed the man's clothes off the floor near the cabin's door, shoved them at his chest, then kicked him in the ass. "Go. I've got paying customers."

"Bitch!" The man stumbled past me, noticed the spirits at my back, and covered his cock with his clothes. "Not you two. Excuse me."

He shuffled past the spirits, looked up bewildered at the fire, then shrugged and jumped into the water. The smooth strokes of a practiced swimmer carried him through the dark water toward another sampan veiled by the fog and smoke.

"What the fuck is that?" Jaga shouted as Yata landed on the gunwale with a croak and loud flap of its wings.

"I'm a three-legged raven," Yata cawed. "Haven't you ever seen a bird before?"

"Blood God, boy, you have any other guests you haven't told me about? Maybe a singing bullfrog? Pull up that fucking anchor," Jaga shouted and pointed at a chain dangling over the side of the sampan. "And you two booby girls sit the fuck down. We're gonna move quick, and if you fall overboard, I am not coming back for you."

"Let me help," Ayo said.

"I said park your asses on the deck!" Jaga had untied a mooring line and was busy coiling it into a basket on the starboard side. "And hurry the fuck up with that goddamned anchor."

"It's already onboard." I pointed at the heavy lead weight and the iron chain coiled next to it. "Anything else you need?"

"An explanation." Jaga pointed past me. "You running from those assholes?"

Marok's sampan threaded its way through the water, a trio of Jade Seekers standing in its prow. Their heavy armor pushed the boat deeper into the water than Jaga's boat, but they'd get here soon enough despite the extra load.

"That piece of shit," I snarled. The pilot had sold me out.

"Yeah, Marok's a cocksucker." Jaga retreated into her cabin with my loot. She hollered at me from her quarters. "If we get too close to any of those stilts, push us off with that pole on the port side."

"Why aren't you out here to pilot this damned boat?" I shouted.

"Because some guy woke me up from a dead sleep, and I need to get some shorts on so my coochie doesn't catch a chill from all this night air blowing through her lips."

Oh, yeah. My bad.

The current carried us below the village, the sampan's prow drifting in a slow circle with no one at the rudder to right it. I grabbed the pole and used it to fend off an impending collision with one of the village's many stilts. The sleek boat turned away from the obstacle and slipped through water turned red by the blaze above us. The fire had spread and would keep on spreading until there was nothing left of the thriving outlaw river port but jagged and charred stumps.

"What the hell did you do, boy?" Jaga asked as she stomped out of the cabin. She wore tight black shorts and a purple vest she hadn't bothered to tie closed over her ample breasts. "They're burning down the whole goddamned place to find you."

"Nothing," I answered truthfully.

"That sounds like what a criminal would say." Jaga laughed and grabbed the rudder. "I don't give a rotten fuck what you did, man. Just trying to keep my mind off how bad it'll hurt if those Jade Seekers catch up to us."

"I'll tell them it's not your fault." I said. "If they catch us."

"Won't fucking matter." The pilot steered us through a narrow gap between a pair of boulders and cursed. "That cocksucker Marok's boat is fast as hell. If he didn't have a ton of armor onboard, he'd have caught us by now."

Despite the weight of his passengers, Marok's boat was gaining on us. If we didn't lose them soon, they'd catch us.

"Ayo," I shouted over the roar of the river. "This is your domain. What can you do?"

I focused my spirit sight on the other pilot's craft, and my heart sank. Twin lines of silver script ran down the sleek boat's keel, and a small core glowed within its cabin. It was hard to make out exactly what techniques were held in the scripts, but they were tied to the sampan's speed and maneuverability. It was no wonder the piece of shit was catching up to us.

"Better do something quick," Yata croaked from the top of the cabin. "I'd hate to have to find another shaman after they kill you all."

"I've got it!" Ayo shouted.

"Don't fuck with my boat!" Jaga cried.

If Ayo had heard the captain, she didn't show it. Her brow was furrowed with concentration, and she'd raised both hands toward the sampan behind us. The strain of whatever she was doing was clear on Ayo's face, and shio danced around her like fireflies as she focused her will on our enemies.

"If she fucks with this boat, I'll skin you alive," Jaga promised me. "The last cocksucker who channeled that shit into my boat snapped the beam right in half."

"She's not going to break your boat." I wasn't sure that was true, but I didn't really care, either. If we didn't do something, the Jade Seekers would catch us, and there'd be a hell of a lot more to worry about than a busted sampan.

"She better not—"

Ayo shouted something in a language I didn't understand. A wave of power burst from her outstretched hands and dove into the river. The energy streaked toward Marok's boat like a school of glowing fish, breaking into smaller and smaller shards of luminescence. By the time the darts of light were thirty feet ahead of the boat on our tail they'd split into a hazy field of power stretched across the river.

For a moment, nothing happened.

Ayo sagged against the side of the sampan, and Aja grabbed the white-haired spirit's shoulder to keep her from pitching over the side into the water.

Whatever the spirit had tried to do, it hadn't worked. I hefted my war club and prepared to trigger the crimson bear's techniques for the melee that was sure to come.

And then, for the blink of an eye, a five-foot-wide section of the river in front of our pursuers just stopped.

Marok's sampan hit the line of motionless water at full speed. The hull shattered into kindling, and the Jade Seekers howled in surprise and rage as wooden shrapnel slashed at their armor. The power held in the sampan's scripts escaped from the ruptured prow in a rainbow spray that lit up the night like a second moon.

The boat's wreckage flipped into the air and tumbled end over end past the trap Ayo had laid for it. Marok was hurled free of the sampan's carcass and splashed into the water with a surprised yelp. He bobbed to the surface a moment later, spluttering but otherwise unharmed.

The Jade Seekers weren't so lucky.

They hit the water like stones, and their heavy armor dragged them to the river's bed. I caught flashes of glowing jade as the current tumbled the warriors through the dark water. Moments later, even those traces of our pursuers had been swallowed by the currents. The armored warriors were gone.

"Holy shit, Ayo," I whispered.

"Told you that shit would break a boat," Jaga shouted from the aft end of the sampan.

The spirits and I sat down on the deck, heads leaned together, and chuckled under the moonlight as we floated down the river with smoke billowing into the sky behind us.

I kissed Ayo, gently, and held her tight. She'd done very well, and now it was time to rest.

Chapter Thirteen

B Y THE TIME THE SUN'S GOLDEN FACE SHONE
through the mist, we were far, far away from the
burning village. Yata had done a quick sky patrol
first thing and hadn't spotted any more boats filled with
Jade Seekers on the river, which was a win in my book.
Against all odds, it looked like we'd escaped.

"Get up, fucker." Jaga prodded my ass with her
bare toes. "Time to get to work."

"I paid you!" I protested. I'd been awake for half
an hour already, but I didn't feel like doing anything.
After the day I'd had yesterday, all I wanted to do was
lie around and soak up what little sun there was.

Jaga, it appeared, had other ideas.

"You did," the pilot agreed. "For the trouble of
getting you away from the Jade Seekers. Now it's time
to pay me for letting you stay on my boat."

"You have to be kidding." I hauled myself
upright, balanced against the swaying of the narrow boat,
and turned to face the pilot. She was shorter than she'd
looked in the bar, though the muscles she showed off
looked bigger than I remembered. The pilot was older
than me, probably in her thirties or close to it, but she'd
held up well despite a career that kept her out in all kinds
of horrible weather and encouraged her to drink herself

into a stupor as often as possible. All in all, she was nice to look at, but a lot less nice to deal with.

"I never kid about money, my man." She gestured toward a small set of clay pots held along the sides of the sampan by lengths of knotted spider silk cord. "It's time to get to fishing for senjin."

"You know it's corrupted, right?" I focused my spirit sight on the dream meridian that ran down the length of the river as far as I could see. Oily black threads crawled through the line of power. "It's basically poison to anyone who handles it."

"I don't give a rat's tight assfuck," she said with a shrug. "There's a magus in Simdelo who'll pay me very goddamned well for jugs of this shit."

"What's he doing with it?" I tried to think of a single good use for the tainted senjin and couldn't come up with anything that didn't involve significant amounts of death and destruction. "Does he purify it before he uses it?"

"Don't fucking know, don't fucking care." Jaga flashed me a startlingly white smile. "Cocksucker can shoot it up his ass, long as I get paid."

"There are more important things than money," I said quietly. My shaman's soul ached at the idea that someone would willingly traffic in the corruption that was destroying the world.

"You don't say, nature boy." Jaga looked at me like I'd grown a third head. "I don't know who you think you are, coming on my boat and telling me what I should or shouldn't do for money. Not all of us have the luxury of living off the land like some kind of animal."

"There's nothing wrong with living like an animal," I growled down at the pilot, the crimson bear's rage burning like a hot coal in my heart.

We stared at one another for a long, tense breath. Jaga's eyes burned into mine, and a dark flush spread across her cheeks and upper chest. My anger was a tight fist in my gut, and I knew I was a few seconds away from either coming to blows or saying something I'd regret.

"Okay, fuck, you win." I took a deep breath and let go of my anger. Fighting with Jaga wouldn't help anything. It was clear I'd never convince her not to sell the tainted senjin, and I needed this boat. Better to swallow my pride and get the spirits back to their mistress as quickly as possible than risk pissing off the pilot any further. "What do you want me to do?"

"Untie a jug from the string there, open the top, hang onto the cord, and stick it in the water. When it's full, pull it out of the water, close the lid, and give it to me." With a snort, Jaga stomped off to man the rudder. Just in time, too, because the stretch of river ahead of us was littered with jutting boulders and splintered tree stumps that looked like they could rip out the boat's flat bottom in the blink of an eye.

"This looks like it'll be fun." Ayo joined me at the rail, her shoulder bumping against my left side as I untied the first jug from the rope that ran down the port side of the sampan's deck.

"Don't get any of that garbage on you," Aja warned me. "Those jugs are scripted to manifest the senjin. Physical contact with that tainted liquid energy might kill you before we can purify it."

"I'll be careful," I promised. "Keep an eye out for any big fish."

The biggest worry I had about fishing for senjin was how much attention it would attract from local wildlife and any spirits who might be in the area.

Manifested sacred energy drew spirits like bees to honey, and they had no reservations about possessing animals to get to the stuff. If a river leviathan came nosing around Jaga's boat, there'd be one hell of a fight.

"You're the boss." Aja grinned at me and leaned on the sampan's edge to let the wind blow through her hair.

"Don't let Jaga hear you say that." I winked at the spirit and went to work.

The jug was a simple red clay pot with a daisy wheel lid. A circle of golden script around the jug's mouth glimmered with shio energy as I opened the lid. One end of a thin spider silk cord was knotted through a pair of brass rings on top of the jug, and the other end of the ring was tied to a wooden peg that jutted from the deck.

"Here goes nothing." I lowered the pot into the water until it was fully submerged and focused my spirit sight on the vessel. I'd never seen anything like this and wanted to know how it worked.

The dream meridian glowed down the middle of the river like a ruler-straight streak of cobalt blue shot through with ebony threads of corruption. It took me long seconds to see past the meridian's power to the rest of the sacred energy around me.

The river's waters were laced with sparks of power the same color as the meridian, complete with their own lines of tainted shadow. Those sparks were drawn to the jug like iron filings to a magnet. When enough glimmers of sacred energy had gathered around the lid, they coalesced into globs of liquid sliver and slipped through the holes in the daisy wheel. In the few seconds I watched, Jaga's contraption captured dozens of those blobs. The script must have been entry only, because the silver didn't leak out of the pot after it went in.

"Huh," Ayo said, her eyes bright. "I've never seen anything quite like that."

"There's a good reason for that," Aja countered. She leaned on my right side and kissed me on the cheek. "No one with any sense would ever use such a thing."

"No one's ever accused me of being sensible." I tossed another jug over the side, then another. Now that I had the hang of it, I only needed a few seconds to get each jug into the water. In the space of a few minutes, all thirteen of the clay pots bobbed in the water alongside the sampan.

Aja was more nervous than I'd ever seen her, and Ayo moved around me to comfort her fellow spirit.

"It's just not safe." Aja pointed at the water that churned around the pots. "Look at that. You think that's how water should act?"

The river thickened around the string of jugs connected to the sampan's side. The water was already as sticky as rice pudding, and jagged bolts of black corruption flickered like lightning inside its clotted mass. Even as I watched the patch of glutinous fluid expanded.

"The senjin's crystallizing the water's essence," I muttered to myself. While the sacred energy was potent, it wasn't the only power in the world. Every living thing, every object, every substance had an essence of its own. As the senjin manifested, it forced the river's essence to mimic the same process. The more senjin that manifested in the jugs, the more of the river that would crystallize around them. Left unchecked, the process would mire Jaga's sampan in a growing field of gel-like water. "Fuck."

"Like I said," Aja muttered.

I pulled on one of the spider silk cords, but the jug wouldn't budge. There was already too much congealed water essence surrounding it.

"Jaga!" I shouted. "Your pots are a fucking disaster!"

With an exaggerated sigh the pilot locked the rudder and hustled around the sampan's cabin. Her face was flushed, and her eyes spat daggers at me as she stomped across the deck to confront me.

"Why the fuck did you put all the pots into the water at the same time?" She stood up on her tiptoes to shout into my face, and her ample chest smashed against mine. "I said to put one pot in the water and bring it to me when it's full, right? One motherfucking pot!"

Oh. Well, shit.

"I figured this would get the job done faster." I pursed my lips and shrugged. "I'm sorry. I'm a shaman. I'll fix it."

"You better." She stormed to the aft of the boat, a stream of "motherfuckers" and "cocksuckers" trailing through the air behind her.

My spirit sight showed me the river's essence consisted of a mixture of mostly blue shio with spots of more energetic crimson rin sacred power. There were threads of black corruption in the water, too, though they lacked the intensity of the ebony lines that radiated from the senjin. If I was careful, I could undo this mess and get the pots out of the water before disaster struck.

"Please make sure I don't fall overboard." I sat down cross-legged on the deck and rested the backs of my hands on my knees. "I'm going to see if I can clean up this mess before the whole fucking boat goes to the bottom of the river."

"What can we do?" Ayo asked.

"I'll free one pot from the river's grip at a time." I pointed to the clay jug the farthest from me. "Starting with that one. When the sticky water's cleared away, haul the jug aboard."

"I'll do it." Aja walked to the prow and looked down at the pot. "Keep an eye on him, Ayo. Make sure he doesn't get himself killed."

"I'm not doing anything dangerous." I let my breath cycle through my body, and the nodes of rin in my core twitched and stirred, eager to be used.

"Says the man who tried to sink the boat with a few pots." Aja grinned at me to take the worst of the barb from her words, but she had a point. I'd made this mess because I hadn't understood the implications of what I'd done. That was the kind of mistake that could get everyone killed if I wasn't careful.

I took a deep breath, let it out, and shifted my vision into spirit sight to get a better look at the sacred energy around me.

The problematic patch of river essence was twice the size of the sampan and growing in every direction at an alarming pace. To my enhanced senses, the crystallized water consisted of straight threads of blue shio held in rigid order by wire-like rods of rin.

The rest of the river was composed of unruly tangles of shio stirred into chaotic motion by the clusters of rin that blazed through the river like a meteor shower.

Be careful. The crimson bear's words startled me. It felt like she was inches behind me. I swore I felt the heat of her breath on the nape of my neck and smelled the rich scent of her flesh. *Energy work is tricky. I'd hate for you to lose yourself in the flow.*

I ached to turn and embrace Mielyssi. I'd been gone from Mount Shiki for a few days, but my heart ached for her as if we'd been separated for months.

This isn't the time. A spectral hand tousled my dream-self's hair. *Save the world you're in, then you can be with me once again.*

You don't ask for much, I thought.

I'm worth it.

The crimson bear's laughter, low and throaty, wrapped around me like a warm blanket. A thousand memories burst through my thoughts and filled my heart with a longing so deep and powerful it ached like a wound. My time with the spirits was amazing, but it had been like drinking water after a lifetime enjoying the finest wines.

I shook my head and pulled my thoughts back to the task at hand. Save the world, save the bear. If I screwed this up, then there'd be no one left to heal this corruption. I wouldn't only lose my life, I'd lose Mielyssi.

She left me to my work, every hint of her presence vanishing save for her rich, wild perfume.

My plan was simple. The problem wasn't the shio, it was the layers of rin that held the water's essence stiff and unyielding. If the rin was gone, the shio would go back to its normal, chaotic self, and the water would flow like, well, water.

Clearing the rin from a large area was beyond my seabound core's abilities, but I only had to purge the sacred energy from the crystallized water closest to each jug. Surely that couldn't be hard.

My little experiment in the Deepways station had taught me that the first step in drawing energy was to clear out some space in my nodes so I wouldn't risk overloading my core. I focused on a single node and released the energy it contained. Because I didn't direct it to a specific technique, the sacred power flowed out of the node and into my body. The vibrant crimson energy traced lines of warmth along the arteries in my abdomen, then found its way into the muscle fibers in my arms and legs. With the node empty, it was time to move on to the next stage of my master plan.

On my next inhalation, I focused my entire mind on the stiff lines of rin that surrounded the pot next to Aja. One of the red wires snapped out of shape and blazed like a star. My breath plucked it out of the surrounding shio and drew it into my core as easily as pulling a splinter out of my finger. One by one, the rin lines emerged from the water and sank into the empty node at the heart of my core.

"Now!" I emerged from my trance and jabbed a finger at the pot I'd freed from the clutches of the crystallized water.

"On it!" Aja reeled the pot up by its spider silk cord, careful to keep the swinging jug from sloshing its contents onto her or the sampan. "Fuck, that's heavy."

Ayo rushed over to her friend and grabbed the scripted jug's handles to steady it on the deck. The two of them wrestled the jug over to me, and I had to brace myself to keep from recoiling away from it.

The manifested senjin within the jug radiated a sickening aura. It filled my nostrils with the rich stink of decay and my thoughts with streaks of vile shadows. My guts tightened into a knot as I closed the daisy wheel.

The jug's script glowed like molten gold and the lid locked closed with a faint click. Sealing the container did nothing to alleviate the queasiness that emanated from it, but at least I wouldn't have to worry about drenching myself in tainted senjin while I freed the rest of the jugs from the river's death grip.

It took me another fifteen exhausting minutes to free all the jugs. My core ached with the effort of continually emptying and refilling its nodes, and the rin I released exceeded the capacity of my flesh and dripped from my pores in scarlet beads that slid through the deck drains and vanished back into the river. I hated to waste energy like that, but the rin that splashed around the sampan's side did help to churn the water and break up the crystallized river essence around the pots, so it wasn't a total loss.

"Pots are full," I called back to Jaga.

"That's nice," she shouted back. "You might want to take a look behind us, though. I think you've got a new friend."

With a groan, I dragged myself to my feet and staggered past the boat's cabin to see what the fuck Jaga was talking about. My skin itched with a prickly heat from all the rin I'd cycled through my body, and the excess energy trapped in my muscles left me feeling jittery and irritable, like I'd had about twenty too many pots of tea. I wanted to punch something, and I wasn't picky about what that something was.

"What the fuck—" I bit the question off as soon as I saw what had gotten Jaga's attention.

The sampan's wake was a smooth V behind us, the water rolling away from the boat's hull in gentle, foamy lines. Beyond that, though, the river was much more turbulent. Something was swimming toward us.

Something big.

Chapter Fourteen

THE CREATURE'S HEAD BREACHED THE WATER AS it approached, and the sight of it made me want to run into the cabin and hide. The beast's mouth was almost as wide as the sampan, and it was surrounded by barbed whiskers as thick as my forearm. Its scaly hide was the revolting red of an open wound, and its eyes bulged from their sockets like a pair of black marbles each the size of my head. The crimson blade of its dorsal fin rose from the water behind it, spines jutting toward the sky. The enormous catfish came on fast, and its hunger was a palpable wave that pushed against me with the force of a storm front.

"Fuck me." My breath caught in my throat as the mutant bottom-feeder sliced through the water with sinuous sweeps of its tail. Its aura pulsed with angry flashes of crimson rin.

It wanted me in its belly. Now.

"Please tell me you're going to do something more than stare at that cocksucker," Jaga called to me.

"I've got it." I wasn't sure exactly how I'd get it, but that had never stopped me from doing something before.

I raced back to the boat's prow and grabbed my war club. The fish was big, but it wasn't so big that I couldn't crack its skull open. One good shot between the eyes might be enough to bring it down.

Maybe.

"You can't be serious." Aja took up a position beside me at the sampan's rail. "You're going to hit that monstrosity with a stick?"

"Thanks for the vote of confidence." I didn't blame Aja for doubting me. She didn't know the full extent of my new seabound core. Hell, even I didn't know just how strong I'd become since the advancement.

We were about to find out.

The monstrosity swerved around the sampan's rudder and surged ahead to draw alongside the boat. The beast stared up at me, and my reflection wavered in the nightmarish darkness of its mirror-smooth black eye.

My spirit sight showed me the beast's core, all ten of its nodes glowing with red rin energy. At least some of that power was mine, shed when I'd struggled with Jaga's fishing pots. That was what had attracted the critter, and it was hungry for more.

A lot more.

The beast's core also glowed with three techniques, one that reinforced its powerful jaws, another somehow tied to its immense hunger, and a third tied to a much, much more powerful creature. The silver senjin thread that floated away from a shadow on the beast's core told me this fucker was the familiar of something very, very dangerous.

Well, fuck. That changed things.

If I smashed this thing in the skull and didn't kill it immediately, it might call out to its master for help. The sampan was a speedy craft, but if the catfish's bigger, meaner boss showed up, I had no doubt we'd be capsized in the blink of an eye.

Fighting was out of the question, then. It was time to do some shaman shit.

"Hey, buddy," I said to the fish. "I know you're hungry and think I'd be super tasty, but trust me when I say that is not how you want this to go down."

The fish tossed its head in response, showering the sampan with a few dozen gallons of water. The spray blinded me for the space of a heartbeat, and I was sure the beast would follow up its trick with another attack. And then I felt a surge of rin in the air and knew the fucker was up to something much more dangerous.

As a shaman, I had a strong affinity for beasts of the wild, even if they were giant catfish powered up by sacred rin energy. That affinity warned me that the river monster had activated two of its techniques, and it was so close to me I felt them thrum to life. My teeth itched with the urge to bite as its first technique kicked in, and my stomach ached with a wash of hunger when the second power switched on. This guy wasn't messing around. He'd come to eat, and he wasn't taking no for an answer.

"I don't fucking think so," I snarled and locked eyes with the giant fish again. I didn't want to fight this asshole and risk angering its boss, but I sure as hell wasn't going to let it eat me, either. "I'm a shaman, you're an animal. Don't upset the fucking pecking order."

The fish didn't seem impressed by what I had to say. It opened its mouth wide, sucked in a bellyful of water, and reared up out of the water.

Before the asshole could spit on me again, I dug into the bag of shaman tricks I'd learned during my time with the crimson bear. We were healers and masters of nature, and that included dealing with the spirits of the wild and all kinds of animals. Even giant ones who wanted to eat us.

My core opened, and a strand of raw rin surged out of me and harpooned the overgrown bottom feeder's core.

Like spirits and other beasts, the catfish's core wasn't ranked, it was just a plain shell with a jumble of nodes inside. Eight of those ten nodes were filled with sacred energy, almost all of which I recognized as coming from me.

Fuck, but I'd shed a lot of sacred power trying to clean up Jaga's pots.

The line of rin snapped taut, and a temporary bond between the catfish and me sprang to life. A sudden surge of blind, animal panic flared through the creature's primitive mind as it registered the strange presence that had just taken root at the heart of its innermost being.

I pushed back against the catfish's urge to feed and its fear, willing it to calm the hell down and go away. As persuasive as I can be, my good thoughts didn't make much headway against its primal drive to eat and eat and fucking eat. In fact, that animal instinct wormed its way back up through the temporary bond and infected me with a primal hunger.

"You all right?" Aja asked. "You're looking a little strange."

"I'm fine. It's just shaman shit." Unlike Yata, the catfish was just a big dumb animal of unusual size. While I could only form temporary bonds with beasts, these connections had benefits I couldn't get from my familiar. For starters, I'd adopt characteristics of the bonded critter, and the longer the temporary bond lasted, the more pronounced those aspects became. At its best, that ability would grant me an eagle's sight, a shark's bite, or a snake's venom. At its worst, it'd grow some barbed whiskers out of my cheeks and make my eyes all googly like my friend the catfish. I crossed my fingers and hoped this little struggle would be over before shit went that far.

As much as the catfish wanted to eat me, it wanted to be free of the bond I'd forged with it even more. The giant fish thrashed and dove deep into the river in a desperate bid to shake my connection loose, and the line of power between us followed it. Frustrated that it couldn't escape into the river's churning depths, the bottom-feeder surged to the surface and threw itself into the air. Its blood-red skin gleamed in the faint sunlight, and its black barbs glistened like oil as it thrashed its tail. At the height of its arc, the creature glared at me with raw, bestial rage and a gnawing hunger. More than anything, it wanted to jump into the boat and eat me and everyone else it could fit into its mouth.

For the moment, though, the catfish couldn't attack me. Our spiritual connection held it at bay, and it could no more take a bite out of my hide than it could chew off its own face. The same was true for me, too. If I attempted to hurt the creature in any way, the connection would snap in an instant.

I needed to do something, though, because the fish's hunger technique was already chewing away at our bond, inflaming the creature's natural instinct to eat into a berserk frenzy. I had a minute or two before that instinct overcame our bond, and then the pissed-off catfish would be free to do whatever the fuck it wanted.

Like smashing Jaga's sampan to pieces and swallowing me whole.

Because hurting the monstrosity was out of the question, I needed another plan. With our cores so close together, the animal's urge to feed was a powerful ache inside my mind. The critter had gotten a taste of my sweet, sweet rin and was now completely bonkers for the stuff. That was the real problem.

If I could heal that insane hunger, the catfish should lose its urge to eat me. I was a shaman. I could handle that.

The hunger technique was fed by a thread of rin energy anchored in one of the catfish's nodes. Removing that power would shut down the technique, and the fishy would be off the hook. The hard part was, I didn't know how to sever that thread.

I focused my will on the node that powered the hunger technique. It was still mostly filled with my rin. The hunger technique looked like it didn't take much energy to power, likely because it was so closely tied to the catfish's natural instincts. There was no way we could wait out the hunger, because it would chew through the bond long before the rin ran dry.

Maybe, though, I could steal the sacred energy and end the technique in a hurry.

I pulled on the sacred energy, trying to coax it out of the fish's node and into my core. It was right there, so close I could feel it. Yet it wouldn't move or respond to my will in any way.

I guess that made sense. Shamans probably weren't supposed to run around sucking the juice out of wild animals to fuel our power. That seemed more like something a sorcerer or necromancer might try.

Fine. If I couldn't leech rin out of the fish to kill its hunger, maybe I could satisfy its need to feed.

Rin rushed out of my core through our connection and flooded the catfish's core. The beast shuddered as my gushing power filled its empty nodes.

That had taken the edge off the critter's hunger, even if it hadn't sated it. Fine. Five of my ten nodes were still filled with rin. I could afford to spend more to end this fight.

"Here you go," I growled and pushed three nodes' worth into the monster catfish's core.

"Who are you talking to?" Aja asked.

"The fish," Ayo said. "It's shaman shit."

"Shaman shit," I confirmed through gritted teeth.

The catfish slurped up every drop of the rin I'd pushed to it. Its core had swelled to almost double its normal size, and every one of its ten nodes glowed as brightly as a lighthouse beacon. The animal cycled the rin through its nodes in a desperate attempt to take in more power. It couldn't. The beast was too full of sacred energy to take in even one more bite.

In fact, it was overfull.

Without warning, the beast gagged and shoved rin through our connection and into my core. The power was different when it came back to me, as if its time in the belly of the beast had imbued it with some aspects of the catfish's essential being.

That was all right with me—the energy felt great as it flooded into me. The power was wild and unbridled, like a brief, glorious flashback to my life with the crimson bear on top of Mount Shiki. I wanted to throw back my head and howl at the sky until my throat was hoarse. I needed to hunt and fill my belly with the flesh of my prey.

"Kyr?" Ayo's voice was small and distant, little more than a whisper on the wind.

Its hunger sated, the catfish dove back to the bottom of the river. It offered a silent thanks for the meal I'd provided and headed downstream with a flick of its tail.

I let it go, and the connection between us snapped with a crystalline chime. The creature's presence vanished from my thoughts the instant I released the bond, but some part of its essence remained within me. My stomach ached with an unearthly hunger. It was time to feed.

I turned to the spirits and licked my lips.

Oh, yes.

They would be fucking delicious.

Chapter Fifteen

AYO AND AJA BACKED AWAY FROM ME, EYES wide, hands held out in front of them defensively. Yata fluttered its wings from the top of the cabin and unleashed a raucous caw of alarm.

A flash of anger raced through my thoughts at their defiance. I needed these fuckers inside me, and their resistance was infuriating.

"Kyr?" Aja's voice was low and dangerous. An uneasy mixture of anger and fear flickered through the spirit's eyes and stoked the fires of my hunger. I wanted her, all of her.

In my belly.

"Come here." The words sounded strange to my ears, as if there was something wrong with my mouth. I crooked my finger toward the spirit to make sure she understood what I wanted.

The redhead shook her head and backed toward the boat's prow, arms held wide as if to protect Ayo, who was behind her.

"What the fuck are you three doing up there?" Jaga shouted from the back of the boat. The pilot's voice was tight and ragged with a violent mixture of anger and anxiety.

"No concern of yours." After I finished with the spirits, I'd deal with Jaga and her foul mouth. She'd make a delightful dessert.

The river's roar ate her reply, and that was fine by me. I was so fucking hungry that nothing other than filling the void inside me mattered. My tongue was swollen with need, and my teeth itched with an overwhelming urge to bite and tear.

"Kyr, stop." Aja had dropped into a ready crouch, her hands raised into defensive claws, teeth bared in a predator's warning. "Let us help you."

"I don't need any help." I let my club fall to the deck and stretched my arms out. I'd never felt stronger or more powerful. There wasn't a damned thing anyone could do to help me that didn't revolve around feeding me.

I stalked across the deck, dragging my nails along the gunwale. The wood held an exquisite texture under my fingers, the glossy lacquer smooth and satiny. Its touch sent shivers racing up my spine. The hunger inside me made everything sharper, clearer. I couldn't imagine how I'd ever lived without this.

Aja and I were a yard apart. Her retreat had trapped Ayo behind her against the prow, and another step would put the spirit into the river.

The thought of losing all that tasty spirit flesh dragged a guttural growl from deep in my chest.

"Don't do this," Ayo pleaded. "There's something wrong."

"It's never been more right." I lunged forward and snatched Aja's wrist in a grip like an iron vise.

The spirit wrenched her arm back, and her struggles rocked the boat, almost knocking all of us into the river's swift current.

"Gods fuck you all!" Jaga shouted. "If you capsize my boat, I'll chase the three of you straight into the Frozen Hells!"

Aja stared up at me with wide, wet eyes. The wind tossed strands of her hair across her face, and the red streaks looked like threads of blood.

The sight sharpened my appetite. I couldn't wait any longer. With a snarl, I dragged her wrist to my lips, opened my mouth, and—

"Stop!" Something bony with sharp claws slammed into my face and slapped the sides of my head. "Stop or I'll claw your eyes out!"

Yata's threat wasn't idle. The three-legged raven's talons flashed in front of my face, and their black razor tips could have plucked my eyeballs clean out of my skull. How dare my familiar attack me?

"I dare because your core is overrun with feral rin, you asshole," the raven cried. "Didn't that bear slut teach you anything other than how to fuck?"

Yata's rebuke was as shocking as a bucket of cold water thrown into my face. I'd saved the sampan by sucking up all the catfish's rin, and I'd gotten more than I expected out of the bargain. The creature's hunger technique had come along for the ride with the sacred energy, and now it was tied up with my core.

Knowing all that didn't keep the desire to feed from pushing its way back into my thoughts. Yata's panicked thoughts brushed against mine through our connection and kept me from falling back into primal hungry-man mode.

For the moment.

With a guttural roar that caused the spirits to yelp with surprise, I tried to push the feral rin out of my nodes.

Unfortunately, that's not where the dangerous sacred energy was rooted. It had flowed through me during my struggle with the catfish, and was now lodged deep in my muscles and bones. The only way to get rid of it was to burn it out with more raw senjin. Lots and lots of raw senjin.

"Help," I croaked to Aja and Ayo. I gestured at my solar plexus with one hand, shaking from the effort of holding the hunger at bay. "Have to purge my rin. Need to cycle senjin."

Aja looked skeptical, but Ayo pushed past her and threw herself into my arms. Her lithe blue body squirmed against my torso, legs wrapped tightly around my waist. She kissed me, hard, her tongue stabbing at mine, and tangled her fingers in my hair. Her core pressed against mine, a cool and comforting presence next to the burning heat of my hunger.

My hands shoved the thin straps of her top off her shoulders and cupped her firm breasts. I pulled away from the heat of our kiss to swirl my tongue around one stiff blue nipple, then the other. The taste of seawater danced on my tongue, and the intimate contact drew our cores together. For a split second my thoughts merged with Ayo's, and our shared sensations inflamed our desire.

Ayo reached between us, her slender fingers cool as they slid down my stomach and under my belt. Her fingers found Aja's fist already wrapped tight around my rock-hard rod, and together they squeezed and pulled me toward the edge of blinding ecstasy. The red-haired spirit kissed the side of my neck, then sucked at my throat and nipped at my skin with her sharp teeth. Ayo groaned as the motion of their hands brushed against her cleft, and her legs tightened around me.

"What in the Frozen Hells?" Jaga asked, one eyebrow raised curiously at what she saw. "First you almost capsize my boat fighting a giant catfish, and now you're rutting on my deck like a bunch of wild animals?"

Yata cawed at that and flapped its wings in a rough approximation of a human shrug.

"Have to," Aja drew in a sudden gasp as my fingers found the nub of sensitive flesh nestled between her legs. She clung to my shoulder, breath hot and heavy against my ear. "Shaman shit."

All three of our cores glowed at the heart of my mind's eye like perfect pearls. Rin gushed out of my nodes and the sacred energy flowed between us in throbbing channels of power. My thumb traced a circle around the edge of Ayo's stiff nipple, and more power flowed from my overstuffed core into her center. The crimson sacred energy combined with the swirling blue shio in her core and produced a sudden burst of senjin that shot through our trio in a shuddering, ecstatic wave. That pushed some of the feral rin out of my flesh in a rush of animalistic passion.

The patch of naked flesh between Jaga's breasts flushed red and her eyes locked with mine. She licked her lips, uncertain of what she wanted, and I reached for her with my free hand. I had no idea what would happen if I brought another person into our magic circle, but I was eager to find out.

The captain hesitated for a moment, breath caught in her throat. The heat from her thundering heart brought a rosy glow to her deeply tanned cheeks, and her mouth dropped open slightly as if she couldn't get enough air.

Ayo pulled herself higher up my body and braced herself with one elbow on my shoulder. She guided the head of my cock toward the hungry opening between her legs, trembling with need. She eased onto me, her weight carrying the slick, tight sleeve of her sex down my length in a slow, languid stroke so exquisite the sensation bordered on the painful.

"Oh, Blood God," she groaned. Another pulse of sweet agony washed through the three of us, drenching our bodies with sweet, pure senjin.

My index and little fingers parted Aja's swollen lips, and I thrust my ring and middle fingers into her depths. My thumb worked at her throbbing pearl, and she whimpered against my throat.

Jaga's eyes went glassy, pupils dilated to cavernous black holes. She shucked her vest off and pressed herself against my left side. Her full lips found mine, tentatively at first, then with increasing urgency. She cupped the back of my neck with one hand and twined the fingers of the other with mine. She pulled back after a long moment, her eyes wild and heart hammering against my side.

"My cabin," she whispered, and nodded her head toward the rear of the boat.

"Here," I demanded, and pulled the three of them to the deck with me.

Ayo rode me in a desperate, fierce rhythm, and I met her strokes with my own thrusts that lifted her knees off the deck. She swirled the tips of her fingers across the deep blue nub of her clit, and her first orgasm sent a blast of senjin rocketing through the four of us. The spirit collapsed against me, her face hot against my chest, her arms cradling my head. She rode my thrusts with faint, dreamy moans, lost in the crashing waves of pleasure that bound us together.

Jaga laid on the deck to my left, her heavy breasts pressed against my arm. She squirmed as my hand found the damp crotch of her tight shorts and groaned wordlessly as I stroked her through the thin fabric. She kissed me, hard and hungry, caught up in a passion she'd never experienced and couldn't yet understand. She thrust her hips forward to grind the damp mound of her sex against my palm. Lost in a desperate, driving need, she pulled at the golden ring through her left nipple, stretching the pink nub taut. The blue serpent tattoo that encircled her breasts heaved with every shuddering breath as if swimming through a storm-tossed sea.

Aja suddenly clamped her thighs around my hand and shuddered. A long, ragged moan emerged from her parted lips, and she threw her head back as she came in a ferocious, muscle-clenching spasm. She ground herself against my fingers, riding the crashing wave of pleasure until shooting stars of senjin blazed through us all.

"What the fuck are you?" Jaga moaned. She shoved her shorts down with one hand and dragged my hand to her dripping slit with the other. "Oh, Blood God, yes, right fucking there. If you stop, I'll tear out your heart with my teeth."

Can't fault a lady for knowing what she likes.

Jaga rose to a kneeling position beside me, legs spread wide, then leaned over to brush the stiff tip of one nipple across my lips.

I got the hint and swirled my tongue around the pink bud, then pulled it into my mouth. My slippery fingers thrust into the tight and yearning juncture of her thighs, stroking her walls with smooth, steady strokes.

"Faster." She humped my hand, head down, long black hair hanging around our faces like a glossy curtain. Her sweat trickled down her breasts and onto my lips, hot and salty. "Faster."

Aja watched the pilot from my other side, her heart racing along with mine, eyes hooded with contented exhaustion.

Ayo's sex clenched around me in convulsive waves, her moans of pleasure growing louder with each of my thrusts. Our bodies moved together in perfect rhythm, pushing us both toward a peak beyond anything I'd ever imagined.

"That's it, there." The pilot clamped her hands over mine and rocked her body against my fingers and palm. She cried out and a shudder ran through her body from the tip of her head down to the deck. "Fuck, oh, fuck."

A sudden flood of her juices drenched my hand and coursed down my arm in sticky streams. Jaga shouted and cursed as wave after wave of pleasure crashed through her. Her enthusiasm was infectious, and I bucked under Ayo with an increasingly feverish need.

I came, twitching and spurting deep inside the blue-skinned spirit. Her skin puckered into goose pimples as my seed splashed inside her, and she joined me in another shuddering spasm. Senjin coursed through our bodies, purging the last of the feral rin from my system.

Jaga sagged to the deck and laid her head on my chest. She brushed her hair out of her face with a calloused hand and blew out a gusty, satisfied sigh.

"Next time, I'm the one getting fucked." She tweaked my nipple. "If your fingers can do that, I have to find out what you can do with that magic stick."

"Next time?" I chuckled and clasped my hands behind my head. "Aren't you getting ahead of yourself?"

"You wanna start swimming?" Jaga clicked her teeth together.

"Speaking of swimming, who's piloting this hunk of junk?" Aja flicked the end of the pilot's nose with her index finger.

"This stretch of the river's wide open." Despite her assurances, Jaga lifted her head and looked out over the boat's prow. "We're fine."

"I've been watching," Yata croaked. "And now I'll scout ahead like I've been doing since we had to run from the fire. Not that anyone notices all my hard work. You four just keep fucking yourselves stupid."

The three-legged raven took flight with a noisy flap of its wings. It vanished into the mist a few moments later, and soon I couldn't hear the sounds of its flight over the gentle pounding of my pulse in my ears.

"I like you." Ayo lifted a hank of Jaga's long, black hair between her fingers. When she saw Jaga's raised eyebrows, she chuckled, a soft and throaty sound that reminded me of the burbling of a brook. "Not like that. You're pretty, but I'm not interested in women like that."

"Good for you." Jaga sat up and combed the tangles out of her hair with her finger. I watched her dexterous hands secure the long dark strands into a tight braid. "My river doesn't run for ladies, either."

"Well, that's good information to have." Aja stood and offered her hand to Jaga, who took it gratefully and stood up on the opposite side of me. "Is there somewhere I can wash up, or do I need to take a dip in the river?"

"Sure." Jaga gestured toward the cabin near the aft end of the sampan. "There's a little toilet in there. It's not much, but it's enough for a whore's bath and a piss without hanging your dainty little ass over the edge of the boat."

"Thanks." Ayo slid off me and scampered into the cabin, leaving me sticky and exposed on the deck.

"Damnit," Aja shouted after the blue spirit.

"Snooze and lose," Jaga chuckled.

She and Aja took my hands and helped me back to my feet. The pair of them bumped into my shoulders, sly grins on their faces. I wasn't sure what had passed between them, but they were definitely up to something. I'd have to keep an eye on the trouble twins or there was no telling the kind of shit they'd get up to.

"Now that we don't have anyone trying to kill us or eat us, and we're all fucked out for at the least next ten minutes, let's talk a little business." I threw an arm around Jaga's shoulder. That earned me a raised eyebrow, as if we were strangers and I hadn't been diddling her into a stupor a few minutes ago. "How far until we get to the lake?"

"You could get there by tomorrow morning." Jaga glanced at the wide river's current and nodded. "Yeah, current's good, river level is just right. We'll need to get a room at Luysi Station for the night, though. Not enough space for all of us in my cabin."

"I can sleep on the deck." I shrugged.

"Good for fucking you, asshole." Jaga punched me in the shoulder harder than seemed strictly necessary. "Maybe your companions and I would like to get fucked in a proper bed. You ever think of that?"

I blushed more than a bit because I honestly hadn't. I'd spent so long with the crimson bear that I almost never thought about shit like that at all. If living in a cave for close to a century was good enough for me, why wouldn't it be good for everyone else, too?

Fuck, I'd been such an idiot.

Pretty much. Mielyssi's voice was light and good humored, despite the words. *Part of being a shaman is your connection to the world. And that world includes people.*

It would have been awesome if Mielyssi popped these little nuggets of wisdom into my thoughts before I made an ass out of myself, but that had never been her style. The crimson bear, like every mentor in every story ever told to a wide-eyed kid, wanted her pupil to figure shit out on his own.

Fine. Be that way.

"I'm sorry," I said, and meant it. "We've got some loot in my satchel. I'll get you the best room we can afford."

"Good to hear it." Jaga wagged her finger at me. "I'm looking forward to it. My knees are still knocking after that bit of finger action you gave me. I'll be laid up for a week if your dick measures up to my imagination."

"My pleasure." I wasn't sure if I should hug Jaga or shake her hand. My arm was still around her shoulder, though that seemed more because she didn't want to bother moving it than because she enjoyed it. "I'll be happy to fill more jugs for you on the second leg of our journey south. It's the least I can do for you after I almost got us killed by a giant catfish."

"Second leg?" Jaga snorted. "I never agreed to take you all the way to the lake, man. Once I get paid for this load in Luysi Station, I'm heading back north."

"What? I thought—"

"You woke me up out of a dead sleep, made me evict my now second-favorite fuckboy from the cabin, brought my boat to the attention of the Jade Seekers, almost capsized us, nearly got me killed by a giant catfish, and somehow made me so horny I didn't even make you wash your hands before you fingerbanged the ever-loving fuck out of me." Jaga glanced at my hand on her shoulder, then blew me a kiss. "Did I miss anything, or should you be glad I didn't already stick a knife in your gizzard?"

The pilot patted my cheek and slipped out from under my arm before I could pick my jaw up off the deck. I'd thought things were going so well, too.

"She is super fucking hot." Aja watched Jaga's naked ass sway as the pilot snatched her vest from where it had fallen and headed toward the rudder. "Too bad she's going to dump us like a load of rotten fish heads."

"Yeah, that's a pain in the ass," I admitted. "I'll figure something out."

If we couldn't find another pilot at the next port, we'd still have days of walking ahead of us before we reached the Lake of Moonsilver Mist. The Jade Seekers had found us in the first village somehow. I wasn't sure we'd have much hope of outrunning them if they found us while we were tramping overland.

I had to convince Jaga to stay with us.

Or we were all as good as dead.

Chapter Sixteen

I NEEDED SOMETHING TO DISTRACT ME FROM MY worries about Jaga leaving us at the next village. Fortunately, I had a built-in distraction courtesy of the senjin that currently sloshed around in my core from the mini orgy. The sacred energy filled me with a warm, comfortable lethargy that made me want to lie down and nap for a week or three. The last time I'd felt like this, my core had advanced from earthbound to seabound. If I was lucky, I might be able to use the power I'd gathered to advance again.

"I need to meditate," I said to Aja. "I'll be up at the prow. If anything happens, give me a shout."

"You'll be the first to know if anything happens," Aja said. "Because you'll probably be the one who caused it."

"Smart-ass." I swatted her on the backside and headed to the fore of the sampan.

The river was much wider here than it had been back at the village. It was a least a mile wide and a hundred feet deep based on the glimmers of sacred energy I spied in its depths. No boulders or trees jutted from its depths, and though the current was still swift it was much gentler than it had been previously.

I sat cross-legged on the polished wooden deck and rested the backs of my hands on my knees. A deep breath filled my lungs, and trickles of rin energy followed it into my core. Or at least they tried to.

All my nodes were already filled with the crimson sacred energy, and the shell that surrounded them bulged with senjin the spirits and I had created with Jaga during our festival of fucks.

"You called?" Yata asked as it landed on the gunwale next to me. "I was out scouting. It better be important."

"I didn't call you, but now that you're here you might be able help me out." I tapped two fingers over my solar plexus. "My core is stuffed with senjin. I want to use it to try to advance to skybound, but I'm not sure of the best way to do it. I was going to meditate, try to will it to happen."

"Well," the three-legged raven said hesitantly. It stared at me with black eyes eyes, tilted its head to one side, then the other. "Your core is a disaster. It's tangled up worse than a bowl of noodles in there."

"What the fuck are you talking about?" I asked. Inside the shell of my core, all ten of my nodes glowed a solid rich red. There were surrounded by a soup of churning silver senjin that looked like a liquid mirror. I didn't see any tangles, though, or anything that could be tangled.

"Your nodes are connected to your core's shell." Yata paced back and forth along the boat's rail, three sets of claws ticking against the wood with every move. The dark bird reminded me of one of the Moonsilver Bat's priests lecturing his congregation during the weekly worship. "Your shell, in turn, is attached to your body through other connections. That's how sacred energy gets from your nodes out into the world. Following so far?"

"Yes," I said sarcastically. "I've been a shaman for a lot longer than I've known you."

But I hadn't really known the details of those connections. I'd assumed there was some way for the rin to do my bidding, but I'd never really given it any thought. The crimson bear hadn't seemed interested in teaching me that particular bit of shaman theory, either. I was starting to worry there might be some significant gaps in my knowledge.

"It's those connections that are all snarled inside you." Yata stopped and jutted its beak in my direction. "When you push rin out of a node, it has to work its way through those tangles before it can activate a technique or strengthen your body. You're wasting lots and lots of sacred energy every time you use it."

"How do I fix that?" I asked. "I know the connections are there, but I can't see them."

"You need to straighten them out." Yata went back to pacing, and its head bobbed up and down absentmindedly as if pecking for an idea, or, more likely, a way to explain its ideas to me. "Try this. Turn your spirit sight inward. Really look hard at your core. Get right in there."

"In other words, you don't know how to do it, either." I frowned, then shrugged. "I'll figure it out."

The slap of water against the hull of the sampan created a gentle, rhythmic pattern. I closed my eyes, then focused on the sound, letting it transport me into a deep trance that Mielyssi had taught me during our time together. The world receded, and my senses narrowed and retreated into my body. I took a mental inventory of myself, starting at my toes, working up through my calves, then into my thighs, through my torso, and finally out the top of my skull. The simple exercise put me completely in tune with my body and centered my spirit sight squarely on my core.

I inhaled deeply once, then again. My core pulsed with silver light as the purified senjin swirled around its shell, unable to find space for itself within me. The sacred power emitted sharp bursts of light that transformed my translucent sea-blue core into a dazzling display of spiritual energy.

After a few seconds of staring at the orb inside me, I was about to give up on finding these connections that Yata seemed certain were tangled up inside me. It was easy enough to see the red nodes of rin energy and the swirling globs of mercurial senjin, but it was impossible for me to spot any connections between the nodes and the shell.

And then, at the peak of my frustration, my sight slipped inside the core and into the very center of my being. After a moment of disorientation, my senses righted themselves at the heart of my core. The red nodes filled with rin orbited around me, the silver blobs of senjin floating around them.

I pushed my attention toward one of those rotating orbs and focused every bit of my concentration on the node. Up close, I realized the node wasn't a solid ball. A fine thread filled with crimson power was wrapped around an empty space to form a hollow sphere. Through the tiny gaps between that thread's core, I saw the heat of red rin energy.

And I saw something else.

Translucent threads unspooled from an almost invisible dot of pale light at the very center of each node.

Those almost imperceptible strings slithered through the narrow gaps in the node's exterior to twist and tangle around the inside of the core like a fish's guts.

"I see them," I said. My voice sounded slow and sleepy, and it echoed through my core as if I were standing at the bottom of a deep pit.

"Good!" Yata said. "You have to be careful, but you should be able to untangle them using the senjin."

"Any other advice before I try this?" I asked. "I don't want to cripple myself in here."

"I said be careful." Yata went silent after that, so apparently it did not have any further useful information.

I stared hard at one thread until it snapped into sharper focus in my spirit sight. I tried to grab hold of it, but my fingers passed through it without disturbing it in any way. The string might as well have been a mirage.

"Use the senjin," I muttered to myself.

There was plenty of the mercurial dream energy around me. It floated in thick blobs, moving in currents I couldn't feel. I reached out and brushed my hand through one of the globs, wincing in anticipation of the sharp pain I expected. Senjin was extremely powerful stuff, and in its pure, manifested form, it could burn flesh like acid. I'd hoped that my spirit sight wouldn't be affected in the same way, but I couldn't be sure and my luck had been running pretty shitty lately.

Instead of sizzling on my fingers, the mirror-like fluid flowed around them. It coated my hand like a shining glove and stuck to me when I pulled my hand out of the bubble.

That was new.

I found the thread I was working with again and reached for it with my senjin-slicked fingers. This time,

I grabbed hold of the thin strand and easily teased it away from its neighbors. I traced the line all the way back to the node it had emerged from, and my fingers left it slick with senjin as they passed down its length. To my surprise, the section of the thread I'd coated with silver energy stiffened and repelled the threads around it, like magnets with their polarities reversed.

Excited by my progress, I coated both hands with the senjin and went to my work. A few minutes later, half of the thread I was working with gleamed with silver energy, though it was still a terrible mess of twists and loops and convoluted patterns that created a horribly inefficient trail through my core. I spent a few more minutes sheathing the rest of that connection with senjin, then stepped back to get a better look at my work.

It was a fucking disaster. The tangle couldn't have been more convoluted if it had been laid out by a monkey drunk on hellfire wine.

Okay, I could figure this out. Now that the connection was covered in senjin, I no longer needed to glove my hands in the stuff to touch it. I grabbed hold of the gleaming thread and looped a length of it under my left elbow and over my left thumb. The thread was firm and slightly stretchy and offered no resistance as I pulled it away from its former path into neat coils around my forearm. After I'd gathered the first half of the silver line, I moved on to the second part of my experiment.

My core seemed like it was ten feet across in my mind's eye, and each of the nodes was roughly the size of my head. The red orbs floated in a perfect circle just inside the core's shell.

I eased the connection's node toward the shell side of the red sphere it emerged from. The node rotated as I tugged on the thread, but it remained stable in its position. So far, so good.

With exaggerated care, I pulled the connection taut from its node and pressed the silver thread firmly against the core's shell.

There was a faint clink, like two glasses touching, and the connection stuck to the shell's wall. I gave it a tug, but it wouldn't budge. That was a good start, though the connection was still ridiculously long and followed a convoluted path from the node to its connection point. Even if I coiled the rest of the connection around my arm, it would still have to go through dozens of tight curves before it reached the shell. The opposite end of the connection was also attached to the shell all the way across my core, which seemed like a spectacularly shitty way for my core to have been constructed.

After I'd saved the world, I was going to track down the Celestial Bureaucracy and ask them what the fuck they'd been thinking when they made me.

I couldn't shorten the connection, and coiling it up would still force the rin through a bunch of tight curves every time I activated a technique. What I needed to do was make it as easy as possible for the sacred energy to flow from its origins to its destination.

I imagined the power moving like a river. Where it had to pass through tight curves or around obstacles, it became more turbulent, and the smooth flow bubbled and frothed against its confines. Through unobstructed straightaways, the current was tranquil even when it moved quickly.

I considered straightening the connection, from one side to the other, then back again until it reached the shell. There would still be a few tight corners for the power to flow through, but overall it would be a straight line from one point to another. That would work for the single connection I was dealing with at the moment, but I'd run into trouble as more and more connections had to be straightened. There just wasn't room through the center of my core to accommodate all of the connections, and soon I'd have to route the threads through twists and turns that would defeat the whole purpose of this exercise.

A sudden pain in my side dragged my attention away from my problem. The stabbing sensation was fleeting, if irritating, and I ignored my body's aches and pains to get back to the challenging work of cleaning up my core.

A curve with a wide enough radius wouldn't constrict the sacred energy or force it to make any abrupt changes in direction that would interfere with its smooth flow. Excited by this idea, I laid the thread of the connection around the inside of the shell in a long, smooth spiral. The gently curved path encircled the inside of my core exactly three times before it reached the point where it connected to the shell.

Fucking perfect.

The success excited me, and I dove back into my project. After the past few days of chaos, this work was soothing and peaceful. I lost myself in the simple motions of coating my hands with senjin and guiding the threads between the nodes and their terminal connection points. The silvery lines cooperated with me and seemed almost to guide themselves into the correct positions with only gentle coaxing on my part.

I still had half of the connections left to route around my core when a rough slap across my cheek dragged me out of my meditative trance. I opened my eyes to find the riverboat pilot towering over me and my cheek stinging and hot.

"Wake the fuck up, you asshole!" Jaga shouted and reared back to slap me again. Her attractive face was twisted into a mask of rage, and her striking green eyes shone like emeralds.

In the split second before her second slap landed against my cheek, a few details jumped out at me.

First, it was almost dark. The pale white disk of the sun no longer struggled through the thick mist that cloaked the world, and the sky had taken on the pink hue of fading daylight. Second, Jaga wasn't just pissed, she was scared. Third, Ayo and Aja stood behind the riverboat captain, their eyes wide with shock, unsure what to do next. Finally, Yata hopped back and forth on its three legs, cawing and croaking with dismay.

"What the fuck is going on?" I shouted and grabbed Jaga's wrist before she could slap me again. She raised her other hand, and I grabbed that one, too. "This better be good. I was on the verge of a breakthrough."

"How nice for you." With her hands restrained, Jaga's temper ebbed, and her sarcasm fired up. "Well, we've got company. Some of your friends are looking for you."

"Blood God," I growled and stood up from where I'd been meditating, careful to keep a firm grip on Jaga's hands. Both my cheeks stung, and I didn't want to get a bloody nose out of the deal, too.

I looked behind us but didn't see any other boats on the river. I scanned the eastern shoreline. There was nothing there, either.

The western riverbank, though, was a whole different beast.

Warriors encased in heavy jade armor rode along the shore on spectral horses that gleamed like molten gold. The strange creatures bore the weight of their riders without complaint and threaded through the dense forest with uncanny ease. The supernatural beasts kept pace with the river's current without even galloping.

Fuck.

"How many of these assholes are there?" I growled and dropped Jaga's hands. "I killed a few dozen of them back at Floating Village, and we left a bunch more behind us when we left Ulishi. Where the hell did these come from?"

The leader of the Jade Seekers emerged from the trees, his golden stallion's hooves splashing in the water at the edge of the river. I'd seen the man plummet hundreds of feet into a ravine lined with jagged rocks. His body should have been pulped inside the cracked shell of his armor. Jiro Kos was supposed to be dead.

And yet, there he stood, as big and scary as ever.

"They're on horses." That, at least, was some blessing. "Without a boat, they can't reach us. As long as we stay on the river, we're safe."

"The river's deep here," Jaga said. "But if they can keep up with us for another hour or so, they'll catch up to us at the next town. Where I'd planned to stop for the night."

Well, that wasn't so bad. I hadn't wanted Jaga to leave us, anyway. The Jade Seekers were a pain in my ass, but if they forced the pilot to let us stay aboard, they'd done me a favor. I was about to explain the bright side to Jaga when everything went to shit.

The mounted warriors drew bows from their saddles, nocked arrows, and unleashed a hissing swarm of missiles at us.

Chapter Seventeen

THE FIRST SALVO FROM THE JADE SEEKERS FELL yards short of the sampan, and the thick arrows splashed into the water. We wouldn't be so lucky once the warriors found their range. It was hard to get a solid count of their numbers as they raced through the trees, but there were at least two dozen, maybe more.

"Get us closer to the middle of the river," I barked at Jaga. The pilot stomped toward the rudder, and I turned my attention to the river spirit. "Ayo, can you do anything to help us outpace these motherfuckers?"

The white-haired spirit narrowed her eyes, and they flashed like sapphires. Ayo focused her spirit sight on the river, then leaned over the gunwale and thrust both hands toward the water. Nothing happened for a moment, and nothing happened in the moment after that one, either.

Another flight of arrows took to the sky, and I watched helplessly as they reached the pinnacle of their arc and plunged down toward us. Yata flew off the deck and through the cabin's door.

Smart bird.

"Cocksuckers!" Jaga shouted. She wrenched hard on the sampan's rudder, and the vessel veered away from the shore. For a moment, I thought she had turned us too far and we'd get flipped over when the current hit us broadside. But she was a better pilot than I'd imagined, and we sliced smoothly across the river to put some lateral distance between us and the hunters on their golden steeds.

The arrows peppered the water where we'd been a moment before, their impacts churning the river into a white froth. Jiro shouted and his archers nocked another flight of missiles. The arrows glowed with an evil, venomous radiance.

"It's now or never, Ayo," I snarled. In my spirit sight, I saw she'd woven blue threads between her hands and the river, a tight skein of powerful connections that throbbed with power. It was an impressive feat, but if she didn't do something—anything—it would all be for nothing.

The glowing arrows took screaming flight, plumes of vile smoke trailing across the dusky sky behind them. The deadly shafts tracked the sampan even as Jaga shoved the rudder violently from side to side in a desperate attempt to avoid them. The missiles had to be scripted with a homing technique that drew them to us with the irresistible force of iron filings to a magnet.

"Hang on!" Ayo screamed. The air thrummed with a sudden release of power, and the river spirit glowed like a blue star.

The sampan lurched forward as if shoved by a giant's fist. The sleek boat's hull burst from the water with the sudden surge of speed, then slammed back into the river with a shuddering crash. The impact threw a wall of water over the boat's prow, drenching us all. I lost my footing and slid across the deck's smooth boards toward the cabin.

Aja and Ayo were both thrown down, too, and shot across the deck to crash against the sampan's gunwale with bruising force. We grunted and dragged ourselves back to our knees, surprised to be alive.

"Everyone all right?" I called. We'd gained a little distance on the Jade Seekers, but they'd be coming for us again.

"I'm fine," Aja called. "Wet as hell, and I'm going to have one motherfucker of a bruise on my hip, but I'm good."

"Sorry for the rough launch," Ayo said, her cheeks dark with embarrassment. "It was only supposed to be a little boost. Guess I don't know my own strength."

"Jaga!" I shouted to be heard over the river's roar.

No answer.

I sprinted toward the back of the boat, feet slipping and sliding on the wet deck. The pilot had been hanging onto the rudder; she'd be fine. She was the only one of us who was an experienced sailor. That little bump wouldn't have even ruffled her hair.

I was sure of it.

But as I came around the cabin, my heart stopped.

The pilot was gone.

"Jaga!" I shouted again. The rudder banged against the hull, and I grabbed it to steady our course.

My eyes scanned the river's choppy surface, desperate for some sign of Jaga.

She was nowhere to be found.

I clutched the wooden handle with both hands and engaged my spirit sight. Schools of fish glowed in the river's depths like swarms of summer fireflies.

Larger creatures, turtles and other denizens of the depths, gave off shadowy light from the riverbed.

There was no sign of the captain or any other life even remotely human in the river. It was as if she'd vanished into thin air.

I shouted her name again, and again. The riders gained on us, their relentless steeds carrying them through the forest at an unbelievable pace. There was no doubt in my mind they'd keep this up all night. Jiro Kos wouldn't let me slip through his fingers again.

"Where is she?" Ayo wailed. "Jaga! Oh, Blood God, I'm so sorry."

Aja closed her eyes, tilted her head back, and took a deep breath. She turned slowly, rotating from side to side as she inhaled deeper and deeper.

"There," she growled, jabbing one finger toward the river behind us.

She was right. Now that I knew where to look, my spirit sight picked out the pale blue glow of the riverboat's pilot. She wasn't swimming, but the light of her core, feeble as it was, told me she was still alive.

At least for the moment.

My heart ached for the pilot. She'd been willing to leave us at the next village, an act that would have made our lives much, much harder than we'd hoped. I'd been angry with her when she told me, but now I couldn't find that cold spark of rage.

I hadn't known Jaga for long, but something told me the captain had only been doing what she'd done all her life: looking after herself as best she could. She was a loner, the kind of woman who prowled through life like a shark, always on the lookout for the next opportunity, always hungry for the next chance to jump ahead of her competition. She wasn't used to having other people look after her, and she sure as fuck wasn't used to looking after anyone other than herself.

The smart thing to do was to leave her to her fate. We had the boat, and while I wasn't an expert at navigating the rivers like she was, I'd be able to manage. If we kept going, we might outpace the Jade Seekers. Another day, day and a half at the outside, and we'd reach the Lake of Moonsilver Mist.

And I'd hate myself for it every minute of the way. How could I save the world if I couldn't even save this one woman?

"Use your powers to make the water grab her!" I shouted to the spirit. "I'll pole us back upriver to get her."

"My core's nearly empty," Ayo moaned. "I don't have the strength."

And there was no time to recharge the spirit's nodes. I was Jaga's only hope.

"Stick to the river." I grabbed Aja and Ayo by the shoulders, stared at each of them in turn. "It will take you all the way to the lake."

"What are you talking about?" Aja asked, her eyes wild and frantic. "What the hell are you doing?"

"Going after Jaga." Before either of the spirits could try to change my mind, I stepped onto the gunwale and dove into the river.

The water closed around me like an icy fist and squeezed the air from my lungs. My body wanted to draw in a breath immediately, but I clamped my jaw shut and forced my arms and legs to propel me back toward the surface. It was hard work to swim against the current, and the effort burned precious oxygen out of my blood as I clawed my way toward fresh air.

Finally, my head burst free of the rushing water, and I gulped a huge breath to fill my lungs. There hadn't been much opportunity to learn to swim in Floating Village, and my strokes and kicks were not as efficient as they could have been. Still, my clumsy efforts were aided by the strength I'd gained from advancing my core to seabound, and the light of Jaga's core grew brighter by the second.

A quick glance over my shoulder showed me that the sampan was getting farther and farther away by the moment.

The riders on the shore seemed confused about what to do next. Their captain wheeled his horse around as if intent on pursuing me, then spun back toward the sampan. The other Seekers milled around him in confusion, unsure what their captain wanted from them.

Good. Anything that slowed those fuckers down worked in my favor.

The tremendous effort of clawing my way through the water burned the sacred energy out of one node. I still had nine more filled with rin, and I hoped that would be enough.

A minute had passed since I'd entered the water, and every second of it had felt like an eternity. The power inside me kept me alive; it just didn't do anything for the aches and pains that built up as I pushed my body to its limits and beyond.

Jaga's body bobbed in the water ahead of me. She was face down, her arms and legs spread-eagled across the river's surface, her dark hair fanned out around her head like a twilight crown. Her core glimmered with pale blue shio, but the spark had almost gone out of her.

With a desperate effort, I kicked forward and grabbed hold of the sampan pilot. Jaga had lost her vest to the river's greedy clutches, and my hands slipped and slithered across her naked torso. She slid out of my hands, and the current nearly swept her away again before I latched onto her wrist. We turned in circles, faster and faster, as the river shoved us downstream with its wild strength.

"Archers!" Yata shrieked from above me. The three-legged raven circled overhead, its wings flapping furiously to maintain its position. "Dive!"

I took a quick breath and followed my familiar's imperative. I looped an arm around Jaga's waist and dragged her below the icy water. She shuddered against me as we descended, but her eyes stayed closed, and she didn't try to gulp a breath. Whatever survival instincts were still kicking around in the back of her brain had kept her alive so far, but it wouldn't be long before she ran out of air and her desperate lungs took their final, deadly breath.

A flight of arrows plunged into the water around us. The river had robbed them of their speed and deadly accuracy, and they hung suspended in the river for a few moments before the current carried them away. We were safe, for the moment, but we couldn't stay down here.

Then I had an idea.

The catfish had proven a challenge, but it had also opened my eyes to part of being a shaman I hadn't really explored yet.

I opened my core to the world and sent a thread of rin snaking through the water toward a curious smallmouth bass who'd emerged from its lair beneath a sunken boulder to see what the fuck was going on. The crimson thread caught the creature before it could escape, and I lashed a connection around its core and gave a little squeeze.

The simple creature only had a single note of raw shio, and I plucked the energy from its core with ease. Confused by what had just happened, the bass struggled against the connection. It wasn't hurt, just bewildered, and I let it go back to the safety of its hole.

The little creature's energy bubbled around inside my core looking for a way out. It wasn't alive, not really, but there was an animal essence to it that made it hate any sort of captivity. One of my nodes flickered and a fine patina of gray-green scales formed across its surface.

Like the catfish, the energy I'd taken from the bass affected me, though much more subtly. When I pulled the remnant of the scaled node and fed it into my arms and legs, it didn't transform me into a fish. It did, however, make my swimming much more fluid and efficient. Even with Jaga under my arm, I could swim faster than the sampan ahead of me. I counted to twenty, then burst out of the water like a dolphin and crashed onto the deck on my back, Jaga hugged tight to my chest.

"Get us the fuck out of here!" I shouted to Ayo. "The Seekers are confused, but they won't stay that way for long."

"Holy shit, you're alive!" Aja brushed tears from her cheeks. "We thought we'd lost you both."

"Not yet," I gasped and eased Jaga onto the deck where I could get a better look at her. I spared a glance toward the shoreline and cursed at what I saw there.

The mounted archers had realized that I'd tricked them and charged through the forest in a desperate rush to catch us. Another minute, maybe less, and they'd be back within bow range. If they had any more of those green arrows, we'd be fucked.

"I need energy," Ayo said. "I burned all I had last time."

Shit, I'd known that. There definitely wasn't time to fully recharge Ayo, but we'd have to make do. I stood, grabbed the river spirit around the waist, and pulled her body against mine. I kissed her, deep and hard, my hands roaming over the firm curves of her ass and then up to the soft globes of her breasts. I bit the tip of her tongue, and she gasped with surprise. A rush of rin burst from my core and flowed into Ayo.

She shuddered and her hand clenched around the bulge in my breechcloth. Our hearts beat quicker at the contact, and her breath gusted hot and humid against my water-beaded chest.

"No time for that now," I said, my voice low and hungry with desire. "Aja, get to the rudder. Ayo, get us moving."

The spirits jumped to follow my orders, and I dropped back to the deck to focus all my attention on Jaga. Her skin was pale, lips tinged blue from the cold and lack of oxygen. Her eyelids were covered in a network of fine red splotches, a sure sign she'd been on the verge of suffocation. I needed to get her breathing again.

"You have to wake up," I whispered and rubbed her hands vigorously. I pulled her body into my lap and hugged her to my chest, praying the warmth would help to revive her. Her core's light was almost gone.

Because Jaga wasn't a spirit or an animal, it was harder for me to touch her core. People naturally built up defenses around their souls, a way to keep the world outside and hide their true selves from strangers and enemies. It was a survival mechanism that separated us from the animals. That defense made us stronger in some ways. In other ways, though, the wedges we drove between ourselves and the world made us much, much weaker.

Jaga curved into the warmth of my body, just a little, but enough to let me know she was still alive. I clutched her tighter, hoping to fan the sparks of life still in her core into a full-blown fire. It hurt to see the fierce pilot so weak. She deserved better.

My hands roamed across her back, trying to rub warmth back into her. Her heart beat against my palm, a faint and thready rhythm that reminded me of a baby rabbit I'd once found in the forest near Floating Village.

"Come on, goddamnit," I cursed. I kissed her forehead. I pressed my lips to each of her eyes, breathed across her face, then kissed her blue lips.

Unconscious, she couldn't have known it was me. But her lips parted, just slightly, and she responded with a faint groan. It wasn't much, but the moment of intimacy was enough of a connection to let me push sacred energy from my core into hers. The thin thread of crimson power curled into her lungs, then slipped deeper through the rigid shell around her spirit.

Her blue shio rebelled against the intrusion, recoiling from my power like a mouse from a snake. Jaga shuddered in my arms, her arms and legs flopping weakly in protest.

She bit my lip, and the unexpected shock of pain made me so happy I could almost cry.

"You ever kiss me without asking again," she snarled, "and I'll cut your balls off and feed them to your stupid bird."

"I was trying to save your life." I leaned away from her. She was still too weak to rise from my lap, but she was alive, and the light in her core grew stronger with every passing breath. She'd live.

Unless the Jade Seekers caught up to us.

Chapter Eighteen

AYO'S COMMUNION WITH THE RIVER DIDN'T EARN us as big of a push as I would've liked. Without a full core, the best she could manage was to double our speed for a quarter of an hour. The boost kept us ahead of the Jade Seekers, but not by much.

While it would've been nice to take the time to fully recharge her nodes with another bout of full-contact carnality, we didn't have time for those luxuries. Jiro and his merry band of fucknuggets weren't about to slow down.

"Thanks for saving my life," Jaga said. "It's a shame your friends are going to kill us all."

"They're not my friends," I said. "And they haven't caught us yet."

Jaga and I were back by the rudder, watching the Jade Seekers on the west shore. The river had narrowed as we went downstream, and we had to hug the east side of the waterway to stay just out of bow range. I'd have preferred to stay on the river until we reached the lake, but maybe it was time to get off the water and head overland. That would put some distance between us and the Seekers. When I raised the idea to Jaga, though, she shook her head.

"There's a bridge at the village ahead, where the river narrows. Those fucking gold horses can cross there and catch up to us before we can escape." She blew out an exasperated sigh. "You really are a pain in my ass, shaman."

I stared out over the rushing river, hoping to find some inspiration. My eyes fell on the spirits seated at the boat's prow. Ayo meditated in a desperate attempt to gather more shio for another speed boost, while Aja watched for hazards on the water ahead of us. It was well into the afternoon by that point, and we were all worn ragged by the events of the day. The spirits, despite Jaga almost drowning, looked the worst of us all. Their energy was flagging, and their cores were nearly empty. If we didn't come up with a new plan soon, they'd start to fade away.

And by we, I meant me.

"There's no branches off this river?" I asked Jaga. "Even if it goes out of our way, it'd be worth it to get the fuck away from those horses."

"I don't think so." Jaga frowned. "We're closing in on the lake, so all the branches we'll find are smaller tributaries feeding into this river. We'd have to paddle upstream, and those assholes would catch up to us in no time."

I racked my brain, trying to think of some way I could use my shaman abilities to get us out of this mess. Unfortunately, even with my now much more orderly core, I didn't have techniques that would be of any use in avoiding our pursuers. My claws would cut the guts out of one Seeker, no problem, but they wouldn't hold off the whole enemy force. My mantle was strong enough to shield me from any arrows that came in, but it wouldn't last forever, and it couldn't protect the spirits or Jaga. My Earthen Darts technique might take down one or two of the Seekers before I ran out of rin, and then the rest of the bad guys would swarm me and carve me into bite-sized shaman chunks.

The dream meridian that flowed along with the river held enough senjin to seriously power me up, as long as I could take the time to purify it with the spirits. Which I couldn't. It was endlessly frustrating to have a font of such immeasurable power that would kill me if I tried to put it to use.

But if there was a dream meridian of this power, then maybe there was another way out.

"The Deepways," I said to Jaga. "Are there any near here?"

"Maybe," Jaga said, a dark look in her eyes. "They don't work anymore, not since the Yellow Serpent Kingdom lost control of them during the War of Shudders. But maybe… Here, take the rudder. Don't run us into a rock or anything."

"Thanks for the vote of confidence," I called after the pilot as she headed toward her cabin.

The Seekers had closed the gap between us to just a few hundred yards. Their supernatural horses seemed to be picking up the pace rather than flagging. We had less than an hour, as near as I could tell, before Jiro and the rest of them drew close enough for another round of pin the tail on the shaman.

Jaga emerged from her cabin, a ceramic slate clutched in her left hand. She sat on the gunwale next to me and turned the slate so I could see it.

The off-white surface was covered in a watercolor map, and it oozed powerful blue shio. I wondered where Jaga had found such a potent item and just how much it had cost her. Before I could ask any questions, she dove into an excited explanation.

"Okay," she said. "We're right here, and there used to be a Deepways station just down here. That's about twenty minutes away with the current."

"That's good." I was relieved that I'd guessed correctly about the location of the Deepways. I'd known they were situated along powerful meridians, but that was about the extent of my knowledge this far from my home village. "We should be able to reach it before the Seekers catch us."

"We may not want to." Jaga tapped a series of symbols next to the Deepways location on her map. "The notes on my maps say it's haunted. Something about crushing spirits."

"I'll take my chances with some ghosts over the Jade Seekers," I said. "If we run into angry spirits, I'll deal with them. I'm a shaman. That's my job."

I didn't want to admit it to the pilot, but after seeing the desolation of the first Deepways I'd encountered, I wasn't sure I could handle more badass corrupted spirits. If the next one was in as bad shape as the last one, dark entities would have an almost limitless reservoir of tainted senjin to power their techniques. Given a choice, I'd much rather stick to the river.

Sadly, Jiro wasn't giving me a choice.

"Your call." Jaga didn't seem pleased about that. "A stream off the river flows straight into the Deepways. It's wide and deep enough to handle cargo ships, or at least it was, so I don't think the horses can follow us in there. I also don't have any idea where the other end of it is."

197

That was an interesting problem. But it was also a problem that future Kyr would have to worry about. Present Kyr's job was to get us the hell off the river and away from the Seekers before they killed us. I needed to recharge the spirits and myself. Maybe with enough senjin, I could advance to skybound.

"We're going in. At the very least, it will buy us some time away from Jiro so I can replenish the spirits' cores. They won't last much longer."

"Is that going to be a repeat of what happened on the deck here?" Jaga asked with a raised eyebrow.

"It depends," I said, "on whether or not you want to join in."

"We'll see," Jaga said. She slapped me on the ass and took the rudder from my hand. "Go up front, watch for any trouble. I'll get us there in one piece."

The stream appeared a few minutes later, and Jaga angled us toward its mouth. Jiro cursed when he realized what we were up to, and his jinsei-amplified voice rolled across the water in an echoing wave.

"You can't escape me!" The words were filled with so much rage, the spirits flinched away from them.

I didn't have a technique to boost my voice, so I made do with sign language. Jiro's horse reared at my obscene gesture, and his mean cowered back from their commander's roar of anger.

He could be as pissed as he wanted to be. It didn't matter. I'd beat the asshole, and there was no way he'd catch me before I reached the lake and returned the spirits to their mistress.

We reached the Deepways a half hour later. Its entrance was an enormous cave that opened like a giant's mouth in the side of a hill. The limestone cavern's opening had been carved into an elaborate archway inlaid with silver scripts and golden plaques. The workmanship was exquisite, though the years of neglect had taken its toll and eroded much of the fine detail into oblivion.

"When was the last time anyone used the Deepways?" I asked Jaga as we drifted under the arch and into the cavern's gloom.

"At least twenty years." The riverboat pilot gestured toward a pole that lay against the boat's side. "Check the depth for me. I can't see a goddamned thing in here."

I snagged the bamboo pole off the deck and lowered its point into the water until I felt the riverbed.

"It's four marks deep." I replaced the pole and leaned against the boat's edge.

The sun's light didn't penetrate far past the cave's mouth. As darkness closed around us, I spotted several glowing stones mounted on raised platforms along the edges of the river. Their weak light revealed the outlines and shadows of a subterranean shipyard, complete with slips for boats of all shapes and sizes to dock. When it was in use, this must've been an impressive place. Now, though, nature had gone a long way toward reclaiming the cave.

"There it is," Jaga said and nodded toward the prow of the boat. "That's the cocksucking Deepways."

After the gloom of the cavern, I'd expected more darkness. Instead, the mouth of the Deepways swirled with flashes of sacred energy like bolts of lightning in a thunderhead. It was brighter here than it had been at the entrance, and the light cast harsh shadows across the water.

"I wonder if it's still active," I said. "If it is, there's no telling where we'll end up once we go through."

"I don't think it's active," Jaga said. "When I was a kid, my mom and dad took me on a trip through the Deepways. You could see clear from one end of the Deepways to the other when they were working the way they ought. There weren't any clouds or that swirly light bullshit."

"All right, then," I said. "Cross your fingers."

My spirit sight told me there wasn't anything threatening hidden in the cloud. The flashes of energy were senjin, but it wasn't tainted. Whatever bindings had been used to create the Deepways had spared at least this part of it from the worst of the corruption.

"If this wrecks my boat, I'll chew your dick off," Jaga promised.

The sampan slid into the churning cloud, and I instantly knew we'd made a terrible mistake.

The cavern vanished behind us and was replaced ahead of us by a long, straight tunnel composed entirely of agitated mist. Jagged strokes of sacred energy crawled through the foggy walls, pulsing and flashing in an eerie pattern that made my skin crawl. A moaning wind echoed around us, and I wondered where the hell this tunnel would take us.

The river under the sampan still flowed, though its surface had turned inky black broken only by phosphorescent glimmers as oddly shaped things swam past us in both directions. My spirit sight showed me lurking shadows at the edges of the tunnel, their eyes red sparks, their mouths lined with electric-blue teeth. With the way my luck had been running, I expected the creatures to surge out of the shadows and attack us.

Instead, they waited, watched, and then closed ranks behind us.

"What the fuck is going on?" Jaga asked.

"I'm not sure," I said. "I'm going up front to get a better look."

The spirits' hunger was palpable. It surrounded us like a wet blanket, heavy on my shoulders, suffocating with its intensity.

"The tunnel's getting narrower," Ayo said. "A little at a time."

"She's right," Aja said. "It's closing around us."

That's why the spirits hadn't attacked. They were waiting for the tunnel to do the heavy lifting and crush the sampan so we'd be stranded in the water with them. Then they'd tear us apart like feeding sharks.

"I'm not dying here today," I growled.

The Deepways were sacred energy constructs. They'd been built to allow quick travel between distant points, and they ran on pure senjin. There was so much raw energy here that it crackled like static on my skin. I wasn't sure what had turned this place into a death trap, and I didn't care. I doubted I could unravel that puzzle before we were smashed to pulpy bits.

I could, however, suck the juice out of the tunnel. With any luck, that would be enough to get it to stop.

"Don't let anything eat me for a minute. I need to meditate." I flopped onto the deck in a cross-legged meditation posture and closed my eyes.

I drew in a series of deep, hungry breaths. Pure senjin rushed into my core. It was powerful stuff, so potent it left me feeling drunk. In only a handful of moments, the untainted mercurial energy had strained my core to its limits. It rested inside me like a lead balloon, the density of its power almost overwhelming.

It also wasn't nearly enough.

The walls were still closing in, and the senjin still surrounded us in dizzying quantities.

"Okay, that didn't work." I stood and paced up and down the deck. "I can't pull enough energy out of the walls to stop them from closing in on us. We'd need some kind of barrier. Something to keep it from —"

Holy shit. A barrier.

I ran into the cabin and grabbed the satchel I'd taken from the other Deepways station. The black book was still where I'd left it, its glossy cover gleaming with potential. I'd only been able to read the table of contents when I'd discovered the book. I'd advanced since then, though, and hoped I could at least make use of the first of its techniques.

I crossed my fingers and flipped open the *Formation Manual of Borders and Boundaries* to the first page after the table of contents.

"The Wall of Sanctity," I read aloud, so relieved I struggled to keep my voice from shaking. "A boundary-formation technique that will exclude all types of sacred energy from entering or leaving its confines. Useful for transporting dangerous practitioners or shielding your domicile from hostile techniques."

I studied the manual's detailed instructions as quickly as I could. The words burned into my thoughts, transforming themselves into strange glyphs and sigils in my mind's eye. My spirit sight blurred, then snapped into focus as the details of the Wall of Sanctity formation etched themselves into my core.

"If you're going to do something, this would be a good time," Aja said, her voice high and nervous.

"Watch and be amazed," I said with a grin. The walls were dangerously close to the boat's hull, but that was all right. I had this.

I transferred a node's worth of rin out of my core and up through my arm. Following the manual's instructions, I formed the sacred energy into a small, crimson pyramid and placed the new construct on the boat's prow. I repeated the process nine more times, and evenly spaced the pyramids around the boat's perimeter. The exercise left me exhausted, but that was all right. With my nodes empty, I could refuel on pure senjin.

"Those better come off my fucking boat," Jaga snapped. "They're ugly, and they'll get in my way."

"They're going to save your life," I said.

"Sure they are."

"Just watch!"

I drew in a deep breath, and pure senjin rushed into my core. My spirit separated the silver dream energy into its masculine and feminine components, transferring the rin into my nodes and shedding the blue shio from my pores. In a few moments, I'd have enough energy to activate the pyramids.

I hoped.

I coaxed a thread of energy from each of my nodes to each of the pyramids in turn. It was incredibly draining because the pyramids slurped the energy out of the node the instant it made contact. The sudden loss of all that sacred energy almost dropped me to my knees. As it was, I had to catch myself with one hand against the boat's cabin and still nearly toppled into the river.

The tunnel's collapsing walls were an inch or so away from the sampan's hull. I clenched my teeth and prayed something, anything, would happen. The pyramids had eaten all my spirit's energy, but they hadn't done anything but glow a sullen red.

It was going to be very embarrassing if I'd been wrong. Fortunately, everyone who'd witnessed my foolish mistake would also be dead before they had a chance to tease me about what I'd done.

Small victories.

The walls closed in around the boat. There was a high-pitched grinding noise like pieces of steel being dragged across each other. The boat shuddered violently, and the river's current slowed suddenly, almost pitching all of us onto our faces. Jaga wrestled with the rudder, while the spirits shouted in surprise and backed away from the prow. I watched, helpless to do anything else, as the tunnel prepared to crush the sampan.

At the last possible second, a curtain of brilliant red power flared from the tips of the pyramids. The brilliant radiance pushed back against the walls of churning senjin, and our boat lurched into motion again. The barrier had held.

But not for long.

A sudden ugly crackling sound slapped against my ears, and the pyramids went dark.

Chapter Nineteen

MY BREATH CAUGHT IN MY THROAT IN THE space between heartbeats. The light had gone out of the pyramids and the flickers of senjin disappeared from the trap's walls. We were blind, and not even my spirit sight could find any light to focus on.

And then, miraculously, radiant red sparks shuddered to life inside each of the pyramids. The formation repelled the trap, at least for the moment, and gave us a tiny sliver of breathing room. By the formation's light, I saw that the misty tunnel was still closing in around us, though at a much slower pace.

I ignored the shouts and cries of dismay from the spirits and the pilot. They seemed certain we were about to die.

Not if I had anything to say about it.

"Do something, Kyr!" Jaga shouted.

While the pylons of the Wall of Sanctity were still ready and willing to protect us, they didn't have enough juice left in their structures to affect sacred energy. That was good enough because it meant I was able to draw more of the raw, pure senjin that surrounded us into my core. I gulped it in, ignoring proper breathing technique in a mad rush to fill my nodes as quickly as possible. The mercurial power battered my core, and by the time I'd processed it into rin and stuffed it into my nodes, my guts felt like I'd gone a few rounds in the sparring ring with the king of kidney punches and body blows

I filled all but one of the pyramids with my sacred energy. That left an opening in the cage for me to process even more senjin, and I used it to refill my empty nodes. I'd never gone through this much senjin and rin in such a short period of time, and it left me feeling punch-drunk. It was hard to hold my head up, and even harder to think clearly. I'd pay for this little stunt tomorrow, but at least I'd be alive.

I filled the last pyramid, and the Wall of Sanctity formation ignited. I maintained my connection to the pyramids, pushing more of my rin into them whenever their lights dimmed. Minutes passed, my skull throbbed, and my eyes burned from the light of the blazing barrier. Even with my eyes closed, I couldn't escape the glare of the cage I'd created. It was impossible to see beyond the wall of sparks that surrounded us, and I hoped we weren't about to run aground.

At some point, I screamed. I was overwhelmed, my mind, body, and spirit taxed beyond their limits. Cool hands pressed against my chest, soothing voices murmured meaningless words into my ears. None of it mattered. I pushed the rin out of my core and into the pyramids until there was nothing left of me to give. My nodes were dark, but still I pushed, wringing sacred energy from my flesh and blood, burning my life force to keep the barrier up and my people safe.

Then I sagged against the boat's cabin, blind and deaf, lost in a darkness that closed around the fitful spark of life that was all that remained in my core.

At least the pain was gone. If this was death, I was grateful that it didn't hurt at all.

In fact, it felt pretty fucking good.

Really fucking good.

Someone kissed me and a tongue flickered across the sharp edges of my teeth. Hands tangled in my hair, and something warm and wet closed around my fingers. Liquid heat enveloped my cock, and that was all it took to drag me out of the darkness.

Jaga was astride me, her back facing me, her feet flat on the deck next to my hips, her knees pulled up to her breasts. She was hot and tight around me, the muscles of her sex squeezing and relaxing in a counterpoint rhythm to her rocking hips. She bobbed up and down, the long, lean muscles of her legs flexing as a dragon tattoo on her back danced along the curve of her spine.

"You could've asked," I said sarcastically. "Didn't your mother ever teach you it's not polite to fuck an unconscious guy?"

"Oh, good, you're not dead," Jaga said over her shoulder. Her dark hair had fallen over her eyes, hiding them. Her full lips were twisted into a wry grin. "This was their idea. Doesn't feel like it's bothering you much."

That was very true. I hadn't exactly been a virgin when I went up to the top of Mount Shiki, but the only sex I'd had since then had been with spirits. They were vigorous and talented lovers, don't get me wrong, but there was something about the feel of another human that was different and exciting.

"You scared the fuck out of us," Aja snarled. She kissed me fiercely and bit my lip hard enough to draw blood. "Don't you ever do anything like that again."

"Or what?" I laughed. "You'll kill me?"

"Yes," Ayo replied. I realized my fingers were deep inside her. With her free hand, she parted the lips of her sex and stroked the swollen pearl above her dripping opening with her middle finger. The motion dragged a low, guttural groan from her, and she swallowed my fingers entirely.

With a start I saw that her core was nearly empty. Aja's was little better. They'd been near death before they'd woken me, and the idea filled me with a combination of anger and regret. I'd been so preoccupied with Jiro and then the problem in the cavern I hadn't noticed how dangerously close to oblivion the spirits had come.

I grabbed Aja by the back of her head and pulled her mouth to mine. She licked the blood from my lip, and I tasted it on her tongue like a hot, bright spot of metal. That flavor ignited a spark of primal lust inside me that urged me to push deeper into Jaga. My tongue flashed over Aja's, searching, desperate, and greedy.

Raw, tainted senjin flooded into my hollowed core, where it boiled and added its heat to the passion running through my veins.

All four of our bodies moved together in perfect harmony. Jaga bounced on me, my flesh invading hers with every deep thrust, filling her with steaming rin even as the crashing waves of pleasure pushed her shio into my core. Ayo cried out and spasmed against my hand, her body convulsing around my fingers as her sacred power combined with mine to purify the senjin. Aja lowered her breast to my mouth, her crimson hair dangling over her face like a veil. A spark of pure dream power rolled through the four of us as if a circuit had been completed, and we shuddered together.

It wasn't enough. I needed more.

The crimson bear's strength surged through my veins, and I slipped my fingers free of Ayo's hungry sex to grab Jaga's hips in both hands. A guttural roar rumbled from my chest, and I stood, hauling Jaga off the deck with me. My cock reached the limits of her depths, and she gasped in surprise at the maneuver. I turned her toward the sampan's port side, then let her feet touch the deck again as I thrust into her in an animalistic frenzy.

"Blood God," she groaned. She clung to the sampan's rail and pushed back against me with feverish intensity. There was no rhythm now, just the desperate grinding need as we chased a stomping dragon of primal pleasure through each others' heaving flesh.

Ayo kissed me with wild abandon, crushing our lips together and thrusting her tongue into my mouth. She let out little whimpers as her swaying breasts brushed against my skin. Her erect nipples ignited sparks of sacred power that jumped between us, raising the hairs on my arms and flickering in the spirit's white hair like shooting stars.

I pulled Aja to me and stroked her dripping cleft with the fingers of my right hand. She sucked at the side of my throat and wrapped her arms around my shoulders. She urged me to go faster, harder, and soon my hand was grinding against her in rapid circles.

Jaga let out a savage moan, arched her spine, and threw her head back. Her hair, damp from the mist, slapped against her shoulders. Convulsive shudders shook her from the soles of her feet to the crown of her skull, until she was left shaking and hardly able to stand.

"Enough," she moaned when I pulled her hips back against me. Another cataclysmic shudder ran through her body, and she collapsed against the railing like every shred of strength had been leeched from her muscles.

The pilot slithered from my grasp and eased herself down to the deck, leaving my prick throbbing and exposed to the river breeze. Her eyes were hooded with exhaustion, and she lolled against the side of the boat with her hands in her lap. Her core glowed with blue shio, a bright marble of light that sent pulses of sacred energy coursing through her body with every beat of her heart.

"Here," Aja growled. She bent over in front of me and reached back between her legs to grab my sticky, twitching cock.

I plunged into the crimson-haired spirit and she yipped like a coyote as the head of my stiff rod plumbed her depths. Her muscles tightened and she howled, again and again, a wild, animal's cry that sent water birds flying through the mist in an explosion of flapping wings.

Ayo straddled Aja's back, facing me, her eyes wild and cheeks flushed a deep, almost violet blue. She kissed me fiercely and pulled my hands off the other spirit's hips to squeeze her breasts. She was lost in a passionate hunger that went far beyond anything I'd seen in her before. She stroked herself desperately, clawing her way toward the divine ecstasy that Aja and I hunted together.

All concept of time and self vanished. I'd become part of a sweating, heaving animal that existed only to satisfy its animal urges. Mielyssi's ecstatic cries echoed in my ears, her voice ragged with emotion and dripping with pleasure as she called my name in an endless litany in time with the slap of my thighs against Aja's ass. Our bodies glowed with the silver radiance of sacred energy, and its power bound us together in a writhing circle of delicious agony.

We came in a string of overwhelming pleasure. Aja's juices splashed down my legs as she melted around me. Ayo cried into my mouth, her lips locked to mine, one arm around my neck, her hand pulling my fingers to the slick nub of her clit to bring her to a shuddering climax.

With a primal thrust, I emptied myself into Aja. Ropes of my seed flooded into her and ran down her thighs with every thrust. A tidal wave of an orgasm plowed through my mind and body and splashed across the three women on the deck with me. Our voices rose in a final, animal chorus, echoed within me by the crimson bear's savage wails of pleasure.

The spirits and I parted reluctantly, our bodies sticky with our shared juices. I lay flat on my back, while the spirits leaned against the sampan's edge next to Jaga. No one said a word, the only sound the synchronized thunder of our pulses in our ears.

"What a fucking mess." Jaga broke the silence at last.

"That's exactly what it is," Ayo giggled.

"I'm not cleaning it up," Aja declared. She pointed at the sticky residue of my cum plastered to the insides of her thighs. "Most of it came out of our shaman. He should clean it up."

"I don't think so. After that performance, I'm not doing anything but taking a nap." I chuckled. "Starting right after you three tell me what the fuck happened and where we are."

"Good, you're done spewing fluids everywhere." Yata landed on top of the sampan's deck. "Now I can chastise you for nearly shattering your core with that little stunt."

"What?" I had no idea shattering my core was even possible. Sure, I'd banged it around a bit pushing myself too hard in the past, but Mielyssi had never told me it was possible to break the damned thing.

"You pushed every dribble of power out of your core at the same time you pulled in pure senjin." Yata squawked and hopped from one foot to the next to the next, wings fluttering. "Your nodes aren't built for that kind of abuse, and the shell definitely isn't meant to have sacred energy incoming and outgoing at the same time. You're lucky you're not dead."

"Which we would have been if it weren't for my little stunt. If I hadn't used the formation, the trap would have crushed us like bugs." I cupped my hands behind my head and wished for a handy pillow that didn't materialize. Maybe there was a shaman technique for that. If there was, I vowed to learn it at the earliest possible opportunity.

"Just because we survived doesn't mean it was a good idea." Yata preened itself and hopped down to the deck next to Jaga. "The good news is that no one died, your core isn't crippled, and we're almost to the Lake of Moonsilver Mist."

"The cave cut through the hills and came out farther downriver." Jaga yawned and stretched her arms overhead, her breasts jiggling in a most distracting way. "We're only a few hours away from the lake."

Aja and Ayo looked very excited by that prospect. The looks of unbridled glee on their faces stirred an unexpected pang of regret in my gut. In a few more hours, they'd be back with their mistress. They'd be home, and that's where they'd stay. After I left to figure out how to save the world, I'd probably never see them again. That would put a very serious crimp in my ability to absorb and use sacred energy.

But, more importantly, I'd miss them.

Suddenly, I didn't want this mission to end. This, the five of us together, seemed right. The very idea of breaking up the group made me want to punch something. Hard.

"So much for the good news," Yata croaked. "Who wants to hear the very bad news?"

"You have to be fucking kidding," I groaned. "Don't tell me the Jade Seekers got ahead of us again somehow."

"Okay, I won't. But this is even worse." Yata flapped its wings and let out a nervous caw. "There's an army camped around the lake. And the soldiers are building boats. Lots of boats."

Well. Fuck me.

Chapter Twenty

YATA SPILLED THE REST OF THE DETAILS IN A torrent of squawks and agitated feather ruffling. Turned out there were a few hundred well-armed and armored assholes parked on the Lake of Moonsilver Mist's south shore. Based on the state of their camp and the amount of work they'd done building barges for themselves, the soldiers had been at the lake for several days, maybe as much as a week.

It wouldn't be much longer before they were ready to launch those barges.

"At least they're on the far side of the lake." I'd take whatever advantages we could get at this point. "And it doesn't sound like they'll be ready to make their move before tomorrow at the earliest. If we head out now, we'll have time to heal the spirits' mistress and get the fuck out of there before they know we've arrived.

"Yes, but no," Yata croaked. "They've got scouts rowing all over the lake on skiffs."

"How the fuck did they know we were coming?" I growled and paced along the sampan's length. We'd dropped anchor out of sight of the lake after Yata had arrived. We were safe for the moment, but if we couldn't reach our goal we might as well have been on the wrong side of the moon.

"What sort of banners were they flying?" Jaga asked.

"Black." Yata preened nervously. "With some kind of golden sunburst design, and a lion or something on them."

"You sure it's a lion?" Jaga asked. "It couldn't have been a tiger?"

"It could have been a fucking house cat," Yata snapped with a click of its beak. "It was a long way away, and the fog is awfully thick. But, yeah, I guess it might be a tiger."

"The White Tiger Kingdom are renowned kickass motherfuckers," the riverboat pilot groaned. "They're awfully far from home. You must have seriously pissed someone off for them to send so many troops all this way to stomp your ass."

"Even if they sent five hundred men, that's a drop in the bucket compared to how many soldiers the kingdoms can field." Every merchant I'd ever talked to in Floating Village had gone on and on about the number of soldiers marching here and there, making life hard for honest, hardworking folk. Things had changed while I'd been away, but I found it hard to believe the Empire would let its armies dwindle. "Their leader could have spared five thousand, if they really wanted us dead."

"That's an interesting way to look at it," Jaga said with a raised eyebrow. "Your numbers are all wrong, though. There aren't more than a few thousand troops in any of the seven kingdoms."

"That can't be right." I sat down on the deck and crossed my legs, Jaga's words reminded me of just how long I'd been gone. I needed more information, and this was as good a time as any to get it. "Let's have a little history lesson."

"Have you really been living in a cave for the past fifty years?" Jaga asked.

"Yes, but it was closer to a hundred years, I think." I tried to grin, but it came off as more sad and wistful than cheery. Fuck, but I missed Mielyssi. "I went into the cave during the nine hundred and eighty-sixth year of the Seventh Age, during the first week of Dragonwinter. I only came back a few days ago."

"Are you fucking with me?" Jaga asked. "This is the fifty-third year of the Eighth Age, and it's the last fucking week of Jadeflowering."

"Do the math for me, because I was gone when the Seventh Age ended." A cold chill ran through my body. I really didn't want to hear this answer. "Just how long have I been gone?"

"Right at a hundred and fifty years," Jaga said. "Honestly, though, you're pretty good at bumping uglies for an old, old man. And here I was worrying I was too mature for you."

"Give me a second." This was a lot to take in, and I still didn't know enough to understand what the fuck was going on. "All right, how long ago was the War of Shudders?"

"That was the end of the Seventh Age." Jaga crossed her arms under her heavy breasts and stared intently at me. "You better not be fucking with me. Everybody knows how that went down. Those crazy priests got sick of the demons rampaging all over the continent and poisoned the dream meridians. That ended the war and pushed all the hungry spirits and their allies back through the nexuses to the Frozen Hells. It also fucked everything up, though. Killed a ton of people, tainted the senjin, and made the Emperor seal off the Deepways to keep worse things than the demons from crawling back out."

That explained what we'd run into on our way here, but it still didn't make any sense. If the dream meridians had been poisoned at the end of the War of Shudders more than fifty years ago, why hadn't Mielyssi freaked out then? She'd been fine, all the way up until the night before she made me leave.

Her words from the top of the ten thousand steps came back to me. She'd known, even then, just how much time had passed. Decades had slipped through my fingers while she taught me how to love and fight and hunt, and decades more had gone by as I descended the stairs. My mind felt like it was about to come unmoored from my body, and my understanding of time and space suddenly felt woefully incomplete. Lifetimes had passed in what felt to me like weeks, at most.

"Holy fuck," I groaned and clasped my head in my hands. "I feel like I'm losing my mind."

"Sorry," Jaga said. She crouched down in front of me, her vest loose enough to reveal the top of the blue tattoo that surrounded her breasts. "If it's any consolation, everybody else pretty much went crazy for a while after the war. The Emperor changed his title to the Midnight Emperor and went to war with the Moonsilver Bat Kingdom. He had his Jade Seekers kill them all, then hunt down every shaman they could get their hands on. Said the bat priests and their spirit seeker allies were the ones who'd poisoned the meridians. Claimed they did it on purpose to try to take over the Sevenfold Empire."

"And that's why those Jade Seekers were camped outside my village, waiting for me." It felt like threads of fate were weaving invisible patterns around me as Jaga told her tale. I'd left before the world went to hell. The crimson bear had kept me on top of the mountain until after the war ended, after most of my people had been wiped out, after all the other shamans had been slaughtered.

At the same time, Aja and Ayo's mistress had known I was returning and sent the spirits to find me. This army had been on the march before I'd even left Floating Village; they'd known where I would be and how to stop me before my journey had even begun.

For a moment, I felt a cold certainty that this was all part of some larger plan. Someone had been pulling my strings, maybe since before I'd left Mount Shiki.

Stop worrying over nothing. That's not how I do things, and you know it.

The crimson bear's voice was harsh in my thoughts. I didn't know if what she said was true or not. There was also no point in worrying about how I'd gotten here. That was something for future me to fret over while he was relaxing in a house of ill repute somewhere with a drink in his hand.

"How bad was it?" I asked Jaga. "The war, I mean. You said tons of people died. How many?"

"Almost everyone." Jaga took in a deep, shuddering breath and plopped down on the deck in front of me. She pulled her knees to her chest and encircled them with her arms. "Before you left, there were what? Ten million people living on the continent?"

"No," I said. Where I'd lived had been pretty sparsely populated, but the traders had told me the rest of the Sevenfold Empire was loaded with people. "Ten times that many. A hundred million, at least. Most of them lived in Sungold Eagle territory, at the heart of the Empire."

It was Jaga's turn to look shocked.

"That's impossible." She scrubbed her cheeks with the palms of her hands and blinked hard as if trying to will my words away. "There are less than a million people left on the continent. Some say there's not even half that many."

My guts tightened into a knot, and my blood seemed to seize up in my veins. It didn't seem possible that any war, not even one involving demons and hungry spirits, could destroy ninety-nine out of every hundred men, women, and children. It was no wonder we hadn't encountered more travelers on our journey.

"Not many left to save," I muttered to myself. My heart ached for the world I'd lost. The more I saw of it, the more it seemed to have suffered while I was gone. If what Jaga said was true, then five hundred men was a substantial portion of the White Tiger Kingdom's military.

They must have really wanted me dead.

That was reason enough for me to want to survive. If the Emperor had sent so many Jade Seekers after me, if he'd impressed so many of another kingdom's troops into his service just to kill me, I must be more important than I'd thought.

I didn't believe for an instant that the priests of the Moonsilver Bat Kingdom had intentionally tried to destroy the dream meridians. Priests were sacred practitioners; they needed the senjin that came out of those meridians to fuel their miracles and commune with their god. The only reason they'd have fucked up the source of senjin was if they'd been pushed into a desperate corner. Maybe they had done something terrible, but they'd done it to try to save the world. I was sure of that.

It was possible that the Midnight Emperor had ordered all of my people wiped out and sent his men to finish the job because he was pissed that they'd fucked everything up.

But it was also possible that the Emperor was the one who'd fucked up. No one got to be the big man in charge of the Sevenfold Empire without a significant amount of skill when it came to channeling senjin. The Emperor had to have known and approved of what the Moonsilver Bat's priests were doing.

If he'd wanted them all murdered when the dust cleared, maybe it was because they knew the Emperor was the one who'd done something terrible and he needed to silence them.

The fact that he wanted me dead told me the reason behind his murder spree was even deeper than that. Maybe my heritage was a key that could help unlock this mystery. Maybe as the last shaman and the last member of the Moonsilver Bat Kingdom, I could undo at least some of the damage that had been done to the world, and the big man didn't want that to happen.

Or, I was jumping at shadows and making connections that didn't exist. None of it would matter if we got caught. I needed to focus on the problems I had in front of me, and solve them one at a time.

"We're not going to be able to cross the lake in the middle of the day," I said. My eyes pored over the spirits' cores and saw that they both had two full nodes of shio. Their little bit of sexual healing had filled us all the way up to the top. Perfect. "We'll wait until nightfall.

This fucking mist and the darkness should help us sneak right past the bad guys. And if we can't get around them, I'll kill them."

"You seem pretty confident about that," Jaga said. "Are you willing to risk my boat on this mission?"

"Your boat won't be in any danger," I said. "I have a plan."

"Are you going to tell us about it?" Ayo asked.

"Yeah," I said. "Tonight."

"What are we supposed to do for the rest of the day?" Aja asked. "Sit around with our thumbs up our asses?"

"There's something else that I'd like to sit on," Jaga said, her eyes hungry.

"We've got a little time," I said. "But keep it down. We don't want the whole army coming to see what all the noise is about."

The spirits laughed at that, and I couldn't help but smile.

Darkness was coming, but, for the moment, we were all together in the light. I decided to make the most of it.

Chapter Twenty-One

NO ONE CAUGHT US IN THE ACT, WHICH WAS SOME of the best luck I'd had so far. Satisfied and relaxed, we all sat on the roof of the sampan's cabin to watch the sunset and fill our empty bellies with the last of the food we'd taken out of the Deepways cargo. Nuts and dried berries weren't exactly filling, but we couldn't afford to draw attention to our position with a fire.

"While you've been stuffing your faces and each other, I was flying around looking for bad guys," Yata said as its claws touched down on the cabin next to me. "We've got three patrol skiffs between us and the island. There are a few more in the area, but I don't think they'll be close enough to spot us."

"Can we slip between them?" Aja asked. "The sampan's a pretty good size, but in the dark with the mist to hide us, we might be able to do it."

"Yes, if we time it just right." Yata flapped up to perch on my shoulder, careful not to pierce me with its talons. "But we can't afford any mistakes. Once we start moving, everything has to be just right or they'll spot us."

"Then I'll kill them," I said. "If we sneak past the scouts on the way in, we'll have to sneak past them on our way out. If we kill them all, that halves our chances of being spotted, and we won't have to worry about being discovered until their watch ends and someone notices they didn't come back to camp."

"Seems risky." Jaga scratched the side of her chin and shrugged. "We get up on them without being seen, then you have to get from the sampan over to their skiff without attracting attention, and then you have to kill them before they can raise an alarm. There are a lot of steps in your plan, and if any of them goes wrong, we're fucked."

"And that is why we're not going to do it that way," I said with a grin. "I have another plan. We'll make our move after sundown, as soon as they finish changing the scouts."

We waited in uneasy silence, our shoulders touching, our toes overlapped in the center of our small circle. An impossible number of enemies was headed our way, and yet, with these women beside me, I was confident we'd win this thing.

"Thank you," I said. "All of you. I couldn't have made it this far without you."

"You wouldn't have come this way at all if it hadn't been for us," Aja said with a nervous chuckle. "You'd probably be in a lot less danger if you weren't trying to get us back to our mistress."

"True." I gave her a wolfish grin. "But if I hadn't met you, then I wouldn't have advanced my core. And I wouldn't have found Jaga, who wouldn't have brought us all this way south. She also wouldn't have given me the history lesson I needed to understand what the fuck I'm doing here. So, I'll say thanks again."

"Okay, asshole," Jaga said. "Enough of this feel-good bullshit. The sun's gone. If we're going to do this, I want to know the rest of your plan."

"I'm going to kill the scouts, you're going to sail the spirits over to the island," I said with a shrug. "It's a pretty simple plan, but I'll be happy to go over it with you again, if it's really necessary."

"It's my boat," Jaga said plaintively. "If it gets blown up, what am I supposed to do?"

"Stick with us," Ayo said. "We'll get you a new boat. A nicer one."

"That's not what I mean," Jaga said with an exasperated sigh. "Look, I'm a riverboat pilot. It's what I do. It's what I'm good at. People almost never try to kill me, and as long as I stay away from city watch patrols and the few guards who roam the rivers, I can pretty much do whatever the fuck I want."

"I'm not going to let anything happen to you," I assured Jaga. "I'll deal with the scouts. It's not a problem."

"Okay," the captain said. "Fine. The scouts won't be a problem. What about the White Tiger army? What about the fucking Jade Seekers? What about the next hundred assholes you pick a fight with who decide to kill me because I happened to be nearby?"

Jaga's eyes were wide and wet. I felt the pain in her heart, the worry about what she'd gotten involved in when I jumped on her boat while Ulishi burned.

"You're right," I said. Ayo and Aja stared at in shock. "This isn't your fight. I never asked what you wanted, and I should have. You were going to leave us upstream before the Jade Seekers showed up and screwed that plan right in the ass. I don't have any right to ask any more of you. You've done more than I could have hoped, and you've only bitched a little bit."

"I'm not bitching," Jaga grumped. "It's called expressing a concern, motherfucker."

"I know." I reached out, took Jaga's hand, and squeezed it between both of mine. "I'm only going to ask one more favor. Get us to the island. I'll clear out the scouts, you can do whatever you want after we land. Turn back, skirt around the lake to find another river, whatever you feel like. No one will know you helped us here tonight."

"God, when you say it like that you make me sound like such a bitch," Jaga moaned. "Fine, it's a deal. I like you, Kyr. I like you girls, too. But I can't risk all I've got for you. No fuck, not even the best fuck of my life, is worth that."

"I understand," I said and kissed her cheek. "But you're going to miss out on a lot more fucks if you leave now."

Yata landed on the cabin's edge with a faint squawk.

"The guards have changed over," it said. "If you two are done playing kissy-face, it's time to fuck some shit up."

"Remember the plan," I said to the three-legged raven. "If you see anything, let me know right away. I don't want any surprises to fuck this up."

Before anyone else could ask me about my plan, I dove off the cabin's roof and into the river. Fish darted in every direction as I speared through the water's depths, and I looped a strand of rin around a speedy little perch before it could escape. Its energy flowed into the node I'd emptied to capture it, and its essential fishiness temporarily became a part of me. My swimming improved, I could hold my breath longer, and my skin slid through the water as if I were greased.

My spirit sight showed me the first guard, his core a pale gray blob just above the water's surface. He only had a single node, and it held just a faint splash of sacred energy to sustain him. He had no techniques, no special skills that would save him.

Good.

I knifed through the water toward my target, the animal energy I'd taken into my core filling me with a bestial urge to hunt and kill. When I was a yard from my target's core, I rose from the water in a silent rush. A final kick shot me up and out of the water, and I landed behind the guard without a sound. He only knew I was there because the skiff rocked beneath us, throwing him off-balance.

Before he could recover and shout a warning or raise a spirit whistle, I triggered my Crimson Claws and Bear's Mantle techniques. I was surprised to find the claws longer, almost knife-like, and my skin was harder and tougher than I'd remembered. Apparently, going up a core level did a lot more than just give me more nodes. It had enhanced my techniques, making them more powerful.

The guard tried to scream, but it was too late. The razor-sharp tips of my claws dug into his throat and scooped his trachea out. Blood sprayed into the air along with a feeble sputter of rin from his shocked core. I caught him before he could fall and then eased him down to the skiff's rough planks. He hadn't had a chance to make a sound, and none of the other scouts were near enough to us to notice what had happened. They were still out there, blind and deaf to the danger that was coming, bored stiff and all alone on the river's black surface.

The next guard didn't fare any better. I surged up out of the water in front of him, grabbed his ankles, and pulled him down into the dark water with the smallest of splashes. A single swipe of my claws opened the warrior from throat to crotch, and his blood filled the surrounding water with a metallic tang that made my throat itch and my mouth ache to bite. I hadn't felt like this since I'd left the crimson bear, and Mielyssi's presence seemed strengthened by my savage attack. Her spirit was all around me, stronger than the blood in the water, stronger than even the scent of my own flesh. She was inside me, where she belonged, and I yearned to be back inside her.

Soon. I swear.

Her fierce spirit goaded me on, and I rose to the surface to take a quick breath before disappearing to hunt down the next foolish scout.

That was when everything went to shit.

I was halfway out of the water when a bolt of red-hot agony shot through my right side. The unexpected blast of pain doubled me over in mid-leap, and I crashed down onto the skiff's deck in an ungainly pile.

"What the fuck?" the scout gasped in surprise. He fumbled for something at his waist, and I knew if he found it we were completely and totally screwed.

The torture in my side made it impossible for me to stand, so I did the next best thing. I raked my claws across the back of the man's ankles, severing his tendons. If I couldn't reach his throat, I'd bring his throat down to me.

Shock robbed the scout of his breath, and he crumpled to the deck alongside me. He'd retrieved the spirit whistle from a pouch hanging off his belt. If he broke it, the siren's hellish wail would call every soldier within a mile straight to our location.

We couldn't fucking have that.

Tearing the man's throat out wouldn't stop him from breaking the thin bone item and unleashing its alarm. Even tearing out his brain might not be able to stop him for calling for help.

I slashed my claws through his wrist, just above the edge of his padded leather jerkin. The severed hand popped off the end of his arm, twisted in the air twice, and splashed into the river. Not even a bubble of air rose to mark the spot where the hand had vanished.

The lance of pain in my side disappeared with the man's hand. I dragged myself back to my feet and glared down at my fallen foe.

The man stared at me from where he lay on the deck. His eyes were so wide they looked ready to pop out of his skull. He didn't seem afraid, or even like he wanted to cry out. When he finally spoke, a simple question fell from his lips.

"What are you?"

"The end of this world." I tore out his throat and he rolled away, convulsing as his life gushed from between his fingers. His body splashed into the river with no more sound than a big bass leaping up to catch a firefly.

"And the beginning of a new one."

Chapter Twenty-Two

THE MIST ABOVE THE LAKE'S SURFACE GLOWED like silver under the moonlight, so dense and thick I didn't realize I'd reached the island until the water became too shallow for me to swim through. I crawled out of the lake and onto dry land, only to find that the mist was much thicker here.

The stink of corruption was everywhere. This island lay at a nexus of dream meridians, all of which were tainted with some hellish spirit poison that I now knew had been used to fight off a demonic invasion decades ago. The defenders had won at a terrible cost. It might've been better to let the demons win, to let this world slip away to be replaced by another.

And then what of me, shaman? I would have gone with it, and you would have died alongside me, your spirit trapped forever at the top of Mount Shiki while the world you'd once known vanished from the pages of history.

"Fine, I'm wrong," I whispered, a faint smile on my lips. No matter what the crimson bear said, I was glad to hear her voice and feel her presence still with me.

I waited on the beach for the others to arrive because there was no way they'd be able to find me any deeper into the mist. A few minutes later, Yata appeared out of the fog, wings flapping, talons extended to land gently on my shoulder.

Jaga's sampan glided up onto the gravel beach moments after the raven appeared, its smooth hull scraping across the fine, water-polished rocks at the island's perimeter. Ayo and Aja immediately leapt out of the boat, our meager gear over their shoulders, eyes dancing with the blue radiance of spirit sight. The boat's captain appeared on the prow, one foot resting on the rail.

"You do good work, Kyr," she said. "I'll miss that cock of yours, but I certainly won't miss the rest of this shit. I'll give you a quarter of an hour to get back from doing whatever the fuck you came here to do. If you catch me before I leave, I'll happily take you with me to my next stop. Otherwise, good luck. Something tells me you'll need it."

I strode down the beach and snatched Jaga off the boat's deck. I held her in my arms, cradling her against my chest like a child, and stared down into her eyes. They were the brightest green, like chips of polished jade in the sun. The faint white scars that cut through the deep tan of her cheeks and forehead shone like faint wisps of silver. I kissed her, gently, and squeezed her tight.

"You're a hell of a woman, Jaga," I said. "You've done more than I could have expected. I'll always remember you."

"You fucking better, asshole," she said with a grin. "It's just my luck we'll meet again, though. My pussy tends to chase after the pricks most liable to cause me fucking trouble. Better hurry; the clock's running on that time limit,"

She wriggled free of my grip and jumped back onto her boat with ease. The spirits joined me to wave goodbye to Jaga, then dragged me deeper toward the island's misty interior. Aja handed me my war club, and grinned up at me.

"Our mistress's temple is at the heart of the island." Ayo seemed positively giddy with the prospect of returning home. I was glad to see her happy, but it pained me to realize that our time together was coming to an end. By morning, there was a very good chance I'd be alone or dead.

I wasn't sure which would be worse.

"Temple?" I asked. "She's a priestess?"

"No," Aja laughed. "She's the Witch Goddess of the Lake of Moonsilver Mist."

Oh, well, that changed things.

"You could've said something about that earlier." I followed the spirits, watching for danger on all sides. My spirit sight didn't show me any immediate threats, but the tainted shadows of corruption were everywhere. They could easily hide dark forces intent on ripping out our guts and chewing off my balls.

I'd pass on both experiences, thanks.

"We could have," Ayo admitted. "But she told us not to until after we reached the island. No sane man would turn down a goddess's plea for help. We only wanted you to do this if it's what you truly felt was right."

"Blood God," I muttered. "You'd have let your mistress, and yourselves, die because I wasn't saving you for the right reason?"

"Yep," Aja said. "Imagine our relief when you turned out to be a real hero and not a complete piece of shit."

"You're welcome," I said. "But I'm no hero. I'm just a half-naked fucking shaman."

The spirits both laughed at that, and their musical voices lightened the mood as we made our way deeper into the island's interior.

The temple emerged from the fog ahead of us, its peaked roof rising far overhead, silver beams of moonlight playing in the thick coils of mist between the tall columns at its entrance. This place had once been beautiful, I imagined, though the shadows and moonlight now made it look sinister.

"She's in there," Ayo said excitedly. "I can feel it. Faint, but she's there."

"Wait." Aja grabbed the white-haired sprite by the wrist and brought them both to a halt. "Something's wrong."

She'd no sooner gotten the words out than a heavy iron club longer than I was tall swooped down, clearly intent on crushing me like a bug.

I threw myself to the side, and the club slammed through the space where I'd just been standing. If I'd been a half second slower, it would've pulped me into a red mist sprayed across the island.

The weapon's wielder was enormous, at least twenty feet tall and too big for me to reach around with both arms. It strode toward me on a pair of ebony hooves at the end of long, hairless legs the color of spilled blood. The creature wore a loincloth around its thick waist, and a pendulous belly covered in open sores and weeping tumors dangled above its heavy chain belt. The humanoid beast's flaccid breasts hung down to its belly, nipples leaking green ichor that stained its skin. The monstrosity's arms were thick with corded muscle, and massive ivory tusks jutted from either side of its slack mouth. Wide eyes, pitch black and surrounded by a faint smoky aura, bulged from its misshapen skull as it advanced on me.

"That can't be Ohsa," Ayo gasped. "It can't be."

I didn't care what the monster was. It was clear only one of us would get out of this fight alive.

It swung its club again, a clumsy backhand strike that missed me by a good yard, and I ducked under the blow and charged in close where the creature would have a harder time smashing me flat. With a savage howl, I tossed my war club away and activated the Crimson Claws technique.

My claws dug a trio of ugly holes in the backside of the monster's left calf. The supernatural weapons sliced through the monster's skin with ease, carving out gobbets of muscle and fat with every swipe. I hacked at its leg with the same technique I'd learned cutting trees for firewood back in my village. Focus on an angle of attack, and chop like a motherfucker.

The creature's black blood splashed the ground around me, its severed veins and arteries gushing like ruptured hoses. Despite the damage, the monstrosity didn't so much as grunt with pain. Instead, the big asshole tried to smash me with a downward thrust of its club.

While the monster was huge, it was too slow and untrained to land a strike on someone with my experience. I darted away from its club and ducked between its legs, slashing and gouging at its ankles with sweeps of my hands as it stomped around in a circle, club swinging wildly.

"Ohsa, no!" Aja shouted at the monster.

The beast swung its head drunkenly toward the spirit, mouth hanging slack. Some spark of recognition flared in its sickly eyes when they fell on Ayo. The giant roared at the spirit and took a step in her direction.

"Don't get its attention!" As long as the diseased monstrosity's attacks were directed at me, I was confident I could dodge out of their way. I wasn't nearly as certain the spirits would survive. Coming all this way to have them die on our destination's doorstep seemed horribly anticlimactic. "Hey, fuckface, over here!"

With a roar, I hacked at the tendon behind its right calf. Each swipe of my claws sent ribbons of shredded, rotting meat over my shoulders. In seconds only a few strands of ligaments held the pus-slicked bones of the giant's right ankle together. Given its size and weight, the damned thing's joint should have come apart and sent it crashing to the ground.

Still, it wouldn't fucking fall.

The creature surprised me with a sudden stomp from its jacked-up leg, and I barely leapt away before the attack smashed me into the mud. The enormous club whipped toward me on the heels of the first attack, driving me back. The rusty spikes that jutted from the weapon's tip swept past my face with less than an inch to spare.

Despite all the damage I'd done to it, the giant hadn't slowed down. In fact, it was getting faster.

I darted past the reach of the rotting monster's club before it could bring it around for another attack. Another slash at its savaged ankle sliced away the last of the connective tissue, to no effect. Filaments of black shadow oozed from the creature's diseased flesh, holding it together.

It was time to change tactics. If I couldn't bring the head to me, I'd go to the head.

The giant roared its frustration, and a rain of pustulant fluid splattered down on my naked back. The monstrosity turned and raised its foot again, howling in rage when it realized I was no longer on the ground.

I scrambled up the giant's raised leg from my handhold on its boot and made it all the way to its knee before the stupid thing understood what had happened. The spirits shouted something from below me, but I didn't have time for anything that didn't involve tearing this fucker to pieces.

The creature was infuriated by my attempts to clamber up its body, and it let me know that in no uncertain terms. It dropped its club and tried to grab me with both hands. The giant's grubby fingers were tipped with thick, black nails crusted with filth, and I had a sneaking suspicion the wounds they would cause would fester into a truly nightmarish pestilence.

Best not get touched, then.

I dodged its first grab by scrambling around to its back, my claws digging into its flesh for handholds. Black blood ran down its body from the holes I left, and I gagged at the horrible stench. I'd smelled dead carcasses before, and the reek of punctured bowels could really turn my stomach, but I'd never smelled anything so foul as the blood leaking out of the giant motherfucker.

The rotting beast's putrid hands tried to scrape me off its back, with no luck. I'd found the sweet spot along its spine where it couldn't reach me with either hand, and I clung there by the claws of one hand like a particularly mean-spirited tick. The creature bellowed with rage and stomped toward the shoreline in a confused, drunken rage. It flailed its arms in the air, desperate for some way to dislodge me from its back.

I scrambled up to the big fucker's shoulder and drove the claws of my left hand deep into the soft tissue behind its ear. With my right hand, I carved away a swath of rotted scalp. The putrid skin sloughed away to reveal the brittle, yellowed bone beneath.

The giant lost its shit before I could push my attack into the rotten stew of its brain. Its upraised fists crashed down, leaving me with no choice but to get the fuck out of there.

I dropped off the monster's shoulder and dug my claws into the mushy meat of its upper back.

The giant's left fist swept through the spot I'd just exited and smashed squarely into the side of its head. Skin splattered off its knuckles, and its weak skull shattered. Shards of bone sliced through the big fucker's brain, slicing through whatever was left between its ears. The critter roared, stumbled, then righted itself.

Unbelievably, that brutal shot to the noggin hadn't killed it.

"If you want something done," I muttered.

I monkeyed back onto the giant's shoulder and took a good look at the damage it had caused itself. Most of its brains had oozed out through the hole in its skull, leaving behind only a gnarled chunk of gray meat at the top of its spine. That little nub of wrinkled jelly was the only thing keeping this cocksucker on its feet.

The monster tried to scoop me off its shoulder, and the flailing attempt crushed the crown of its skull. Moonlight poured down through the mist, bathing my target in silver light.

"Nighty-night," I growled, and carved the last bit of brain out of the giant's head.

Its knees buckled, and the giant fell. I rode its shoulder down, and we hit the ground with a meaty thud and a liquid squirt.

I rolled free of the impact and bounced back up on my heels, looking for my war club.

The spirits rushed up just as I retrieved my weapon from where I'd dropped it in the grass. There was goop smeared all over me, and chunks of rotten meat were glued to my chest and shoulders. That didn't stop Ayo or Aja from throwing their arms around me and smothering me with kisses.

"I'm okay," I said. "You two must have seriously strong stomachs to come anywhere close with this gruesomeness all over me."

That got a chuckle from the two of them. The humor didn't last long, though, as Ayo lowered herself to her knees next to the monstrosity's pulped head. She brushed her fingers across the ruin of its brow, and a quiet sob shook her shoulders.

"Ohsa," Aja said with a quiet sigh, "was a friend. She was one of our mistress's guardians."

"Your mistress kept that thing as a guardian?" It was hard to see the creature I'd killed as anything more than a hideous monster incapable of anything but destruction.

"She wasn't like this when we left." Ayo stood, brushed her hands clean on her armor, and reached out to take my hand. She reached out for Aja, who took the other hand. "Things are worse now. We have to be careful."

Great.

"We need to go to our mistress." Ayo pulled us along with surprisingly strong strides. Close to the end of her quest, she was eager to finish this thing.

The temple was built from white stone, and it was covered with thick vines. This close, we saw that the pillars were cracked, some of them fallen, and there was a gaping hole where the door should have been.

"Oh, no," Ayo sobbed. "What happened?"

"This was sealed when we left," Aja whispered.

The main door, a thick stone slab twice my height and at least eight feet wide, had been destroyed. The white rock rubble lay on the ground in front of the temple, the jagged stones already surrounded by growing grass and coated with a thin layer of mossy slime. The temple was wide open and looked more like a tomb than a place of worship.

My heart raced as I stepped forward and raised my war club.

Someone had beaten us to the spirits' mistress.

Chapter Twenty-Three

THE SPIRITS WERE SO DISTRAUGHT OVER WHAT we'd seen on the island so far that I wanted them to wait outside until I could survey the damage inside the temple. Ayo's face was streaked with tears, and Aja's jaw was clenched so tight I heard her teeth grinding over the splash of the lake's waters against the shore.

"You can't go in there alone," Aja said. "We can't lose you, too."

My heart ached at the defeated resignation in the spirit's voice. She'd already decided her mistress was dying, and the grief had nearly broken her. Ayo sobbed when she heard her companion's words and buried her face in her hands.

"He's not going alone," Yata cawed. "I'll keep an eye on him. We'll be back. Soon."

And, with that, my familiar flapped its wings and flew through the shattered door into the temple.

"If you see anything out here, yell," I said. "I'll come running."

Ayo nodded, and another sob racked her shoulders. Aja said nothing. She shrugged and turned toward the south side of the lake, peering into the gloom as if she could see our enemies through all that mist.

My nerves jumped and my muscles tightened as I entered the temple. Someone, or more likely something, had done a lot of damage in there. The entryway's walls had once been decorated with intricate inscriptions and an ornate frieze near its ceiling. Now the walls were cracked and crumbling, the decorative tiles shattered and scattered around the floor, inscriptions fractured into indecipherable shards of jagged stone.

"Whatever did this was seriously pissed," Yata said. "You think it's still here?"

"I sure as fuck hope not," I said. "One monster fight a day is more than enough."

We moved through the entryway and into the temple's sanctum. The six-sided room held two ranks of three polished wooden pews that had all been shattered into splintered ruins. A small dais across the room from the entrance held a golden altar that had been hammered into a misshapen lump by something extraordinarily strong. Braziers that had once flanked the altar had been cast down, their dead coals now scattered across the dais, charred streaks showing where they'd smoldered after they fell.

Even more disturbing than the raw destruction was the aura of decay that clung to everything. Black vines had pushed through the temple's wooden floor and coiled around the ruined furnishings. Blossoms that looked like bulbs of raw meat sprouted from the intruding vegetation and filled the sanctum with the foul stink of rot.

This is what you left me to fight.

Mielyssi was right, and her words weighed heavily on me. Since I'd found the spirits, I'd been focused on delivering them to their mistress. That quest had been a simple, straightforward objective. As long as

I'd concentrated on saving them, I'd been able to ignore the real problem staring me in the face.

Now I had to face the reality of the situation, and I didn't want to. At all.

What I wanted was to go back to Mount Shiki.

But if I abandoned my true purpose, the corruption would spread and, eventually, everything would die. Including the crimson bear.

If I pushed on, there was a very good chance I'd die much sooner than later.

Once again, I was reminded that everyone wants to be a hero until it's time to do the actual hero shit.

"Stairs," Yata cawed from where it had landed on top of the wrecked altar.

I took a deep breath, ignoring the rotten-meat stink, and squared my shoulders. It didn't matter what I wanted to do, this was what I'd been meant to do since the day I'd ignored everyone's advice and decided to become a shaman.

"All right, motherfuckers," I grumbled. "Let's see what you've got."

A spiral staircase behind the altar led down into a darkness deeper even than the pitch-black depths of Cragtooth Station. My war club glowed where Mielyssi had kissed it, brighter and brighter as I descended, and yet the light couldn't push the dark back more than a few feet. The blackness clung to every surface and burned my eyes with its intense nothingness.

"Shake it off," Yata croaked. "We've got a job to do."

"Thanks for the support, dickhead," I told my familiar. "You could be a little more understanding here.

The rug just got yanked out from underneath our little quest."

"Boohoo, life sucks," the three-legged raven said with a click of its beak. "Let's get this over with. This place is giving me a case of the piss shivers."

"You're a bird. Don't pretend like you've ever pissed."

"It's called an expression, you savage," Yata snapped. "Try not to be so literal all the time."

"Yeah, yeah," I said. After close to a minute of hiking down the spiral staircase, we reached its base. My club's light didn't show me much, just a small room at the bottom of the steps with a single passage that led off into, you guessed it, more darkness. "I guess we're going this way."

The raven, perched gingerly on my shoulder, flapped its wings and ruffled my hair with its feathers. I'd expected a smart-ass comment, but the bird kept its peace. It was every bit as freaked out as I was.

The short passageway led away from the staircase and into a circular room so wide my light didn't even come close to its center. I listened for any sounds of life, and heard nothing. My spirit sight couldn't reach any farther into the darkness than my war club's light. If there was anything in there, I wouldn't find it by standing at the door.

I walked the room's perimeter, and it took me most of five minutes to return to the passage I'd entered through. There was a pattern engraved into the stone floor, something like a spoked wheel, or a compass. I took great care not to step on any of the etched lines, any one of which could have held some hideous trap.

There was only one hallway leading in or out of the room, though the circular wall was broken by evenly spaced alcoves. Each of those spaces held items that had once been precious and, judging by the glimmers of sacred energy that still clung to them, very powerful.

Now, all they held was ruined garbage.

The only part of the chamber my walk hadn't revealed was the center, which was still cloaked in darkness. If there was anything to see, that's where I'd find it.

"No sense putting this off any longer," I grumbled to myself.

I'd resisted using my spirit sight while walking around the room because my gut told me I'd see horrible shit that would haunt me for the rest of my days. But my survival instincts told me I couldn't afford to blind myself like that. There could be sacred energy traps, or corrupted shadows waiting to ambush me. I steeled myself and opened my spirit sight to the world around me, positive I was going to get freaked the fuck out.

And I was completely and totally right.

The pattern inscribed on the floor glowed with writhing wisps of black. Each of its lines marked the path of one of the dream meridians, and they were all corrupted beyond anything I'd ever seen. Even the Deepway station hadn't been this badly blighted.

This wasn't simply a tainted area.

This place was a source of the corruption that tainted the world.

I took care not to step on any of the lines as I neared the center of the room. Those writhing tentacles looked ready to tear my soul apart if I gave them half a chance.

"I don't want to look," Yata croaked from my shoulder. "I'm going to cover my eyes with my wing, and you tell me what happens."

"Oh, I get it," I quipped. "You're not a bird, you're a pussy."

"Ha," the raven cawed. "You're fucking hilarious."

"I know."

The banter helped steel me for what I was about to see. With every step, the light from my war club pushed the darkness back and revealed more nightmares. Blood stained the floor in deep red puddles that still gleamed wetly in the cold silver light of Mielyssi's kiss. Small bits of white poked up from the puddles. I peered at one of them, and it took me a long moment to realize what I was looking at.

They were teeth.

A few more steps revealed long, twisted strips of flesh and hanks of hair with the bloody scalp still attached. Whatever had happened here, it had been ugly.

"Whoo," Yata groaned. "That smell."

"Thanks for reminding me," I said.

The slaughterhouse perfume of old blood and rotting meat had grown stronger as we drew closer to the room's heart. Every breath tasted like a bite of carrion left in the hot summer sun. It took every bit of willpower I could muster to keep going.

Sometimes, I still wish I hadn't.

A few steps more brought me to scattered bits of armor. My heart skipped a beat when I recognized the broken plates as the same gear the Jade Seekers wore. Greaves and pauldrons lay next to dented breastplates and helms that had been caved in by some tremendous force. Despite enough armor to protect at least a dozen men, there were no bodies that I could see. The armor was destroyed, but it wasn't smeared with blood.

What in the everloving fuck had happened here?

"I do not like this," Yata squawked, ruffling its feathers.

"Welcome to the club."

I found the missing bodies a few yards closer to the room's center. It wasn't pretty.

They were mashed together in an arc of pulped gore. It was impossible to tell where one of the corpses ended and the next began. My stomach churned at the sight, and I paused to catch my breath. There was no way the goddess had survived whatever the Frozen Hells I was looking at here. I could turn back, tell the spirits she was dead, and wait for the White Tigers to show up and kill us all.

That seemed like a better idea than pushing ahead.

"Fucking hero shit," I grumbled and stepped over the line of death.

The next few yards were a mess of tattered skin and shards of red-stained bone. Dots of corrupted senjin smoldered on the floor like splatters of acid, wisps of shadow rising from their hearts. The only good thing about the mess of mangled corpses was that it was proof, finally, that the goddamned Jade Seekers were dead.

I stepped around the worst of the carnage, but still managed to get nasty shit stuck to the bottoms of my feet. If I ever got out of there, I was going to take a bath for days.

A mound of something wet and red lay atop the intersection of the dream meridians at the center of the room. The pile of slop was surrounded by a spiral of bones that started very small and gradually increased in size until they reached the heart of the bloody mess. The largest of the bones was a cylinder the size of my clenched fist, and the smallest was no bigger than the last digit of my pinky. It was a bizarre sight, all the more horrible because I couldn't make any sense of what I was seeing.

My traitorous foot took another step, knowing full well I really, really didn't want an up-close-and-personal look at the massacre.

A woman's face stared up from the center of the gore, eyes wide, mouth hanging open as if in shock. Streaks of blood sliced her face into a hundred pale patches between their crimson lines. A dagger, black and glossy, had been plunged through her open mouth as if to nail her to the floor.

That tied my stomach into knots. I had no idea what kind of motherfucking beast could do this to anyone, and I didn't want to find out.

"Oh, gods, no." Ayo's voice broke the silence. She unleashed a wailing sob that punched through my heart like a crossbow bolt. "Nononono."

I'd been so horrified by what I'd seen that I hadn't noticed the spirits enter the chamber behind me. They were too far away to see any details, but the light from my lantern was more than enough to show them the glistening red heap of flesh in front of me.

"Don't look," I shouted, far too late.

I raced across the room. I no longer cared if I stepped on a crack or slipped in the gore. Ayo was hurting. That was all that mattered.

I crossed the floor in seconds and swept her into my arms.

"You weren't supposed to come down here," I whispered into her ear, not sure she could even hear me over her inconsolable wails.

Aja stood mute before me, her eyes half-lidded, pain etched in cruel strokes across her face in the small shio light in her hand. If I'd had any doubt that the dead woman in the center of the floor was her mistress, it shattered into icy crystals under the weight of the spirit's cold, dead stare.

Chapter Twenty-Four

I URGED THE SPIRITS TO RETURN TO THE SURFACE, BUT they were having none of it.

"Take us to her," Aja demanded. Her tone was unyielding as steel. "We have to know what happened."

I guided them between the meridians and helped them avoid the worst of the carnage, but there was nothing else I could do for the spirits. Whatever dangers had been there, they were long gone now.

The spirits needed space to grieve for their mistress, and I needed space to think. After warning them to stay away from the lines on the floor, I headed back to the surface.

I took a short stroll to the south beach and threw myself down on its rocky shores. The pain of gravel biting into my ass and thighs sharpened my thoughts, and I welcomed it. I had to figure out what came next.

The dead woman at the bottom of the temple was a terrible tragedy, but she was only one problem on top of a very large pile of shit that needed my attention.

There was a goddamned army on the lake's south shore, and they were building barges to come and kill the fuck out of me. By dawn, that problem would be so far up my ass I'd need a stick and a quart of oil to dislodge it.

At least I wouldn't have to worry about the Jade Seekers showing up again. They'd taken their shot at the goddess and paid the price for it.

The island I was standing on was so badly corrupted, its stink was permanently lodged in my nostrils and the hum of its evil in my thoughts made it hard to concentrate on anything else for more than a few seconds at a time.

I wrestled my thoughts back into some semblance of order and reviewed the list of things that needed fixing.

Oh, yeah. The spirits were low on shio, their cores were still fucked, and they'd be dead before sunrise if I didn't recharge them. I wasn't sure they'd ever be in the mood to bump uglies again after what they'd seen down there. They'd been that woman's familiars. There was a very real chance they'd want to die now that she was gone.

I tried not to imagine how I'd feel if I were them, and failed. If I'd stumbled onto the crimson bear's body, savagely mutilated like that...

You'd kill whoever did it. And that's what you should do now.

She was right, I supposed, but I had no idea who'd done this, or even where to start looking for the murderer. The Jade Seekers were involved, but I didn't suspect there'd been any survivors of the slaughter down there.

"I need your help," I whispered, hoping Mielyssi could hear me. "I've come all this way to save these two, and now I'm trapped in a dead end, and we're all going to die. I don't know what to do."

The damp wind off the lake slapped my cheeks, coating them with mist.

"That's a shitty answer."

A goose honked, and a peep frog squeaked in a desperate search for a mate.

I guess that was the best answer I was going to get.

"Fine," I muttered. "I'll figure it out on my own."

My resources were pretty fucking limited. I had a war club that lit up thanks to my sexy spirit animal's kiss. I had a satchel with a few herbs left in the bottom, a couple of core-stabilizing pills I'd made back in Jiro Kos's camp, two low-level techniques, and the bedroom skills to make humans and spirits alike weak in the knees.

None of those assets seemed capable of pulling my ass out of the swiftly growing fire I'd landed in.

With a sigh, I sat up, opened my satchel, and looked inside to make sure I hadn't missed anything.

Turned out, I had. *The Formation Manual*, its sleek cover so glossy it almost glowed, was right where I'd left it.

I opened the manual and took a closer look at its contents. The Wall of Sanctity was still the only formation I could read.

"I don't think any light reading is going to save your ass." Yata returned from its scouting mission and landed on the beach next to me. "The White Tigers have almost finished their boats."

"Well, fuck." I closed the book and shoved it back into my satchel. "I've only got one thing to try. Might as well get going on it."

I paced the circumference of the island and discovered it was a small circle in the middle of a very big lake. The temple itself was a fifty-foot square in the island's center, with thirty feet of land between it and the island's shore on all sides.

I retraced my steps, though this time I dropped a pyramidal pylon of rin energy every few steps. When I reached the end of my jaunt around the island, the barrier was almost ready to light up. One more jolt of rin and it'd throw up a barrier that might just keep the bad guys at bay.

For a little while, anyway.

Unfortunately, my core was empty and there was no way for me to refill it. Any senjin I drew from the island would be tainted, and the spirits were far too grief-stricken to help me cleanse the power. That would leave me with nodes filled to the brim with corrupted energy that would quickly eat me from the inside out.

Don't die, or the world dies with you.

"I'm trying to stay alive," I promised Mielyssi. "But there are a lot of assholes fucking things up."

"Talking to yourself is a sign of insanity," Yata said. "Nice pyramids. What are you going to do with them?"

"Nothing," I confessed. "They mark the boundaries of a barrier, but I don't have any rin to fire them up."

"Want some of mine?" The bird hopped off my shoulder and landed on the ground next to the last pyramid I'd placed.

"You can give me sacred energy?" My jaw dropped. "How long have you been holding out on me?"

Yata hopped back defensively, and I realized I'd raised my war club. I must have been more stressed out than I realized to lift a hand to my familiar.

"You didn't need it before now!" Yata crowed. "And I don't have all that much. I was saving it for a special occasion."

"I needed it when we ran into that trap in the river Deepways," I grumbled.

"You were fine. I would have jumped in if it looked like you were going to die." Yata preened and flicked a tattered feather onto the ground. "You want it or not?"

"I can't believe you were holding out on me." I stared at the raven's core with my spirit sight and saw that it held seven nodes filled with pure senjin. "How fast do you fill up?"

The raven squawked and paced back and forth in front of me.

"No idea." It flapped its wings. "I've been full since before we met. Didn't have anything to spend the juice on."

I cursed myself for an idiot. I should have known to check my familiar for a reserve of power. I'd been playing with tainted senjin when I could have used the pure stuff stored in Yata.

"I'm going to try something. You'll probably hate it."

"I hate everything you do to me," Yata squawked. "Remember that time when we met and you almost killed us both? Good times."

"No promises." Before the raven could protest any further, I imagined one node of its senjin draining through our connection into me.

"You were right. I hate this." Yata let out a loud caw, then ducked its head under its wing.

A strand of senjin flowed through the bond between us, slow as cold honey, and eased into my core.

It didn't hurt, nothing exploded, and we weren't on fire, so I was off to a good start. It took most of five minutes to transfer the single node from Yata to me, but we were both alive at the end of the process.

My core quickly broke the mercurial dream energy down into rin and shio, absorbed the rin, and let the shio ooze out of my pores in tiny beads of azure light.

"That worked." My words came out in a rough croak, and I cleared my throat. Must have been getting dehydrated. "Now we wait to see how long it takes for your senjin to come back."

"What if it never comes back?" The bird hopped nervously from foot to foot to foot.

"Then I'll thank you for your sacrifice." I yawned. The long day had finally caught up with me. "Don't be so dramatic."

"Says the sacred energy thief who may have just crippled me for life," Yata squawked and dodged the pebble I threw at it. "Bastard."

"Whiner." I took a deep breath, hoping the cool lake air would revive me a little. No such luck. I meditated, hoping that would help me find a better route through the maze of hazards that was closing in on me from all sides.

After three hours, I hadn't discovered any new insights that would save my ass, and the raven's senjin hadn't refilled.

"Crippled," it groaned. "I'll spend the rest of my life with an empty node."

"How was I supposed to know!" I shouted at the bird. "Maybe it's not refilling because the senjin here is tainted."

"Or maybe I'm crippled." Yata jumped into the air and circled around me. "You're the worst shaman ever."

It flapped its wings indignantly and landed on the top of the temple.

"For fuck's sake—"

"Kyr!" Aja shouted as she burst from the temple's doorway. Her crimson hair trailed behind her in unruly tangles, and her eyes glowed with a feral light as she stumbled toward me.

Her core was nearly empty, the nodes flickering weakly as she struggled back to her feet.

I rushed to the spirit's side and scooped her into my arms.

"I'm so sorry," I said. "I should have tried to—"

"She's alive," Aja gasped, skin pale, nostrils flaring. "Our mistress is alive, Kyr."

"How?" I asked, almost certain that Aja was delirious.

I'd seen the remnants of her mistress, and there was no way that messy pile of shredded meat was alive. The spirits had to be mistaken.

"Ayo fed her energy," Aja insisted. "She bled herself and our mistress revived. She's hurt so badly, Kyr. She needs you."

"You need me, and Ayo definitely needs me if she sacrificed her shio to feed your mistress," I said. Suddenly, I hated the mutilated woman below the earth. If the spirit died in a vain attempt to save her mistress's life, I didn't know what I'd do.

"We're not important," Aja insisted. "Go down there. Save her."

My pulse surged with new hope. If their mistress was alive, there was a chance I could heal her and the spirits.

I raced into the temple, the rising sun throwing its first copper rays through the mist behind me, Aja in my arms, and prayed I was up to the task before me.

Don't die.

"No promises," I muttered to myself.

A baying horn sounded from the south side of the lake.

The White Tigers were coming.

Chapter Twenty-Five

I POUNDED DOWN THE STAIRS AS FAST AS MY LEGS would carry me, careening off the rail at every corner, heedless of the bruises and bumps I picked up in my rush to reach the gory room. My club dangled from my right hand, banging off my shins with every step, throwing out just enough light to cast confusing shadows in every direction.

Aja's life was fading before my eyes. She felt lighter by the second, as if her body was fading away with the last of her rin. In a very few minutes, she'd be lost forever. Ayo had to be at least as bad off, maybe worse. I couldn't imagine their mistress was in a better place, either, and I had no idea how much time it would take to heal them all.

More time than I had, to be sure.

If that horn had been the army casting off its barges to head for the island, we had less than an hour before they arrived. That might give me enough time to recharge the spirits and figure out what was wrong with their mistress. There was no way it would be enough time for much of anything else.

Still, I had to try. I hadn't come all this way, suffered through so much, to give up now.

I found Ayo slumped over her mistress. The woman at the heart of the pattern was still every bit as bad off as she had been when I'd left her. Her body was mutilated, torn open and its pieces rearranged like some disgusting art project.

But she was also undeniably alive.

Her eyes fixed on me as I approached the nexus of the dream meridians. Someone had pulled the knife out of her mouth, and her jaw worked soundlessly for a moment. She blinked and furrowed her brow, and something stirred inside the mound of torn meat beneath her face.

A bony finger, its flesh flensed away, emerged from the carnage. Its bloody tip pressed into Ayo's cheek, and the woman stared hard into my eyes. Her thoughts blazed bright in my mind for a moment. She needed the nexus cleansed, and she needed me to do it.

"I don't know if I can," I gasped. "I'll do my best."

Aja was weak, but Ayo was unconscious and her core held so little shio I couldn't even see the sacred energy. I laid the redhead down away from the remains of her mistress, careful not to let her touch the lines, then carried Ayo over and laid her down next to her companion. They looked so small and weak like that, their flesh pale and washed out in the silver light of my war club. Their eyes fluttered and tried to focus on me, and they stirred weakly, struggling to reach out to me.

"Heal us," Aja whispered, her words faint and trembling. "Save us."

I knelt down above their heads and kissed each of them gently on the lips. Faint sparks passed between us, the barest flicker of power from the one node of rin still in my core. The spirits started restlessly at its touch. It was a start, but they needed more. There was an endless source of sacred power in the dream meridians on either side of us, but I hesitated to draw from it.

Using that power would fill me with corruption. If the spirits were too weak to complete the purification ritual, we would all die.

But if I did nothing, the spirits would definitely die, and I'd probably be killed by the army when it rushed ashore by dawn's early light. There was nothing for this but to throw the dice and gamble they came up in our favor.

I didn't have time for fancy breathing techniques or meditation to cycle the corrupted power into my core. Instead, I shoved my fist into the churning current of the dream meridian that ran through the channel inscribed on the floor beside me.

The instant my knuckles touched the sacred energy, it flowed into me. Tainted senjin rushed up my arteries, found my heart, and exploded through every inch of my being in a cataclysmic flash of black fire.

A seizure racked my body, and I fought it with every fiber of my being. The corruption wanted to drag me down into the meridian and consume me. It was more powerful than anything I'd ever experienced before, and it dared me to defy its might.

Clearly, it didn't know it was dealing with the stubbornest shaman in the world. The crimson bear had taught me to never back down from a fight, and I wasn't about to start wimping out now. I held my ground, and let the energy pour into me.

With a guttural groan, I finally dragged my hand out of the current. Sticky rivulets of corrupted senjin dripped from my fingertips and splattered like drops of oil on the cold stone floor. My core was filled to bursting with the tainted energy. If I didn't purify it, right now, I was dead.

Ayo's eyes burned into mine as I lowered my mouth to hers. She gasped at the instant of contact, and her back arched as power flowed between us. Her skin glowed blue and her armor burned away as the power overflowed her core and illuminated her essence. She cried out and her arms curled around my neck. She sucked greedily on my tongue and yelped in surprise as crashing waves of intense sensation rippled through her muscles.

All I wanted was for that moment to go on forever. Ayo's trembling tongue lashed around mine, her teeth pressed against my lips. She tasted like lightning.

The corrupted energy began to break down inside us, the purified shio into Ayo, the rin into me. It wasn't much, yet, but it was enough to revive the spirit and pull her back from the brink of death.

"Aja," she gasped, and pushed me away. Tears stained her cheeks, and I didn't know if they came from grief or joy. "Aja."

The tainted senjin within me had ignited a primal survival instinct that wouldn't be denied. I hungered for the spirits' touch, I needed their flesh to join with mine and purify us all.

With a guttural sigh, I let Ayo push me toward the other spirit. My tongue dipped between the redhead's lips, rousing her from her stupor with a taste of the power that raged inside me.

Aja latched onto my shoulders with both hands. She pulled my mouth against hers and bit my lips and tongue, the sharp nips sending tingles of pleasure and pain coursing through my body. She turned under me, sudden strength twisting her around until her hips were beneath mine and her legs hooked around my back. Her hand darted through the gap between our bodies to rip aside her leather skirt and reveal the crimson thatch of curls at the juncture of her thighs.

A need rose inside me, hot and fierce and undeniable. I couldn't resist the scent of Aja's lust, raw and wild as the hunt itself. I buried myself inside her with a single, savage thrust that lifted her hips off the floor. We cried out in unison, the contact so intensely pleasurable I was lost in its warm and sticky depths for long breaths.

The nearness of death pushed our lust to new heights. Aja screamed beneath me, her nails raking my sides as I plowed into her with relentless strokes that drove us closer and closer to the edge of ecstasy. Ayo pressed herself tight against my side, her mouth hot on my throat, her hands guiding the fingers of my left hand to her dripping cleft.

Aja bucked against me, ankles digging into my hips and urging me deeper, harder, faster. She bit my lip, then my shoulder. She gasped into my skin, her breath hitching in her lungs as the wet walls of her sex spasmed around my rigid length. Pulses of sacred energy passed between us, setting our nerves on fire and urging us on. Aja's body trembled, shaking as her pleasure peaked, then peaked again

"Me," Ayo whimpered. She licked the side of my neck and swirled the hot tip of her tongue around the edge of my ear. Her hands roamed over my body as if she couldn't decide what she wanted—no, needed—to touch most. "Please."

Aja slithered out from under me, a wide smile on her full lips. She reached between us as she slid off me, her fingers lightly scraping the underside of my aching cock. The tingle of pleasure at her touch raced up my spine like a spark on a fuse, almost enough to detonate the pent-up need that burned inside me.

I rose onto my knees and grabbed Ayo's hips. She yelped in surprise as I pulled her over in front of me, then moaned and shoved her hips back against mine. My prick, still slick with Aja's juices, slid along the crack of the spirit's ass before a quick tilt of her hips guided me into her.

Ayo howled, and the strength of her wild desire tugged at the crimson bear's attention. Mielyssi was there, inside me, inside Ayo, binding us together with unbridled animal lust. The bear's essence surrounded us, a crimson whirlwind that urged us to lose ourselves in one another.

I couldn't get enough of Ayo. With every thrust my hands explored her body, stroking the smooth ridges of her ribs, cupping her breasts and squeezing them, greedy for the feel of their springy softness under my palms, the taut nubs of her erect nipples between my fingers. Every touch sparked an electric tingle that drew a panting groan from us both.

The spirit's head sagged between her shoulders, hair dragging on the floor, and her hips rose to meet me. We crashed together, again and again, pushing one another faster and faster toward the light that burned just out of reach. Her fingers slid to her groin, working in furious circles as the end charged toward us with a wolf's howl.

A wave of unfathomable pleasure crested, and then crashed down. Ayo unleashed a visceral groan as her muscles tensed and relaxed, milking thick sprays of cum from me.

The strength of that moment ripped every thought out of my mind. I was lost in the sensation, spent by our efforts, and blinded with pleasure. I pulled Ayo onto me and held on, unwilling to let this end. Outside of that instant, the world was a dark and shitty place. Inside the spirit, I was safe. Nothing could touch us if I just held on.

Let go.

Mielyssi's voice rang in my ears and eased me back from the darkness that I'd retreated into. My muscles were weak and throbbed with power at the same time. My nodes were filled with rin, but it wasn't pure. It was tinged with a dark and feral strength, an aspect of the crimson bear who'd joined us in our final moments together. I didn't even know how that was possible.

"Ayo," Aja's voice, trembling with fear, roused me instantly.

"What's wrong?" My muscles tensed, and the wild rin in my core urged me to activate my techniques and prepare for battle.

"She's gone," Ayo responded, her eyes locked on the bloody stain that was all that remained of their mistress. "After all we did, she's gone."

"Surely you know better than that," a woman's voice, stern but not cruel, rose from the center of the nexus.

Startled, I scrambled across the floor and grabbed my war club, ready to knock the shit out of whoever had intruded on this place.

"Be at peace, shaman," the woman said. "You've done me a great service by returning my familiars. And an even greater service by reviving me."

I raised my club high overhead and peered into the ring of shadows that surrounded us. A faint shadow slithered beyond the edges of the light, and a sound like snake scales on cold stone rasped in my ears.

"Mistress?" Ayo said, the word almost a sob. She stood and rushed toward the edge of my light.

"Come no closer, child," the voice continued. "I am no longer ruined, but neither am I well. I would rather not be seen in this delicate state."

"You took the purified senjin from us," Aja said. "That's what healed you."

"Only a sip," the woman confirmed. "Enough to help me undo the worst of what was done to me. But there is still much healing ahead of me."

"Tell us what we can do," Ayo pleaded. "Whatever you need, Kyr can help—"

"That man has more pressing concerns than an old woman's aches and pains," the woman chuckled. "I am grateful for your service, honored shaman."

Her formality made me nervous, and I shuffled my feet, unsure of how to respond.

"It's nothing," I said at last, realizing just how dismissive I sounded after her show of respect for me. "I mean, ah, it's nothing, honored witch goddess."

"You are too kind, shaman. I am but a simple witch. Few know or care about the goddess part of my title, now." The woman's voice was heavy with sorrow. "I owe you a great debt. Sadly, the Midnight Emperor's treachery has laid me low. I don't know how his Jade Seekers found me, or what foul magic he used to turn them into the monster they became in their attempt to destroy me. I fear I am not so certain I can aid you in the next step of your journey."

My heart sank. I'd come all this way because the crimson bear had been so sure I'd save the world. I'd escorted the spirits to this shitty island in the middle of this motherfucking lake, and now the one person who could give me a little bit of goddamned help was telling me I was already fucked.

"You have to at least try," I said. "Tell me what I can do to help you help me."

"There is a ritual—"

"We're out of time," Yata called out in a raucous voice as it descended the spiral staircase in a thunder of black wings. "The bad guys are on the doorstep and they don't look like they plan to knock politely."

As usual, there wasn't time to figure anything out before I had to act. I still had no idea what the hell this woman wanted, or how she thought I'd save the world. What I did know was that if I didn't get topside and deal with an army of White Tigers, we were all going to die in the next few minutes.

"Whatever the ritual is," I said to the shadowy woman, "fucking do it."

"It will take time," she said. "I am very weak, and the senjin here is corrupted. I have no idea how long I will require to purify enough power to fuel the ritual—"

"I'll buy you time," I snarled. The threat of battle ignited the rin in my nodes, churning its animal fervor into a battle frenzy. My core was full, and I was so pissed I'd have gladly chewed through a whole flotilla of barges and the soldiers on them. "Get it done."

Before anyone could say another word, I hurled myself toward the staircase, Yata chasing after me.

"They're coming hard," Yata croaked. "Twenty barges, at least. They've got swords and crossbows. Even fucking horses, not that those will do them a damned bit of good."

"How far out are they?" I bounded up the stairs three at a time, my long legs carrying me toward the surface one effortless step after another.

"Close," Yata crowed. "Five minutes."

"Plenty of fucking time."

My heart thundered in my ears, adrenaline pushing it hard. The fight was hopeless, I knew that. I couldn't beat ten well-armed men, much less five hundred.

That wouldn't stop me from trying.

Make them pay.

"In blood," I howled, hurtling through the sanctum and out the temple's doorway. The crimson rays of the rising sun flashed over my enemies, and I roared a challenge as they neared my beach.

Claws burst from my fingertips and dense red hair sprouted across my shoulders and down my chest. The crimson bear was with me.

These assholes wanted a fight?

I'd give them a slaughter.

Chapter Twenty-Six

BEFORE THE BOATS COULD REACH THE SHORE, I slammed a node's worth of rin into the nearest pyramid. The barrier instantly sprang to life, a blazing red field of power that burned through the mist with a violent hissing. The sacred energy that flowed through the barrier writhed in strange swirls of crimson that turned on themselves like snakes eating their tails.

The power I'd unleashed was different than the rin I'd channeled before. It was more concentrated and potent than anything I'd experienced before. It seethed with a vibrant anger that would not be denied. I didn't know if it was because the enormous amount of corruption on this island left an imprint that even the spirits couldn't purify, if the crimson bear's rage had fused with it, or if I was just so pissed at these motherfuckers that I'd transformed the rin.

"You think that's going to hold them?" Yata asked.

"We're about to find out." The first boat was mere yards away, its cargo of soldiers eager to rush the shoreline. The white tigers on their banners flapped in the moist breeze, and their armor gleamed like sharpened knives. In their minds, they'd already won this battle.

The boat's hull scraped across the island's shore, and the first wave of soldiers burst over its gunwale in a crashing wave of armor and weapons. Their boots kicked up wet gravel and gritty sand, gouging an angry trail across the shoreline. The commander shouted from the rear, urging his soldiers forward, sword raised overhead, voice booming like thunder.

I couldn't tell if the soldiers didn't see the barrier, or just didn't care it was there. To be fair, it was only meant to stop sacred energy. I wasn't sure what effect it would have on charging troops. Maybe their leader knew it would be utterly ineffective. Or maybe he didn't care whether his men slammed headlong into a wall of sparking rin.

I held my breath, and Yata remained still as a stone on my shoulder. I hefted my war club, ready, waiting.

The first wave of soldiers rammed into the barrier. Their suits of armor rang like struck bells, and the scripts engraved on the protective plates erupted in coruscating crimson patterns. For a moment, it looked as if they'd push through the formation, and I willed the barrier to hold them back.

Miraculously, it did.

The soldiers who'd slammed into the wall were hurled backward against their charging companions. Their metal-clad bodies smashed into the troops behind them, turning the charge into a chaotic avalanche of falling soldiers. Most of them lost their weapons as they tumbled over one another, and the soldiers bringing up the rear were too slow to react and tripped over their fellows. In a handful of seconds, the first boatload of warriors was down on the beach, struggling to right themselves under the weight of their armor.

My spirit sight flashed over my enemies, taking in the details quickly so I could formulate the next phase of my plan. The scripts on their armor helped reduce the suits' weight and increase their flexibility. When they'd struck my barrier, the sacred energy held in those scripts had been disrupted and violently repelled. Without that power, the armor was too ponderous for the soldiers to manage on their own. They'd either have to recharge their scripts, which would take time, or ditch their armor, which would leave them defenseless.

Of course, even defenseless men could overwhelm me if they had the numbers, and these assholes definitely had enough bodies to throw into the fray. More boats were already piling up on the shore. The commanders disembarked to discuss their next steps while the other soldiers helped the fallen men to their feet.

That impact hadn't used up the entire node of rin energy that I'd fed into the barrier, but it had taken a good chunk out of the power. The pyramids were only half lit, and I'd have to watch carefully to know when to refill them. Too soon, and I'd waste some of my limited reserves of power; too late, and soldiers would take down the formation and be on top of me before I knew it. Once they started beating me about the head and neck with their swords, it would be all but impossible to get the barrier back up. I'd be overrun and hacked to bits in the space of a few heartbeats.

Fortunately, the army gathered on the shore was dithering about, trying to decide what to do next. Their eyes burned into mine, but they didn't approach the barrier again. Several of the men who'd been knocked back were still down, arranged on their backs in neat ranks above the waterline, their swords laid across their chests.

Good. If I'd killed a few of the fuckers maybe they'd think twice about running into my barrier again.

In the meantime, I probed the dream meridians that converged on the island. My core hungered for more power, a craving I'd never experienced before. The empty node inside me wanted to be filled, and it wanted to be filled right that goddamned second.

I shook my head and pushed back against the desire to cycle more senjin into my core. If I gave in to it, even for a second, the tainted power would poison me and tear my core apart. I knew that.

Knowing that did not reduce my desire for power. Not even a little bit.

Thankfully, the White Tigers distracted me from the gnawing ache in my empty node by charging the Wall of Sanctity again.

They'd formed themselves into a long line that stretched halfway around the island. On their officers' commands, they sheathed their weapons and hurled their bodies at the crimson wall that stood between us. In the instant before impact they dropped their shoulders and put all their weight behind their heavy pauldrons.

It was a good plan, and it scared the shit out of me. By hitting the barrier across a wide front all at the same time, the soldiers put the maximum possible strain on its ability to push them back. They also wouldn't have to worry about being tossed back into their own troops and trampled into the sandy gravel if they didn't make it through.

I watched the nearest pylon with an intense focus. I couldn't afford to make a mistake. Time seemed to slow as the crash of boots became an endless, terrifying roar.

The soldiers slammed into the barrier almost simultaneously. The formation blazed blood red and spat curls of sacred energy into the scripts emblazoned across their armor. The fire of my violent rin against the stable senjin trapped in those engravings ignited a lightning flash that dazzled my spirit sight and drew surprised shouts from the charging warriors.

The pylon nearest me went dark.

I slammed another node's worth of rin into it, terrified I'd been too slow. If any of those soldiers got through, even one, I was deader than shit.

In the split second before any of the troops could spill through the faltering formation, my power kicked it back to life. The soldiers were thrown back from the formation's perimeter, feet off the ground, arms flailing. Several of them tumbled through the air, landing on their heads, necks twisted at impossible angles. Others staggered back and landed hard on their asses, their armor smoking, their helmets blown free by the power that had repelled them. Still others slid across the beach on their backs, leaving trails of churned gravel to mark their passing.

I'd beaten the warriors again.

Though not without suffering for the win. My energy didn't just power the formation, it bound the wall to my core. Every impact was a bruising blow that left my spirit a little more tired and a little weaker. While the White Tigers lost men with every assault, they also whittled away my reserves of strength and stamina. Even if they didn't exhaust my rin, their relentless attacks could still beat me down.

The commanders stared at me from beyond the formation, their eyes narrowed with rage.

I straightened my shoulders and stiffened my spine. Never let the assholes see you sweat.

"You might as well turn your toy boats around and get the fuck out of here," I shouted. "I can keep this up all day. You'll run out of men long before you get through my defenses."

"The Midnight Emperor has declared you a heretic," one of the commanders shouted back. His helmet must've had some sort of script woven into it, because his voice cracked through the air between us at an impossible volume. "We won't leave without your head."

"Then send his ass over here," I said. "He and I can settle this man to man."

Several of the soldiers chuckled at that and got screamed at by their sergeants for their insolence. The commanders glared at me but didn't respond.

We stared at one another for a good five minutes before they decided they couldn't melt me with their collective anger and retreated to huddle up near the barges. I took that opportunity to take a deep breath and cycled my breathing to relax my muscles and help my body recuperate before the next round of attacks. It would take those dickweeds time to prepare their troops for battle.

You need a better plan.

Mielyssi appeared in my mind's eye. She stalked through the darkness of my thoughts, her naked body gleaming like ivory under a full moon. Slashes of red war paint stained her cheeks and forehead, and a feral gleam burned in her eyes.

"I'm open to suggestions," I said. My heart ached to hold her. She felt so real, as if she stood right in front of me, ready and willing to be taken. I wanted to go back to the time before all this shit had started, back to our time together, alone.

That's not how this works.

I didn't know whether she meant my wish to return to Mount Shiki or my request for advice, and she didn't clarify. She was inches away from me now, at least in my mind, and she studied me so intently it was hard to bear.

I've given you gifts. Use them or die.

I couldn't hold back any longer. I wrapped my arms around her waist and pulled her lithe body against mine. My lips found hers in a frenzied crush of passion, and the kiss burned itself into my soul.

"Don't go," I begged. "Together—"

We are already together. Do not waste what I've given you, Kyr.

"What the fuck does that mean?" I shouted.

But Mielyssi was gone.

The troops had gathered on the other side of the barrier. This time, they'd formed up into ten columns, each four soldiers wide. The long formations snaked back into the water beyond the boats, and each soldier leaned forward against the soldier ahead of them. They advanced, slow and steady, their sergeants barking out a cadence that kept them in lockstep.

As they approached the barrier, I saw the grim determination in the front ranks' eyes. I felt their righteous rage at my existence, and their willingness to die for this cause as surely as I'd felt Mielyssi's lips on my tongue. Whatever their new plan was, they were confident it would work where the others had failed.

This time, they were coming through.

And I didn't think there was a damned thing I could do about it.

"Hurry up with that ritual," I muttered. "We're going to need it."

The warriors reached the barrier.

Live or die, the end of this fight was at hand.

Chapter Twenty-Seven

THE POOR FUCKERS IN THE COLUMNS' FRONT RANKS never had a chance. The instant the scripts on their armor touched the barrier they were doomed. The senjin held in those engravings burned more slowly this time because less of the scripts' surface area was exposed at once. Instead of a single explosion of brilliant light, the senjin oozed from the engravings in white-hot rivulets. Manifested sacred energy melted through the White Tigers' armor with the ease of a hot coal dropped into a bucket of lard.

The soldiers screamed as their defenses turned against them and the unfettered power burned through their flesh. The pain broke them, and they pushed against the barrier with their hands, only to find that their comrades behind them had other ideas. The rear of the long columns advanced and pushed the pinned soldiers forward into the barrier. Men screamed as they were flattened against the red wall, their voices choked by steaming senjin that melted away their vocal chords. The soldiers died knowing they'd been sacrificed by their commanders.

The second node's worth of rin was gone, burned up by the slow and steady advance. I unleashed another node, refilling the pyramids. It worked, for a moment.

Then the first row of dead and mutilated soldiers were forced through the crimson wall and collapsed onto the beach.

I braced myself for a sudden rush that never came. The corpses had passed through the barrier because there was no sacred energy left in their armor or their bodies. It had all been repelled by the barrier. My defenses had held.

I let out a roar of victory.

My excitement was short-lived. That ordeal had inflicted a beating on me, and my core was sore and exhausted. There were still nodes of rin left inside me, and I could still spend them, but my muscles burned with the effort of holding me upright, and my thoughts tumbled and fell across one another. I couldn't keep this up for much longer.

The soldiers on the other side of the barrier, however, just kept on coming. Those who were now in the front ranks wailed and screamed for the advance to stop, while the men behind them marched forward with grim determination. Every man who wasn't smashed up against the formation knew that if they didn't break it, they could be the next to die. Given that horrible choice, there wasn't a man on Earth who wouldn't sacrifice someone else to save his own skin.

"We're coming for you," one of the commanders snarled at me. "We're coming through this fucking trick of yours, and we will skin you alive for the pain you've caused."

"You'll never get through," I growled.

My rage had swelled inside me with every word that man spoke. His pompous attitude, his callous disregard for the men who served under him, and his willingness to serve a corrupted tyrant who'd destroyed my people and laid waste to the world filled me with a bone-deep loathing. I'd never done anything to deserve this. All I'd wanted was to grow closer to nature and heal its wounds. I'd wanted to be a shaman to fix things; I'd never wanted to fight.

What do you want?

The crimson bear's voice was fainter, a mere whisper now. But her presence burned inside me, a guiding star in the wilderness.

What did I want?

I wanted her. I wanted the spirits. I wanted the world healed, and my life back the way it belonged.

Another rank of bodies fell through the barrier, and I burned another node of rin to keep the barrier alive. The screaming never stopped. The soldiers at the front of the columns turned away from the barrier, howling for release, their morale shattered. They'd expected an easier win.

Instead, they'd watched dozens of their allies in arms die screaming, and they were next.

The soldiers that hadn't reached the wall rammed the panicked warriors ahead of them into the barrier like siege engines of flesh and metal. Senjin burned, and the air filled with the smell of fresh lightning strikes and burning meat.

The commanders screamed at their men to keep pushing, that they were winning, that this was almost over. They vowed to honor the sacrifices of the fallen with statues and monuments to their glory, promised to take care of their families and make sure the widows never wanted for anything.

A wordless roar burst from the throats of the soldiers. Lines of senjin curled around them from their commanders' helmets. It wasn't just words that came out of their leaders' mouths, it was a compulsion. The soldiers had to keep going, they had to fight, because their lives weren't their own. These men were under the thrall of commanders who didn't give a shit about them, who in turn wore the leash of a distant ruler who would gladly throw their bodies into the meat grinder to see me dead.

"Turn back," I howled. "Save yourselves, you fucking idiots. You'll gain nothing from my death."

"Your death is reward enough, savage," the commander shouted back at me. "With you gone, the Emperor's great plan can proceed."

"Fucking fools," I snarled.

My barrier pressed against my core from all sides. Another node of rin held the soldiers but did nothing to alleviate the pressure around my spirit. The bond between the Wall of Sanctity and my spirit had grown stronger the longer I'd been attached to it. When it fell, I would fall.

More bodies tumbled through the barrier, and my soul shuddered at the weight of the columns pressed against it. The link I felt to the formation was so powerful it might as well have been a part of my own body. So far, I'd been a passive observer, fueling the defenses and hoping they'd protect me.

That wasn't going to win this fight.

The crimson bear was right. She'd given me the gifts I needed to survive, and I suddenly understood how to use them to defeat these fuckers. I roared, unleashing two more nodes of rin into my Crimson Claws and Bear's Mantle techniques. But I didn't manifest them in my fingers and shoulders as I had before. I pushed the technique out from my core, through the bond I shared with the barrier.

The soldiers in contact with the formation exploded in fountains of blood. My claws erupted from the wall of sacred energy and sliced through armor and flesh with ease. The barrier stiffened and grew harder, its surface armored against any blows.

I roared again and pushed back against the invaders. The effort cost me, my body sagged to its knees, but everything I had went into the barrier around the island. Crimson claws tore soldiers apart, scattering their shredded bodies in every direction. The columns broke, panic shooting through their ranks when they realized the danger.

The commander nearest the formation opened his mouth to roar a command to his fleeing men, and my talons ripped off his helmet and the top half of his head. He fell to his knees, mouth open, wordless gibberish pouring from his lips as he drooled through his final breath.

"Holy shit, Kyr," Yata crowed. "What the fuck."

My rin was almost gone, my core exhausted. It took every ounce of willpower I could muster to maintain the formation as the broken White Tiger army retreated. They piled into their boats, and I unleashed my Earthen Darts technique through the barrier.

The rocky ground near the formation's base exploded outward. The missiles from my technique hammered into the backs of the fleeing warriors. Armor shattered under the barrage, and men fell into the lake with their bodies punctured and their spines snapped. The water around the lake foamed red with the blood of the fallen as the survivors shoved off and rowed as fast as their weary arms could manage.

"Go, fools," I roared. "And never return. Take word back to your Emperor that I'll do the same to any others who come here."

I held the formation until the boats had disappeared into the mist. The last node of my rin was gone, my core and all of its nodes empty. I was hollow and starving, desperate for more sacred energy, yearning for another jolt of the power I'd purified from the meridians that converged on the island.

"Don't do it," Yata barked. "Here."

The raven pecked the side of my head, distracting me from my breathing technique. It forced a node of senjin through our bond and replenished one of my nodes.

The sacred energy pulled me back from the edge, but only just. The desire to take in as much senjin as I could muster, including the corruption it contained, was still there, but I could control it.

"The shit I do for you," Yata scolded. "Now I'm down two nodes."

"Thanks," I groaned. "Let's finish this."

I staggered to my feet, leaning on my war club like a cane. The spikes bit into the ground, turning up rich, dark earth teeming with wriggling insects and worms. The temple's door seemed a thousand miles away, and every step was an extraordinary effort. I'd pushed myself far beyond the limits I'd previously known, and the power I'd taken from the island, even purified, had left its mark on me. I was hurt in ways I didn't understand, and my aches seem to multiply by the second.

A sharp pain lanced through my side, and I fell to one knee. The hot poker of agony burrowed beneath my ribs, twisting and turning, ripping a terrible roar free of me.

"What's wrong?" Yata screeched, fluttering about my head, eyes wild with panic. "What happened?"

I couldn't talk through the pain. It grew more intense by the moment, and I was sure I was about to die.

The pain passed at last, and I dragged myself back up to my feet. The sudden realization settled over me, and I knew exactly what had happened.

I'd felt the same way in Ulishi.

And again on the river, before the Jade Seekers' attack.

Jiro Kos had put more inside me than just corrupted sacred energy back on that bridge. He'd marked me, and that pain was his way of finding me.

"They're coming," I groaned. "They're close."

"Who?" Yata demanded.

"The Jade Seekers." My head sagged, my hair dangling around my face. "Jiro fucking Kos."

Chapter Twenty-€ight

THIS WAS IMPOSSIBLE. THE JADE SEEKERS WERE dead. I'd seen their bodies scattered around the nexus chamber, broken and shattered by their battle with the spirits' mistress.

"Isn't he dead?" Yata asked.

"Fucking thought so," I said. "But apparently fucking not."

I hadn't seen Jiro's ridiculous blade down there, had I? I'd assumed the Jade Seeker bodies I'd spotted down there had been the same ones who'd been chasing me across the countryside for the past few days. I'd been blinded by the hope that the spirits' mistress had killed them all.

And I'd been wrong.

"Going to need more juice," I said to Yata. "As much as you've got."

Another wave of pain ripped through my side. It was nauseatingly strong and sucked the breath out of my lungs. It didn't last long, fortunately, but it was much harder, more intense than the first one. Jiro was closing in on me.

"Are you crazy?" the raven cawed. "What if it doesn't come back? I don't want to be empty for the rest of my life."

"Your life is going to be pretty goddamned short if I get killed." The pain had frayed my temper. I shouldn't have snapped at Yata, but I couldn't bring myself to apologize. There'd be time for that after I finished.

"Yeah, okay, good point." The raven screeched and unleashed its reserves of senjin through our connection. The mercurial power hit my core like a gut punch, and I sucked in a deep breath as I processed the raw energy. Blue shio dripped from my pores as the red rin soaked into my nodes. That hadn't helped my pain, not even a little bit, but it had made me stronger. I straightened up, shrugged off the agonizing pain buried in my side, and lifted my war club over my shoulder. "That's better."

"For you," Yata squawked. "What do you want me to do now?"

"Get the fuck out of here," I said. "Downstairs. Find out how far along they are on the ritual. I don't know if I can beat Jiro, but I can hold him off for a while. Tell them to finish what they're doing, right fucking now."

"Pretty sure that's not how magic works," the bird croaked. "But I'll tell them to hurry."

The raven's wings flapped as it launched itself off my shoulder and into the temple.

I took a deep breath in an attempt to settle my nerves.

My thoughts flashed back to our battle on the bridge, my lucky shot that had knocked him over, and the fact that he had survived a fall hundreds of feet onto the rocks below. If that hadn't killed him, I wasn't sure I'd be able to finish the job alone.

Never alone.

Mielyssi's words were comforting, but not in the way she thought. She was still out there; she could find a replacement for me if I fell. Maybe the spirits and their mistress would help her. In the end, what mattered was that I'd tried. Win or lose, I'd given this fight my all.

Another wave of pain tried to bring me to my knees. I fought it and stood tall.

Jiro Kos arrived on his golden horse. Its hooves splashed across the water until it reached the shore, and then it vanished from beneath him. The Jade Seeker didn't miss a step as his feet hit the gravel, and he came toward me with an easy, confident stride.

"Why didn't you just come out on the river if your horse could fucking walk on water?" I asked Jiro. "Probably would've ended this right then and there."

"My power was spread thin supporting my troops," Jiro said. "I could have banished their horses and come alone to face you, but after what happened on the bridge, I didn't want to chance another of your savage tricks. You were lucky once. It wasn't a good gamble to give you a chance to be lucky again."

"It doesn't seem like it mattered," I said. "I dumped your ass into the ravine, and yet here you are. Still a pain in my fucking ass."

"The Midnight Emperor treats his valued ally well," Jiro snarled. "Your trick hurt me, but he brought me back."

Well, shit. Maybe that explained the empty nodes I'd seen in Jiro's core. Maybe the Jade Seekers weren't really alive; they were just animated shells piloted by the spirits of warriors. If their bodies got fucked up, the Emperor could make new ones.

"Neat trick," I said. I was too tired. It was time to end this. "Are we going to spend any more time jerking each other off, or do you want to fight?"

The Jade Seeker's only response was to draw his sword.

The enormous two-handed blade hummed with power, and its voice, feminine and throaty with bloodlust, wailed as he approached.

"I'm going to make you eat that sword," I said. "You'll spend an eternity in hell with it singing."

"You're going to die," Jiro said.

He was still three yards away from me when he swung his sword. Silver senjin flashed around the blade as its technique ignited, and a wave of pure, limb-severing force streaked across the distance between us.

If my core hadn't been advanced, that would've ended the fight.

Too bad for Jiro I was faster than he'd expected, and pissed as hell. I twisted my body away from the attack and sidestepped toward him, club raised to bash his fucking brains out.

Jiro danced back, sword held in a high defense. His blade was heavier than my war club, and I had no idea what other scripts it held. I needed to get in close where the ludicrously oversized sword wouldn't help him.

That was easier said than done. When I advanced, Jiro step back. If I attacked, his sword unerringly flicked into the perfect defensive position to parry the strike. If I dropped my guard for even a second, he unleashed another wave of deadly force at me.

"Are you going to keep dancing, or are we fighting?" I sneered. "Get the fuck over here so we can finish this. I'm sick of looking at you."

"I'm not giving up my advantage because of your insults," Jiro said. "I'm a trained warrior, my weapon is one of the most powerful in the Empire. You're a savage piece of shit who fucks bears. You've already been worn ragged by the White Tigers. I can do this all day, but you'll run out of sacred energy long before that. And then, I'll take your head."

"You'll give me head?" I taunted. "I thought we were fighting. Now you want to suck my dick?"

I hoped the crude jibe would pull Jiro out of his shell, but his steely resolve deflected my words as easily as his blade parried my club.

Sensing my aggravation, Jiro launched a brutal series of attacks. An arc of his sword technique screamed toward my body, and when I dodged to the side, he stepped forward and swung the blade itself at my neck.

I got my club up in time to keep my head attached to my shoulders, but only just barely. The impact jarred me down to the soles of my feet and shoved me back a good twelve inches before my heels dug in. He was stronger and faster than I was, and his weapons and armor were more powerful than anything I had at my disposal. If I was going to win this thing, it would have to be with a trick.

Just like the last time we met.

I backed away, retreating outside the reach of his sword. The techniques were deadly, but the blade was sharp enough to end me on its own if I slipped up. My steps carried me back down the beach toward the water, and it lapped gently against my heels.

Jiro scoffed at my move and shook his head.

"No training, savage," he said. "You've retreated downhill and put your back to the water. You've surrendered the high ground to me and trapped yourself with no space to retreat.

I shifted my feet uncertainly and glanced back over my shoulder at the water behind me. It was shallow here, but a few feet away from the shore the water became much deeper. Jiro was right. If I backed up too far, there was no way I'd be able to fight.

Emboldened by my mistake, Jiro advanced quickly. His sword was held at the ready, prepared to protect him from my war club.

But not from my techniques.

With a thought, I dumped a node of rin into my Earthen Darts. Shards of stone burst from the ground at Jiro's feet, slamming into his armor, pounding against the front of his helmet, knocking his visor askew and momentarily blinding him.

Outraged by that trick, he swung his sword in a wild arc. I'd been expecting that, though, and hadn't moved. The instant his blade twisted his body away from me, though, I charged.

Sacred energy flowed into the Crimson Claws and Bear's Mantle. The techniques ignited a feral bloodlust within me, and I let the savage beast take hold. If Jiro thought I was a savage, I'd show him what a savage could do.

I slammed into the Seeker's waist and latched my arms around him. He brought one elbow down hard between my shoulder blades, but the Bear's Mantle shielded me from the impact. Before the Jade Seeker could react, I lifted him off the ground, threw my weight backward, and slammed him, shoulders first, into the lake behind me.

Jiro's shout of surprise was drowned by the water that rushed into his helmet.

I twisted out from underneath the Jade Seeker, grabbed his belt, and dragged him away from the shore. His armor's scripts made it feel lighter and more maneuverable while he wore it, but it was still a bunch of heavy metal strapped to his body, and it pulled him down beneath the water. When I was waist deep, I pounced on Jiro, landing with my knees on either side of his body. I ripped his helmet aside with my claws and locked my hands around his throat. I squeezed until I felt the crunch of cartilage in his trachea, and a gout of bubbles tinged pink with his blood rose to the lake's surface.

I kept squeezing until my hands cramped and the water's chill left them numb as blocks of wood. Jiro had long since stopped struggling, but the berserk rage inside me didn't want to let him go. I wanted to squeeze until my fingers touched and his head floated free of his body. I wanted to squeeze until the monster who directed him to come after me felt it, trembling through the connection they shared.

"I'm fucking coming for you," I growled. "Nothing will stop me. No one can save you now."

I clawed Jiro's head off his shoulders. I tangled my fingers in his hair, rose from the lake, and walked back to the temple.

If the Emperor raised the Seeker again, the cocksucker wouldn't have a head.

"Fucking asshole," I grumbled. "Stay dead."

Chapter Twenty-Nine

I DIDN'T WANT TO CARRY JIRO'S HEAD WITH ME, BUT I also didn't want to let it out of my sight. I was afraid that if I didn't have the head where I could see it, the Midnight Emperor would steal it away and bring the Seeker back to life.

The stairs seemed longer as I descended. Every turn felt like it should be the last, only it wasn't. Around and around I went, and my thoughts went round with me.

I'd killed dozens of men that day. They had been more than ready to do the same to me, of course, but that didn't make me feel any better about what had happened. I hadn't become a shaman to slaughter my enemies. No one had told me that was part of the job.

I did.

Okay, point taken.

When I finally reached the bottom of the stairs, I found the nexus illuminated by balls of blue shio energy. The spirits were at the heart of the chamber, seated on either side of their mistress, whose eyes were closed.

And, much to my surprise, she had no legs. Her waist tapered to a long serpentine tail that coiled around the spirits. I realized that's what those bones I'd seen before had been: pieces of her spine and tail arranged in a mockery of life.

The dream meridians were still tainted, but the darkness seemed much more constrained now than it had been before. I wasn't sure if that was a result of the ritual, or if I was just too tired to see things as they really were.

I also didn't care.

"Kyr?" Aja asked. "Is it over?"

"My part is," I confirmed. "How about you?"

"She needs time yet," Ayo responded. "She can purify the corruption, but it will take her longer than we anticipated."

"Are we talking hours or days?" I asked.

"Weeks," Aja said meekly. "It's more work than we could have imagined, and her core is still damaged."

"I don't know if we have weeks," I said. "I sent the White Tigers packing and killed Jiro as a bonus, but there's no telling when the next wave of fuckers will show up to finish what they started. Will you to be all right while she works?"

"With your help," Aja said, a lascivious grin playing at the corners of her lips. "You wouldn't leave us alone, would you?"

I sat down at the entrance of the ritual chamber, resting the head on the floor behind me. Nobody needed to see that.

"I'll stay as long as I can," I said. "I need to talk to her."

"And she needs to talk to you," Aja said. "After."

"After," I agreed.

Whatever the ritual was, it was quiet. The snake woman didn't say a word; she didn't even hum. Her breathing was quiet and regular, and I sensed the flow of spiritual energy through her. She drew corrupted senjin out of the nexus, channeled it through her core, and ejected purified dream energy back into the meridians. It was an impressive stunt, not the least of which because I'd never seen anyone channel pure senjin without breaking it down into rin and shio. What she was doing was very advanced energy work, and I desperately wanted to know how she pulled it off.

My core wanted to know, too. Half my nodes were empty, and they desperately wanted to be filled with the power I sensed around me. There was so much energy, just waiting to be taken. I could suck it all up, fill my core to bursting, and I might even advance. Hell, with as much power as I sensed here, I could advance two or three times.

No one would be more powerful than me. I just had to accept the corruption, and I'd be good to go. My thoughts drifted to more pleasant times, when my core would glow like the sun. I'd be so powerful no one would dare to stand in my way.

A sound like breaking twigs came from behind me. The sudden series of cracks had me on my feet in the blink of an eye, my war club clenched in both fists. I shook my head, and cursed myself for letting some bizarre power fantasy distract me.

The head. The goddamned head.

Insectoid legs had burst from Jiro's ears and the stump of his neck. They were long and black, their segmented links articulated on swollen joints that clicked and cracked as the head scuttled toward me.

"You cannot stop me." A deep, sepulchral voice emerged from Jiro's slack jaw. The insect legs had grown longer, thicker, until the thing towered above me. Filaments of shadow unfurled from its neck and wrapped around the legs, forming a body of sleek, glossy darkness. "My eyes are everywhere, I am everywhere. You cannot evade me, savage."

"Fuck you, too." I pushed a node of sacred energy into my arms and slammed my weapon into the monstrosity's legs with battering-ram force.

One of the legs shattered like a stick of glass, but the rest remained unmoved by my attack. An undamaged appendage lashed out and struck me full in the chest. The blow sent me sprawling, and I skidded across the floor, rolling through tendrils of corruption before coming to rest on the cold stone.

"You have cost me much, shaman," the deep voice boomed again. "I sacrificed an entire squad of Jade Seekers to kill the witch. You shattered the army of the White Tigers. You slaughtered Jiro Kos, one of my most trusted lieutenants. You will pay for the suffering and expense you've extracted from me, shaman. You will watch as I despoil the spirits you have protected, you will listen as I destroy the witch myself. If you are very lucky, I'll let you die when I have finished with you."

"If you're lucky, I won't pluck off all these fucking bug legs and shove them up your ass," I snarled and summoned my claws and mantle again. "I'm just about sick of all this bullshit. Leave me and mine alone, or I will destroy you."

"I am the Midnight Emperor," Jiro's head intoned. "I am the voice of the Celestial Bureaucracy. It is by my will that the world shall be remade. Kneel before me, shaman. Tremble before my might, and know that today, you stand in the presence of greatness."

"You talk so fucking much," I groaned and swung my club again.

The spikes ripped another leg off, but two more had already taken the place of the first one. With a snarl of frustration, I leapt up, grabbed hold of a knobby knee, and twisted around until I was standing on top of the leg. Threads of shadow tried to weave around my feet, but I jumped over them and scrambled up higher to where a carapace had begun to take shape.

Jiro's head was nestled between two chitinous plates, its eyes rolling wildly and a black tongue wriggling from between its parted lips. The presence had come through that head; I felt the connection between Jiro's skull and somewhere far distant. If I could sever that, the Emperor wouldn't have any way to reach us. Without one of his servants handy to serve as his dark host, we'd be safe.

I scrambled forward, claws digging into the carapace, and crouched above the skull. Physical damage wouldn't be enough to break the Emperor's hold over Jiro's remains. I'd need something else. I let my spirit sight take over and focused on the thread of power that emanated from a spot between Jiro's eyes. That was the connection, the bond I needed to sever.

Unfortunately, my claws passed through it as if it weren't even there. I needed something else.

I willed the dregs of rin energy in my core to pass through my arm and out my claws. The blood-red energy flowed along their length, coating the razor-sharp edges with sacred power.

"Fool," the Midnight Emperor growled. "You think I'll be so easy to stop?"

"Yep," I said.

I lashed out with my rin-soaked talons. Their edges snagged the black thread, and, one by one, tore through it. The bond between the Midnight Emperor and

Jiro's skull fell neatly into three pieces, and then dissipated like windblown smoke.

Well, almost all of it dissipated.

The biggest part of it stuck around.

It wrapped around my claw.

And burrowed into my mind.

Chapter Thirty

THE CONNECTION TO THE MIDNIGHT EMPEROR rampaged through my thoughts and put down roots faster than kudzu from hell. The power of that bond drowned out the world around me and plunged me into a chaotic maelstrom of violence and destruction. I found myself standing in a wasteland of bubbling lava on a pitch-black obsidian plane. There was no sun; the entire sky burned behind a cloud of roiling black clouds that raced ahead of a blustering storm front. Pillars of stone burst through the ground around me, only to disappear in swirls of black shadow a moment later.

"This is the world your people made," the Midnight Emperor said. "This is the devastation the Moonsilver Bat's priests would have brought to fruition had I not stopped them."

His feet, wrapped in golden boots beneath an ornate black robe, floated above the glossy obsidian. He wielded no weapon, save for the glowing orbs of energy that surrounded both of his hands. Despite the horror stories I'd heard about him, he didn't look like a monster. He was quite handsome, with almond-shaped eyes, a long black beard waxed to a precise point, and jet-black hair slicked back against his scalp. A crown of black crystal rested on his brow, and his jade-green eyes flashed with intelligence and a hint of cruelty.

"My people didn't make shit," I said. "Unless you allowed it. Or commanded it."

"You know nothing, boy," the Emperor said. "You were gone long before the hungry spirits invaded, and you've only returned long after the War of Shudders that dispatched them. The years between are lost to you."

The Emperor stopped ten feet away from me, his hands at his side, his head cocked slightly to the left as if he couldn't decide what he was looking at.

"You expect me to believe that in less than a generation my people turned into a bunch of chaos-worshipping cultist freaks bent on destroying the world?" I said. "That's bullshit, and you know it. They did what they thought was necessary to save the world, right? And they didn't do it without help."

"It doesn't matter what you think," he spat. "What matters is what I say. I declared them the cause of our woes. Yes, they attempted to defend us from our enemies. In the end, though, they failed. And that failure cost us dearly."

Raw power radiated from the Emperor in palpable waves that tried to push me to my knees. There was something about him that demanded reverence and obedience.

"Us?" I said through gritted teeth, muscles tensed to keep from bowing before him. "You seem like you made out all right."

Talking to this asshole was a waste of time. He wanted me dead, and he wouldn't rest until he got what he wanted.

"The wise always prosper in times of danger and turmoil," he said. "If you understood —"

I burst into motion mid-soliloquy. The Emperor was so caught up in trying to explain his righteousness to me that he didn't notice my attack until it was too late. Before he could react, I was on him, my claws still manifested, a savage howl tearing itself loose from inside me. I slashed at him, and ribbons of his robe fluttered away on the stormy breeze. Another slash drew blood, opening his cheek to the bone to expose the twin rows of his teeth through the bloody gash I'd opened.

His hand flashed out and bejeweled fingers slammed into my chest. The blow looked casual, barely more than the effort you'd used to swat away an annoying fly.

It sent me sailing across the obsidian plane. My back slammed into a stone pillar, shattering the rock, and I fell to the ground, stunned. Worse than the physical damage, the asshole had done something to my core. One of my empty nodes filled with a vile purple power.

Pain tore through my spirit, a splash of acid that devoured whatever it touched.

He wants to change you. He wants to own you."

Well, that was fucking great. I wrestled with the pain until it subsided, then staggered to my feet. The violet node in my core throbbed like an open wound, its influence struggling to spread through my body. If I didn't keep a lid on it, the infection would spread to my other nodes. If that happened, there was no telling what this fuckstick would do to me.

An image of Jiro Kos's disembodied head shambling around on insect legs, a black tongue lolling between its lips, made me shudder. No, I wasn't going to end up like that. No matter what else happened, I wouldn't become his slave.

"No?" the Emperor asked as if he'd read my thoughts. "My slaves have more advantages than you'll ever know. Their bodies can wither and die, but their souls live on. I craft new shells for them, younger, stronger, faster. Jiro knows this, and he will rise again to hunt you to the ends of the Earth for how you hurt him."

"You think so?" I asked. Wherever we appeared to be, I knew we were still in the ritual chamber. I felt the surging energy of the meridian nexus surrounding us. It was as rich and wild as an untamed river, the flow of corrupted senjin stronger than I'd ever felt before. "You're strong, but I can take you."

The Emperor laughed and vanished from where he'd been floating. He reappeared behind me and drove his fist into my shoulder with terrifying power. The blow sent me staggering forward, numbness spreading from the point of impact, my core trembling as yet another node emptied of rin and filled with the purple haze of the tyrant's influence.

"I will have you," he scoffed. "I will keep the world's last shaman as my pet. You will remind the others who would stand against me of the cost of their belligerence."

"I can't believe you think that's how this is going to go down," I said with a shake of my head. I forced myself to straighten and pulled my shoulders square, despite the fact that I couldn't feel my left arm at all. "I'm here to unravel all the damage you've done. I want to put the world back the way it was."

"The way it was," the Emperor mused. "Ripe for plunder at the hands of the hungry spirits. Ready to be raped by the hordes of the Frozen Hells. That's what this world was before I remade it."

"Oh, now you're responsible for all this," I said. "And here I thought my people had done it. You can't have it both ways, asshole."

"Clever boy," the Emperor said, his voice as silky smooth as a freshly sharpened blade. "It doesn't matter what I say here, the people know the truth. And they know their only hope is to let me continue the work I've begun. To fashion this world into something stronger, something more powerful than it was before."

"Oh, wait, I think I know this one," I said, raising one finger as I advanced toward the Emperor. My spirit sight showed me the blazing darkness of his core. My stomach tightened into a knot, and I realized I was looking at the highest possible level of sacred energy advancement. The Emperor had transcended to the voidbound core, a mythical state so far above other practitioners he might as well have been a god. I pick the worst fights. "The world will only be perfect when you're in charge. Am I close?"

"Don't be a fool," the Midnight Emperor scoffed. "Of course this world needs a ruler. Someone must control the senjin, to keep it from running wild and attracting enemies from beyond the realms of mortals. I am the one to harness its power. I can protect everyone. Just submit to me, and the world becomes a place of peace and prosperity."

Everything made sense now. The Emperor had used the invasion to trick my people into poisoning the dream meridians. That horrible mistake had driven the demons out, and it had destroyed most of the sacred energy practitioners. Only those who had prepared and shielded themselves from the danger, like the Emperor, or who hadn't been around, like me, had survived. The rest had been wiped out in the blink of an eye.

While I'd been gone, this asshole had been bending the world to his will. If he had his way, he wouldn't be like a god. This world would be his, and he would be its god. He would become the unstoppable master of corrupted senjin.

That corruption would choke the life out of the great spirits like the crimson bear. It would kill off the lesser spirits, too. Ayo and Aja would die without sacred energy to sustain them. The world would become a dead place, its inhabitants slaves to the Midnight Emperor.

"No," I said. "I don't think so."

For all its faults, the world I'd left behind was a better place than this one. I had a chance to save its inhabitants from becoming slaves, to show them how to live free again. I could heal the corruption, and bring the sacred practitioners back into this world.

All I had to do was kill the most powerful motherfucker in the world.

"Then you must die," the Midnight Emperor howled. His mortal mask peeled away to reveal the ugliness beneath. Purple malignancy bubbled through his skin, shredding his flesh as it sprouted into its true form. Beams of hellish radiance poured from its body like spears hurled at me. Even as it changed, it attacked, tentacles lashing at me, spines thrusting.

I dodged, jumped, twisted around the attacks, wishing I had more than one node of rin left to push into my legs. I avoided every assault, but only by the skin of my teeth. I didn't have enough sacred energy left in my core to continue, and the two nodes he'd infected were fighting against me. I was just about out of the power I needed to have any chance of beating this piece of shit.

There was more power, though. A source so potent it called to every fiber of my being. Sure, it was corrupted all to hell, and taking it in would almost certainly kill me. The question was: Would it kill me before I killed the Midnight Emperor?

If I dealt with this piece of shit fast enough, the connection between us would be broken before I died. I'd wake up back in the nexus, with Ayo and Aja right there with me. Together we could purify the stain on my core. I could do this.

I am not strong enough.

Mielyssi's words came to me as I ducked under a rain of obsidian splinters and rolled to temporary safety behind a dune of ashes. When I realized what she meant, I winced at my stupidity.

The corruption had nearly killed her during her short time in this world. And every time I'd taken more of it into me, she'd felt it through her bond. Every time I'd been poisoned, she'd also been poisoned. And now she was at the end of her rope.

A man chooses the world he lives in.

Mielyssi's voice repeating my grandfather's words gave them a different meaning. I'd assumed the old man had meant that the choices I made would shape the world as I moved through it. But that hadn't been what he meant.

I had to make a choice between two futures.

I could choose to wait on the slim chance the witch would finish her ritual, purify the nexus, and fill me with awesome power before the Midnight Emperor killed me.

Or I could sever my connection to Mielyssi, fill myself with corrupted power, and hope I had the strength to slaughter the Emperor before he did the same to me.

Heal the world.

Return to the crimson bear.

That's what I'd thought the deal was.

I'd never expected saving the world meant leaving Mielyssi. The only way I could pull more corrupted energy into my core was to sever my ties to her. Otherwise, it would kill her.

If I broke our sacred bond, there was no guarantee I'd find her again to rebuild it. I yearned for the crimson bear to speak to me again and give me the advice I needed to move ahead.

Silence.

This was more shaman shit I had to figure out on my own, no matter how much it hurt.

There wasn't time to think about it. There wasn't time to consider all the options and weigh the pros and cons. The Midnight Emperor's assault was relentless. His attacks ripped lava-filled furloughs in the earth under my feet, cast shards of obsidian at me, and rained bolts of lightning from the sky. If I didn't do something, right that second, I was a dead man.

My heart shattered.

I made my choice.

"Goodbye," I moaned.

It took more effort to say those two syllables than it did to break a connection I'd thought would last my lifetime.

Before grief could overcome me, I reached out for the power that roared within the heart of the nexus.

Corrupted senjin poured through me in a burning tide. My core screamed as the dark forces filled me with their horrifying essences.

The Midnight Emperor's attack slammed into my body at the same instant, powerful purple blasts that searched for a foothold inside my core. But the corrupted senjin I'd sucked in had filled me to overflowing, and there was no room for the Emperor's weaker force. His power spilled away from me, as harmless as water, and his eyes widened in horror.

"You'll die," he spat. "That energy will destroy you, like it destroyed all the others."

"Maybe," I said. "But not before I destroy you."

I flew at him like a storm. My feet barely touched the earth as the power inside hurled me across the plane. We slammed together with a thunderclap that sent a shock wave racing away from us in all directions. The obsidian ground shattered and chunks of glossy black flew into the sky, then crashed down to earth with a hellish racket.

I landed on my feet.

The Midnight Emperor landed on his ass.

He stared up at me, his nose broken, teeth missing, blood running from his ears.

"Impossible," he spat. "I am a god."

"Not today." I seized one of the stone pillars and snapped it loose from its base. My muscles burned, my body was on fire. Black lightning jumped out of my skin and stabbed at the bellies of the clouds overhead. I raised my ponderous weapon over my head and swung it down at the Emperor with all my strength. As my makeshift weapon descended toward my enemy, I took more and more power into my core. It flowed through me and into my muscles, filling me with an unholy strength that threatened to burn my body to ash.

The stone pillar slammed into the ground. It shattered into gray powder and shards of stinging shrapnel on impact. The Midnight Emperor screamed in rage and pain. Purple blood sprayed in a mist, and something bitter and reeking of corruption surged around me.

I stayed on my feet long enough to kick away the rubble I'd created.

There was nothing beneath it.

The Midnight Emperor was gone.

For the moment.

But he'd be back.

And I'd be ready.

Chapter Thirty-One

I F, OF COURSE, I DIDN'T DIE IN THE NEXT HANDFUL OF seconds.

The corrupted senjin I'd gulped down so greedily had blasted the lesser evil of the Midnight Emperor's influence out of my nodes and replaced it with a corrosive force that chewed at my core like a pack of rabid weasels.

The connection the Midnight Emperor had forged between us dissolved, and the world it had shown me melted into oblivion. I was back in the nexus chamber, shaking and shivering, convulsions racking my body as my core tried, and failed, to process the power I'd stolen from the badly corrupted dream meridians.

The senjin's potency was the only reason I was still alive. As fast as the corruption could tear me down, the senjin repaired the damage. The pain was unbelievable, but my gamble had paid off. I wasn't dead.

Yet.

"Aja," I croaked. "Ayo."

The spirits jumped to their feet and bolted toward me. They were so close I could almost feel their bodies when a scaled tail looped around them and barred their path.

"Don't touch him," the serpent woman snapped. "He is beyond your help."

"Get out of their way, you snaky bitch," Yata screeched. "He's going to fucking die if they don't do something."

"I said he is beyond their help," she said with a smile. "Not that he is beyond all help."

She slithered around the spirits and lowered her face to mine, her eyes glowing a brilliant magenta. She was beautiful, in a stark, ethereal way, despite her slit pupils and the tips of the fangs that peeked over lips that matched her eyes. Her breath smelled faintly sweet when the tip of her forked tongue traced the outline of my lips.

"Be gentle," she whispered. "Until it is time to be fierce."

Our first kiss was tentative and awkward. My muscles were too wracked with tremors from the dark power I'd ingested for me to do much, and she was so out of practice or inexperienced she wasn't sure which way to tilt her head to keep our noses from bumping together. Despite that, the touch of her soft lips on mine was enough to ignite a connection between us. It wasn't much, just enough for the first thread of tainted senjin to flow out of my core and into her.

But it was a start.

"Oh," she gasped. "I've never felt anything quite like that."

"More," I groaned. The kiss had relieved the pressure before it could kill me, but I was far from out of the woods. The corruption was still killing me, and until we'd purified the senjin, very bad things could still happen to either of us.

"Yes," she said, and laid down next to me. She brushed her hair aside, revealing the golden globes of her breasts and the dark circles of her violet nipples. She pressed her body against mine, her flesh warm on my side and chest. Her tail was cool and sleek where it touched the outside of my thigh. It was a strange sensation, but not an unpleasant one.

I had enough control over my body to turn my head and kiss her again. This time, I teased her lips with my tongue, then probed past her teeth with a quick, darting motion. Her teeth bit down, lightly, as I penetrated her mouth. Her kisses weren't subtle, but her passion increased with every one. What she lacked in skill, the witch made up for in enthusiasm.

We kissed for long minutes, slow and fast, hard and easy, teasing and urgent. My partner savored each moment, absorbing the experience, experimenting with her responses. Her tail wrapped around my left leg, its coils squeezing around me in an undulating motion that was both terrifying and exhilarating. She shoved her tongue into my mouth, then pulled back, a smile on her lips, before doing it again. She bared her neck for me to kiss and groaned when I sucked hard enough to leave a mark above the heat of her pulse.

"Perhaps I shouldn't have waited so long to do this," she whispered.

My thumb, which had been circling her nipple in slow, teasing strokes, froze.

"Waited so long since the last time?" I asked.

"For the first time," she said with a throaty chuckle. "Don't stop. You'll die. Or I'll kill you."

She grinned at me, eyes wide, pupils dilated into deep ovals of darkness, and nipped my lip with her fangs.

"I didn't know." I hesitated. "Your first time shouldn't be with a virtual stranger. It should because you want to, not because you have to."

"I don't have to do anything," the witch said, her voice low and dangerous. The pulsating rhythm of her tail around my leg quickened, her breath suddenly shallow and rapid. "I want this. I want you. Hurry, before I lose my mind and we both regret what happens."

"You sure know how to sweet-talk a guy," I said with a grin of my own.

I lowered my head and rolled her nipple between my lips, grazing its smooth edges with the tips of my teeth. She arched her back, pushing herself into my mouth, and I sucked until she cried out and her tail spasmed around my leg.

She groaned and rolled onto her back, one hand toying with my hair, the other moving hesitantly over my loincloth. She clutched my shaft through the fabric, and her breath hitched in her lungs. Her hips swiveled next to me, eager for the next step.

It occurred to me I had no idea how to move on to more intimate contact. I stroked the taut, golden skin of her stomach with my fingers, then trailed my hand down past where her navel would have been until I found the line where her skin gave way to a layer of fine scales. Lower still, the scales were sleeker and thicker, like overlapping armored plates.

"Lower," she moaned, and her tail unlashed from around my leg. She squeezed my cock so hard I gasped and pulled my head close to her. "Almost. Almost. There."

Her scales parted under my fingers, revealing a soft, wet opening that quivered at my touch. Her tail slapped the stone floor violently as my finger slid inside her, and her breath gushed into my ear in eager pants. Her pulse hammered against my fingers, impossibly fast.

I couldn't wait any longer. I rolled over, braced myself on my elbows, and eased into the witch.

Or tried to.

I wasn't more than an inch deep when she wrapped her tail around my waist and pulled herself onto me with a single, smooth motion. Her muscles clamped around me, pulling and relaxing with the motion of my hips. It was a strange and exhilarating feeling, and the witch seemed to agree.

Aja and Ayo moaned nearby. I spotted them sitting a few yards away, their arms hooked over their knees, their eyes closed, rocking slowly. With a start, I felt them with me, their minds enraptured by their mistress's experience.

"All one," the witch gasped. Her sharp teeth pierced the skin on my chest, just hard enough to draw blood.

The unexpected jolt of pain heightened the moment. I pushed deeper into her, pressing her back to the floor, grinding our bodies together. The sweet pressure of her sex combined with my memories of Ayo and Aja, and they added their voices to our gasps and groans. We really were all one, our bodies and minds wrapped together as our cores joined to share every intimate sensation.

"I never knew," the witch moaned under me. Her tail was hooked around my hips and coiled around my left leg. She writhed around me as if trying to make sure every inch of her touched every inch of me. "It's so much more than I ever imagined."

She was right. This experience was more profound than I'd believed possible. The pleasure was insane, but the intimate connection between all of us was beyond even that. I slowed my pace, wanting this to last forever, pushing into her with long, slow strokes that left her gasping.

Just before I reached the point of no return, I reached out to the nexus. I wanted more. More power. More of this experience.

Tainted senjin poured into me in a rush that knocked the wind out of my lungs and ignited a spasm of lust and fear inside me. The witch and her spirits shouted and arched their backs, thrusting up to meet me, groaning together.

"What are you doing to me?" the witch gasped in a breathy voice, chest heaving against mine, head tossing from side to side as pleasure gushed through her. "It's too much, Kyr. Too much."

"No," I groaned. "Never."

The four of us raced toward a new height, lights in our minds flashing in time with our pulse, our breaths cycling in and out of our bodies in time with the steady thrust of my prick into the witch's tight, wet depths. The spirits had fallen onto their backs, legs spread wide, muscles trembling as they rode the waves with their mistress.

Finally, it was too much for me to bear. I came in blinding pulses, thrusting deeper into the witch, riding her as she erupted with me, again and again. The cries of the spirits rose over their mistress's groans, and the sound pushed me over the edge again. I never wanted it to end, and I kept at it until we were both sticky and our muscles quivered uncontrollably.

I collapsed on top of the witch, her arms around my shoulders, her tail looped loosely around my hips.

"Kyr," she whispered. "It's happening."

Before I could ask the witch what the hell she was talking about, it happened.

An endless wave of pleasure tore through me. My body went stiff, and the witch cried out as I thrust into her a final time. The world burned with a brilliant silver radiance that obliterated every thought in my head.

In a single, ecstatic moment, everything changed.

Chapter Thirty-Two

I WOKE TO AN AUDIENCE GATHERED AROUND ME, AND their concerned faces almost convinced me that I was a dead man.

"I'm fine." I sat up, and found myself in a large, round bed in a cozy, wood-paneled room. Tall, narrow windows let the light in, and golden bars fell across the heavy blanket that covered my legs and stomach. "Where the fuck are we?"

"My home," the witch said with a faint smile. "Surely you did not think I lived in the sanctum or the nexus?"

Ayo and Aja tittered at that, then eased onto the bed on either side of me. Their hands closed over mine, and they planted kisses on my cheeks. They'd changed clothes while I slept, replacing the armor we'd scavenged from the Deepways with simple white gowns that clung to their curves in all the right ways. For the first time since I'd met them, they looked relaxed and at peace. Their easy smiles lit up my heart.

"What happened?" I had a vague memory of fucking the witch, an even vaguer memory of touching the nexus, and then...

Nothing.

"You cleansed the nexus," Aja said.

311

A glimmer of something came back to me. Power pulsing through the four of us like a blast of lightning that wouldn't stop. A flare of light so bright it put the stars to shame. And then…

Fuck. Nothing after that.

"Why'd I get knocked the fuck out, and the rest of you are just fine?" I leaned against the wall behind the bed.

"Not all of us advanced." The witch smiled at me, her eyes twinkling with mischief. "And not all of us became a king."

The spirits giggled and turned their faces aside at that. The witch's eyes, though, stayed fixed on me.

"You're fucking with me," I said, casting a quick look at my core. Well, fuck me running, it had advanced to skybound. Still, that didn't mean everything the snake witch said was true.

"As much as I'd like a repeat performance of yesterday's activities, I'm afraid I'm still a little too sore for that." The witch leaned past Aja to kiss my forehead. "And you most certainly are a king."

"That makes no fucking sense." My thoughts whirled and I tried to remember any scrap of what had happened after the flash of light. If they made you a king, surely there'd be something to remember. A ceremony, someone putting a crown on your head, or some fucking thing.

"Come with me." The witch offered her hand and helped me out of bed. My legs were still a little wobbly, which was annoying. If I'd been in bed all day, my fancy new core should have patched up whatever damage the Midnight Emperor had done to me.

Unless I'd been a hell of a lot closer to the grave than I'd thought.

The witch led me through a narrow door, and the spirits followed behind us. A vivid memory of her anatomy rose through the murk surrounding my memories, and I couldn't help but wonder whether she was more like a snake or a human in other regards. That was a puzzle whose depths I'd have to plumb more thoroughly at a later date.

I was surprised to find the passage from her living quarters passed through the sanctum. We entered the ruined chamber from the east, and I was positive I hadn't seen a door there before. I looked behind us, and didn't see a door then, either.

She was a witch, I reminded myself. Invisible doors were clearly witch shit of one sort or another.

"We'll fix this place up," I promised. It seemed the least I could do after the witch and her spirits had saved my life. Though, to be fair, I'd saved their lives first, which should count for something, right?

"I am quite sure we will," the witch said, and the spirits giggled again.

"What's so fucking funny?" I growled. The constant snickering was starting to get on my nerves.

"You," the witch said, honestly. "You still do not know what you have become."

"Someone could explain it," I grumbled.

"Come, see," the witch said and slithered through the temple's door.

I followed her through the doorway, down the steps past the rubble, and onto the soggy ground.

Only it was no longer soggy.

And the sun was bright and gold as a freshly minted coin in the sky.

The mist was gone.

"What happened?" I couldn't believe it. Since I'd come down from Mount Shiki, I'd been forced to breathe swampy air that smelled like the inside of a dead rat's asshole.

Now, though, the air was clean and clear, the only moisture what blew in off the lake.

"You happened," Aja said. She took my hand and pressed my knuckles to her lips. "You did this, Kyr. You cleansed the nexus. You healed the land."

"That's it?" I asked, dumbfounded. "The corruption is gone after one round of hide the sausage with a witch?"

If someone had told me saving the world was that easy, I'd have taken on the job with a lot more enthusiasm.

The witch rose up on her tail and circled around me. She draped her arms over my neck and kissed me, long and deep, eyes open and burning with magenta fire. The kiss went on until we both needed a breath, and when we parted a smile quirked her lips.

"You have won a battle, and it was a great victory, but the war is far from over, shaman." She turned and guided me toward the shore to the west. In that direction, the lake was divided neatly in half by an invisible line. The north side of the lake was dappled with the sun's rays, the waters clean and clear, the air free of the cloying mist.

The south side, though, was still wreathed in shadow. Perpetual twilight ruled there, and the fog churned against the invisible barrier, eager to spread out and corrupt the area I'd just cleaned up.

"Fuck," I groaned. "I only saved one chunk of the world."

"A sizeable chunk," the witch said with a good-natured laugh. "The entirety of the territory that was once known as the Moonsilver Bat Kingdom. What is now your territory to name as you please."

My head throbbed and my jaw dropped. I wasn't fit to rule over a chicken coop, much less an entire kingdom.

"No, no way." I shook my head vehemently. "What the fuck would I do with a kingdom?"

"Defend it," Ayo said. "You've done a great thing, Kyr. Thanks to you, this area is now purified of the taint. Practitioners can draw energy from the land again. They can use the dream meridians without being driven mad or destroyed."

"But…" There was always a fucking but.

"But you have made powerful enemies," Aja said. "The White Tigers will take some time to recover from the reaming you gave them, but they'll be back."

"And the Midnight Emperor will not forgive you for what you did to him," the witch continued. "His wounds are most grievous thanks to you, and his plan has been set back by your actions here."

"I didn't want to start a war, and I don't want to be fucking king." I shrugged and pointed at the witch. "I quit. You're the queen now."

The witch's face darkened, and her eyebrows knitted together in a concerned scowl.

"Take it back," she hissed.

"I don't—"

"Take it back." Her words slammed into me, panic and rage wound through each syllable.

"Okay, fuck, I was just kidding around." I sighed and my shoulders sagged. "I'm still the goddamned king. Though I have no idea why."

"Oh, oh," Ayo said. "I know. Can I tell him?"

The witch nodded, her features shifting into a genuinely pleasant smile. I didn't know exactly what I'd done to set her off but made a silent promise to myself to never do it again. The snake lady was downright scary when she was mad.

"In the time before man," Ayo began, obviously reciting a bit of history she'd memorized, "the seven sacred beasts ruled over the great continent. They divided their territories as was their wont, and their subjects lived in peace within those boundaries."

"And then humans showed up and fucked up everything," Aja interjected. "They don't know how to follow rules."

"Yes." Ayo shot an annoyed glare at the other spirit and continued. "When men came to the great continent, the sacred beasts knew their age had come to an end. They were no match for the speed and cunning of humans—"

"Or for the way they'd breed themselves into an army," Aja said.

"—and so they decided they would retreat to the sacred hunting grounds where they could live in peace."

My heart ached at the mention of the crimson bear's home. I missed her more than I'd thought possible.

Save the world. Find the bear.

Fucking priorities, Kyr. Don't be an idiot.

"But the sacred beasts didn't want just any humans to rule over their former dominion." Ayo pursed her lips and glanced at the witch. "And so they created scions, who would watch over their lands and set forth divine tests for those who would be king."

I'd known each of the kingdoms in the Sevenfold Empire had been named after one of the sacred beasts.

The rest of this story, though, was new to me

"You could have fucking told me your mistress was in charge of handing out crowns," I grumbled to the spirits. "That could have smoothed out a lot of rough patches."

"How?" Aja asked.

"It would have been a lot easier to hire a riverboat for starters."

"You'd have told one of those cutthroats who our mistress really was?" Aja shook her head. "Come on, Kyr. You're smarter than that."

I wasn't so sure about that but didn't see any reason to correct the spirit's appraisal of my abilities.

"Also, I forbade them to speak of this until we found a suitable replacement for the king who was lost," the witch said, her magenta eyes sparkling. "Which I now have."

"I'm not a goddamned—"

"I am Ryasina, the Wave Serpent, guardian of the Moonsilver Bat throne," the witch said in a voice that rang across the waters as loud and clear as a temple bell. "You have proven yourself worthy, and by my hand are you crowned Lord of the Northern Reach, king of the lands of the Moonsilver Bat."

"Oh, for fuck's sake, I don't even have a—"

A light weight settled on my brow.

The spirits laughed, and the Wave Serpent wrapped her tail tightly around my legs, her bare breasts against my back. She gave me a hug and kissed my ear.

Nick Harrow

"Welcome home, my king," she whispered.

Chapter Thirty-Three

DAYS AFTER I BECAME KING, I WAS STILL WOBBLY. The Wave Serpent insisted it was just the aftereffects of my battle with the Midnight Emperor.

I knew better.

My techniques were still in place, and more powerful than ever. My Crimson Claws were so sharp they could cut stone with a single swipe, and Yata couldn't dig its claws through the Bear's Mantle no matter how hard it tried. Even my Earthen Darts were so powerful I was sure they'd punch right through the next Jade Seeker who got in my way.

No, the weakness wasn't something that had been done to me, it was something I'd brought on myself.

My core ached where I'd severed my bond to the crimson bear. The pain was always with me, a hole in my soul. Even the connection I now had with Ryasina couldn't heal it. Only time, the one thing I never had enough of, would bring me back to full strength.

"Boat coming," Yata croaked.

"A little late on the warning," I said sarcastically. The boat the raven had warned me about was less than twenty feet from shore. By the time I'd raised my war club and stood up, the sampan was already sliding across the rocky shore.

"You motherfucking piece of shit cocksucker," Jaga shouted as she leapt off the boat. It skidded to a stop behind her as she charged up the beach toward me, fist raised like she wanted to punch my head off my neck.

"That's King Motherfucking Piece of Shit Cocksucker, peasant," I said, and snatched her fist out of the air before it could land across my jaw. "Glad to see you're all right too, Jaga."

"Fuck you, asshole!" She tried to yank her hand free, but she wasn't nearly strong enough for that. Wobbly or not, I was far stronger than a normal human since my advancement.

"What did I do?" I asked.

"You ruined my cargo, you cum-slurping gutter whore!" She twisted her body around her imprisoned wrist and tried to use her feet to lever herself free.

"Oh, my apologies. I had to save the world. So sorry your shitty tainted-senjin trafficking project got fucked up." I gave Jaga a shake and slapped her ass with my free hand. "I'm going to let you go, but if you try to punch me again, I'll let Yata pull out one of your eyes."

"Seriously?" Jaga asked in a quiet, much calmer voice. "I was just fucking with you, Kyr. Don't do that."

"Gods, you're infuriating," I growled and swept her up a tight hug. I squeezed her until she yelped and kissed her until she pushed away to gasp for air. "I'm really glad you're not dead."

"It was a close thing," she said. "A storm kicked up not long after I left. Damnedest thing. I had to pull onto shore until it passed."

"That was probably when I was fighting the Midnight Emperor," I said. "I kicked his ass."

"You are so full of shit." Jaga kissed me again, her hands roaming across my back, her mouth hot and hungry against me. "But, as the second-best fuck I've ever had, I am also glad you're not dead. What's this king shit, anyway?"

"Long story." I lowered her to the ground and hugged her again. I was surprised at how much I'd missed the ornery pilot. "Come on, let me introduce you to my new girlfriend."

"Oh, shit, I almost forgot!" Jaga pulled away from me and dug her hand into the pouch at her belt. "Some dirty chick with blonde hair and a bad attitude came to the sampan during the storm begging for a place to stay. Nice tits, I guess, as long as you weren't comparing them to mine. Anyway, she knew you. Asked me to give you this."

Jaga handed me a gold necklace with a medallion hanging from it. It was warm to the touch, and the simple coin shifted and twisted in my hand. A moment later, the disk had become a stylized bear's head.

"Neat trick," the pilot said. "Just how many women are you fucking? Seems like a new one pops up every time I turn my back on you."

"Just four, now." The medallion had a bold inscription hacked into its back. The letters were thick and crudely formed, and my eyes stung with unshed tears when I read them. "Used to be five."

"Is that four including me?" Jaga asked, wiggling her eyebrows.

"Only if you think you can keep up," I said. "Last time you punked out on me. So frustrating."

"Fuck you," she muttered.

"Later." I took her hand and pulled her toward the temple. My heart was lighter than it had been since I'd left Mount Shiki. Despite everything, my life was looking up. "Come on, I've got people for you to meet."

At the temple's entrance, I introduced Jaga to Ryasina, and was surprised when the two of them seemed to get along like bees and honey. I had no doubt they'd be plotting against me in no time.

Aja joined me at the temple door, her eyes shifting to the necklace in my hand.

"What's that?" she asked. "Jaga trying to buy you with trinkets?"

"Shaman shit," I said with a chuckle.

"Mm-hmm." Aja kissed me. "Be that way, then."

I turned and looked north, beyond the hills, searching for Mount Shiki. My thumb rolled over the letters on the back of the bear's head, and I straightened my shoulders and puffed out my chest as I felt each of them in turn.

The message was pure and clear, just what I needed when I needed it most.

Don't be a pussy.

A cool breeze ruffled my hair and tickled my ears. I could have been lying to myself, but I swear I heard the crimson bear laugh.

Books, Mailing List, and Reviews

If you enjoyed reading about Kyr and the rest of the gang in *Witch King* and want to stay in the loop about the latest book releases, awesome promotional deals, and upcoming book giveaways be sure to subscribe to our email list at:

www.BlackForgeBooks.com

Word-of-mouth and book reviews are crazy helpful for the success of any writer. If you *really* enjoyed reading *Witch King 1*, please consider leaving a short, honest review—just a couple of lines about your overall reading experience. Thank you in advance!

About the Author

Nick Harrow is a former game designer and gold miner who now spends his days telling stories about daring men, dangerous women, and devilish villains.

You can find him at www.nickharrow.com, where he tells frequent fibs to keep his editor happy. For free stories, book previews, and other tasty tidbits, visit www.nickharrow.com/tastybits.

Books from Black Forge

If you enjoyed *Witch King 1*, you might also enjoy other awesome stories from Black Forge, such as War God's Mantle, American Dragons, Dungeon Bringer, Witch King, or Full Frontal Galaxy. You can find all of our books listed at www.BlackForgeBooks.com.

Aaron Crash

War God's Mantle: Ascension (Book 1)
War God's Mantle: Descent (Book 2)
War God's Mantle: Underworld (Book 3)

American Dragons: Denver Fury (Book 1)
American Dragons: Cheyenne Magic (Book 2)
American Dragons: Montana Firestorm (Book 3)
American Dragons: Texas Showdown (Book 4)
American Dragons: California Imperium (Book 5)
American Dragons: Dodge City Knights (Book 6)
American Dragons: Leadville Crucible (Book 7)

Nick Harrow

American Dragons: Alaska Kingdom (Book 8)

⊥

Robot Bangarang (Full Frontal Galaxy Book 1)
Space Dragon Boogaloo (Full Frontal Galaxy Book 2)

Nick Harrow

Dungeon Bringer 1
Dungeon Bringer 2
Dungeon Bringer 3

⊥

Witch King 1
Witch King 2

Books from Shadow Alley Press

You might also enjoy books from Shadow Alley Press, such as Viridian Gate Online, Rogue Dungeon, the Yancy Lazarus Series, or the Jubal Van Zandt Series. You can find all of our books listed at www.ShadowAlleyPress.com.

James A. Hunter

Viridian Gate Online: Cataclysm (Book 1)
Viridian Gate Online: Crimson Alliance (Book 2)
Viridian Gate Online: The Jade Lord (Book 3)
Viridian Gate Online: The Imperial Legion (Book 4)
Viridian Gate Online: The Lich Priest (Book 5)
Viridian Gate Online: Doom Forge (Book 6)

⊥

Viridian Gate Online: The Artificer (Imperial Initiative)
Viridian Gate Online: Nomad Soul (Illusionist 1)
Viridian Gate Online: Dead Man's Tide (Illusionist 2)
Viridian Gate Online: Inquisitor's Foil (Illusionist 3)
Viridian Gate Online: Firebrand (Firebrand 1)
Viridian Gate Online: Embers of Rebellion (Firebrand 2)
Viridian Gate Online: Path of the Blood Phoenix (Firebrand 3)
Viridian Gate Online: Vindication (The Alchemic Weaponeer 1)
Viridian Gate Online: Absolution (The Alchemic Weaponeer 2)

Nick Harrow

⊥

Rogue Dungeon (Book 1)
Rogue Dungeon: Civil War (Book 2)
Rogue Dungeon: Troll Nation (Book 3)

⊥

Strange Magic: Yancy Lazarus Episode One
Cold Heatred: Yancy Lazarus Episode Two
Flashback: Siren Song (Episode 2.5)
Wendigo Rising: Yancy Lazarus Episode Three
Flashback: The Morrigan (Episode 3.5)
Savage Prophet: Yancy Lazarus Episode Four
Brimstone Blues: Yancy Lazarus Episode Five

⊥

MudMan: A Lazarus World Novel

⊥

Two Faced: Legend of the Treesinger (Book 1)
Soul Game: Legend of the Treesinger (Book 2)

⊥

eden Hudson

Revenge of the Bloodslinger: A Jubal Van Zandt Novel
Beautiful Corpse: A Jubal Van Zandt Novel
Soul Jar: A Jubal Van Zandt Novel
Garden of Time: A Jubal Van Zandt Novel
Wasteside: A Jubal Van Zandt Novel

⊥

Witch King

Darkening Skies (Path of the Thunderbird 1)
Stone Soul (Path of the Thunderbird 2)

Gage Lee

Hollow Core (School of Swords and Serpents Book 1)
Eclipse Core (School of Swords and Serpents Book 2)

Aaron Ritchey

Armageddon Girls (The Juniper Wars 1)
Machine-Gun Girls (The Juniper Wars 2)
Inferno Girls (The Juniper Wars 3)
Storm Girls (The Juniper Wars 4)

⏚

Sages of the Underpass (Battle Artists Book 1)